# What the

# Heart Wants

**Dawn2Dawn Publishing**

**Dawn2Dawn Publishing**
**8810c Jamacha Blvd #136**
**Spring Valley, CA 91977**

Published by Dawn2Dawn Publishing 06/2014

ISBN-13: 978-0-9914000-6-5 (sc)

ISBN-13: 978-0-9914000-7-2 (e)

A blaring house mix shook the foundation of the entire building, eliminating even the possibility of interpreting any conversation. Yet everyone there still carried on as if the music wasn't loud. Cliques huddled around the dance floor, shaking their assets, while others on the sidelines devised plans to catch someone else's attention. A few couples erotically grinded their bodies against each other, signaling that their tangos would definitely continue well into the night. Everyone was having such a good time that no one seemed to mind the one-hundred-fifty-degree temperature. If they did, they didn't show it. Sweat-stained garments were everywhere, but no one cared except Meme.

Candice and April were heading out for some fun and had invited Meme to come along. However, they had no idea she'd still be a third leg eight hours later. They had left her brother Marlon's wedding reception and dropped in on a barbecue. All three women were overdressed, but the men didn't seem to mind. Their sophisticated attire immediately attracted much attention. There wasn't a single man in the house who hadn't approached them. The right combination of looks, body, and money approached them, and that lead to happy hour. But true to form, a poor, unsuspecting, clueless jerk had to be the one to hit up Meme. He wasn't all that bad. Another woman may have been happy to have him, but he was barking up the wrong tree with Meme. She'd sworn off men, preferring a less volatile woman over any brute, misogynistic man. This same hatred of men had seriously confused her at Marlon's reception.

Eight hours after leaving the reception—where her presence was clearly unwanted—she was still with Candice and April. Meme was tortured by sitting through what they clearly thought was fun. She'd gotten up several times to leave, only to be pulled back into her seat by Candice or thrown into some strange man's arms by April and hauled off to the dance floor. There wasn't a doubt in her mind that both of them knew she batted for the other team, but neither seemed to care.

Any other time, Meme would've just left, but she didn't want to risk offending anyone else in her life. The way things had been going, her choices were coming back to bite her. The people she cared about could barely stand the sight of her. So instead of calling up friends who understood her, she opted to sit and be cordial. They weren't the best of friends. They weren't even considered associates, but their connection to her brother was a beam illuminating a path back into his life. Feeling like an outsider amongst her family at the reception was too much to bear, but could she really take advantage of April and Candace? Could she use the friendship they were offering to get close to her brother?

*No, and even if I could, I don't think I could endure more nights like this.*

She knew they'd both protest if she chose to leave, so Meme decided to excuse herself to use the restroom. That hope was quickly shot down by the buddy system. *Why can't women go to the bathroom alone?* As soon as she excused herself to the ladies room, Candice announced she had to go, too. Meme trekked across the crowded room with Candice in tow, contemplating her next move. They were almost to the restroom when someone tugged on Meme's arm. Meme turned toward a woman, looking her up and down. There was a vague familiarity, but she couldn't put a name to the face. Meme excused herself and stepped to the side. She couldn't let this opportunity slip past her.

"I see you're not partying at the Golden Stone tonight."

The Golden Stone was a small, trendy club where closeted professionals could mingle discreetly. Though Meme had only recently been dragged out of the closet, she never worried about being approached by someone who recognized her from one of the clubs. Truth was, outing others was something frowned upon. Most people, although proud of who they were, didn't want their business out there like that.

"I could say the same for you." Meme's smile was sweet, but her eyes said, *don't start nothin'.*

"Sorry, I didn't mean to put you out there like that. I was just watching you dance earlier, and you seem as miserable as I am. Thought you could use a break. My name's Sahara. We've partied together a few times, but have never been formally introduced. I'm having a girl's night out with my sisters. Since they don't know about my sexual preference, I have to spend the evening pretending like I'm having the time of my life. What's your reason for being here?"

"I'm just hanging with some friends. I'm pretty sure they know my preference, but they just seem hell bent on trying to convert me."

Sahara cringed. "Your situation is much worse than mine. Let me buy you a drink. It'll make you feel better."

Meme sized her up as the offer hung in the air. Sahara was definitely appealing, but Meme wasn't one to swoon over looks alone. Sure, physical attraction made her heart thump like any other sensual woman, but it wasn't everything. Even when she was dating men, she'd find herself lusting after their physical traits. However, she no longer swam in the shallow end of the pool. There had to be something beyond the physical. She wasn't foolish enough to believe in love at first sight, so she understood finding that special someone was going to take time. After the mess she'd just made of her and Marlon's life, she was hesitant about getting involved with anyone.

"You are a beautiful woman, but the timing is bad."

Sahara laughed. "Relax, it's just a drink. I am not trying to hop into bed with you. It's just a drink, no strings and no expectations."

Meme shook her head, chuckling at herself. Her cheeks warmed with pink embarrassment. "Sorry."

"It's all right." Sahara's smile was easy. She seemed friendly and harmless, and Meme intended on using that in her favor.

"I'd love a drink, but let's go somewhere else. It's too loud and hot in here."

8

Meme managed to sneak out without being noticed by April or Candice. She hopped in the car with Sahara and headed off to somewhere peaceful to have a drink and talk.

They chatted casually as they drove around looking for a spot to hang. Normally, Meme would have driven, but she'd left her car at the reception hall and rode with April. Riding with someone gave them too much control. They had the final say in where you went, when you arrived, and when you left. Driving yourself also prevented awkward conversations like the one they were currently having. Sahara hit play on her CD player. She must've also been tired of the awkwardness.

Maxwell's voice crooned through the speakers.

*I should be crying, but I just can't let it show.*

Meme rested her head on the back of the cool leather seat. She squeezed her eyes closed, trying to ward off the emotions that threatened to burst forth. Her mind mulled over the last twenty-four hours, her conflicting emotions, the last three months of trying to rebuild her relationship with Marlon, and the months before when she'd selfishly destroyed their relationship. *Maxwell was right, this woman's work is never done.* She'd come along way, but still had further to go.

Meme had caused irreparable damage to the ones she claimed to love. And since she was still alive to tell the story, they obviously must've loved her. As soon as her brother returned from his honeymoon, her main goal would be winning back his trust. How she was going to do that remained a mystery—one of such magnitude she'd need the craftiness of Sherlock Holmes to help solve it.

Sahara could sense Meme's sadness and placed a hand on her knee. Before Meme could enjoy the solace of her caress, Sahara snatched her hand away, remembering the apprehensive look Meme had shot her at the club. Rigid awkwardness combined with the thoughts already swirling around in Meme's head was too much to bear. "On second thought, I'm really not up for a drink. Do you mind taking me to my car? It is only about five to ten minutes from here."

"Look." Sahara pulled to the side of the road. It was dark and there weren't many cars out. Meme had no idea what was about to go down, but whatever Sahara had planned, she wasn't going out without a fight. Meme slyly slipped her hand into her purse and wrapped it around the small can of mace, took off the safety lock, and prepared her mind to fight. She'd been attacked before and vowed never to be the victim again. "I can't lie. I've been attracted to you for a while. I've always been scared to approach you, but seeing you tonight, I thought it was fate. I can love you the way you need to be loved if you just give me a chance."

"Like I said before, it's just not a good time." Meme wanted to kick herself for falling for the *I just want to buy you a drink* speech. "I'm flattered, but it wouldn't be fair to you or me if we started something I can't put my heart into." Meme held her breath, hoping her excuse was enough to end this evening.

Sahara shoulders slumped with resignation as she started the car.

Meme released the breath she was holding but still gripped her can of mace as she gave directions to her car. Before Sahara could even put her car in park, Meme had removed her seat belt, flung open the door, and rushed toward her car without as much as a goodbye. She revved up her car and sped out of the parking lot. Getting in the car with a complete stranger was a bad idea, but she'd hopped in without considering the consequences. That same *act now, worry about the consequences later*

10

attitude is what had started the rift between her and Marlon. She had to start making wiser decisions before she completely alienated everyone in her life.

Once she closed her apartment door, she finally exhaled. She showered in an attempt to wash away the last nine months of her life. However, she would settle for the last twenty-four hours, which included her brother's wedding ceremony she wasn't allowed to attend, the reception where she wasn't invited to sit with the family and the bathroom tryst with Mike—a random man who'd sat across from her. In the last real conversation she'd had with her brother, he said that he forgave her and wanted to work on rebuilding their relationship. Then, he got engaged and found out he was going to be a daddy. He'd been so preoccupied that he didn't have time to devote to their relationship. He also excluded her on the happiest day of his life, so it appeared that they were right back at square one.

Cold sheets awaited her as she climbed into bed. The silence of the apartment was drowned out by the chaotic clamor of confusion in her mind. The torrential storm of emotions continued to rage out of control as she tussled about the bed trying to find a comfortable position. In spite of everything else she was dealing with, thoughts of the stranger she'd encountered at her brother's reception crept to the forefront of her mind. Images of Mike's face, the rough caress of his hands, and his scent were so powerful; it felt as if he were in the room. The deep timbre of his voice had caressed her so seductively that she temporarily forgot about her hatred for men, the pain they'd caused her, and her vow to stay away from them.

She'd been sucked so far into his aura that she brazenly led him out of the room and foolishly offered herself to him. She leaned back against the counter—in the bathroom of all places—ready to spread her legs for him, only to have him grow a conscience. He backed away and ran out the bathroom so fast you would have thought the building was on fire. If she had thought about her actions before leading him out of the room, maybe she would've been spared the tortuous embarrassment.

That embarrassment was the reason she'd ran into Candice and April. She was leaving the reception, so she didn't have to sit across the table from that man all evening. That's when she saw the club-hopping duo in the parking lot. It was obvious they thought she was leaving early because of her issues with her brother, but at that point he was the furthest thing from her mind. She was angry about Mike's rejection, but her body was still pulsating from his touch. It had been years since she allowed a man to touch her. Because of the last man's actions, she'd sworn to never let another man touch her again.

She'd been successfully thwarting all male seduction attempts, but there was something about Mike that she couldn't describe. It could've been all the love floating in the atmosphere. The room was filled with happy couples cuddled up and gazing into each other's eyes, rehashing their own nuptials. Whatever it was, took her breath away. His dark eyes had caressed her skin from across the table. When he came around the table to talk to her, she could feel heat radiating from his body. His hand touched her thigh and she lost her mind. That's how she wound up in the bathroom. Temporary insanity was the only explanation for her behavior.

Even now as she lay in bed, the thought of him warmed her. A low, smoldering heat grew into a blazing inferno, leaving her desperately gripping the sheets. She needed her fire doused quickly. There was nothing like a little firefighting to help a girl relax and get some sleep. She squeezed her thighs together, vainly attempting to quell her inner-fire. The throbbing intensified and she had no choice but to pursue other means of finding relief.

## <u>2</u>

**M**eme woke up early Monday morning to the sound of someone banging on her front door. She'd spent all Sunday in bed trying to avoid reality by watching movies and sleeping. She wanted things to go back to normal. Whoever was at the door seemed determined to ruin her plan. She marched to the door and yanked it open without even checking to see who it was. "How did you find out where I live?" Her voice drawled with exaggerated annoyance. She stretched and yawned, making it clear she was tired and not in the mood for company.

"Good morning to you, too. I brought breakfast." April smiled, holding up a bag full of food from the Pancake House. Meme's stomach growled.

*Now that, I am in the mood for,* Meme thought. Her stomach took control of her brain. She sat her thoughts aside, so the food could enter.

"Good morning, April. How and why are you here?" Meme nonchalantly led her into the kitchen, too preoccupied with digging through the bag to really care about a response. Her Sunday vegetative state didn't include food, and her stomach was demanding to be filled.

"You forgot that my cousin is married to your cousin, so tracking you down wasn't hard. You disappeared Saturday night. I wanted to make sure you were all right."

Meme eyed her suspiciously while April laughed.

"Don't worry, I am not trying to push up on you. I don't get down like that, trust me. I just thought we could be friends. Saturday you looked like you could use a friend."

They ate in silence while Meme contemplated her offer. Another friend was always nice as long as they were drama-free. Hanging with April seemed cool, but Meme would have to be careful. A seemingly innocent friendship is what had ruined things with Marlon. She would definitely tread lightly with April, and if at any point it seemed like she wanted more than friendship, their relationship would be nipped in the bud. "Although I do have a few friends, another would be nice."

"Good. Now finish eating and put some sweats on, so we can work out."

About three hours later, Meme limped back into her apartment, seriously rethinking her friendship with April. By no means was she out of shape—she had the body to prove it—but working out with April was on another level. Meme was naturally slender, so it only took half an hour on the elliptical, sit-ups, and push-ups to keep her body tight. But April had the kind of body that made grown men drool, and she worked hard to maintain it.

April barked out orders and yelled in Meme's face at the slightest sign of weakness. A couple of times, April had almost got herself punched in the face. They stood toe to toe, both refusing to back down. Men had even stopped their workouts to watch with excitement, no doubt hoping to see a catfight.

"Wow, I didn't take you to be a quitter," April taunted. That statement alone lit a fire under Meme. She retook her stance at the squat machine and matched April rep for rep, pushing harder than ever. They completed an hour and a half of cardio, using machines Meme had never considered touching.

Every muscle in her body rebelled, and when it was time to climb the steps to her apartment, her legs went on strike. She barely made it to the top, practically crawling and whining with each movement. Her body demanded a hot bath and her brain obeyed. She peeled off her sweat-soaked pants, and her muscles cried out as if they weighed a ton. Thank God for the bag of Epsom salt in the bathroom cabinet. Dumping the remnants of the bag into the tub, Meme slid into the hot water and let it minister to her ailing body.

Although the workout was sheer torture, it kept Meme's mind off her problems. Not once had she thought about her brother, her past, or the guy from the reception. But now that she was back in the quiet loneliness of her apartment and her body was beginning to relax, the wretched thoughts came back with full force. It had been months since she'd betrayed her brother's trust. Even if Marlon never truly forgave her, it was time she forgave herself. Instead of trying to push those thoughts to the back of her mind, she welcomed them. In the past, she had unsuccessfully tried to analyze why she had done what she did. She was done trying to figure out why. She just wanted to get past it. Maybe she could if she just focused on the end result of her mistake. Her actions had led her brother to meet and marry Latrice. He was happier now than he'd ever been, and they had a baby on the way. Hopefully, he focused on that as well, and maybe he'd forgive her.

She sat in the tub for over an hour, refilling the water every time it got cold. Her fingers and toes were wrinkled, but her muscles were relaxed. She could've stayed there all day. The only reason she decided to get out was because her phone was ringing. She ignored it the first time it rang, even the second time. After the third call, she was a little worried and decided she better answer.

Moving faster than she was before her bath, Meme padded her way into the bedroom, leaving a trail of water behind her. She plopped down on the bed, answering the phone before the voicemail clicked on.

"Hello?" Meme gripped the phone between her shoulder and ear as she shimmied her way under the blanket.

"What's up, baby girl?" The voice on the other end of the line was music to her ears.

"Hey, Marlon, is everything okay?" She was excited to hear her brother's voice. Something had to be up for him to be calling her while on his honeymoon.

"Does something have to be wrong for me to call my little sister?"

"Of course not, it's just been a minute."

"I hear you, really I do. Like I said, we will work on that, but as for right now I need a favor."

Meme couldn't help but smile.

"I need you to run down to the restaurant. I have a delivery coming tomorrow afternoon and I forgot to tell Cole about it. He is going to need to be there to let the people in. He is not answering his phone. I left him a message, but I'd feel more comfortable if you went down there." Marlon had taken over as the executive chef of Pavoli's and made Cole his sous chef. Since the day Marlon started running things, Cole had been by his side, supporting every decision. Together, they had built a reputation for serving high-quality food.

Things weren't so great in the beginning, only because Cole had a passion for cooking and didn't want to see some new guy come into the restaurant he'd been slaving in for months and mess it up. Marlon proved that he was assertive, able to stand under pressure, and a darn good chef. They'd been friends ever since.

"Okay, just give me a few minutes and I'll run down there." Meme hung up the phone still sporting a wide grin. She felt like she'd just been given an opportunity to audition for the role of devoted sister, and no matter how miniscule the task, she didn't want to mess it up. Meme pulled her hair into a sexy style, threw on something appealing, and dashed out the door. No matter how much of a rush she was in, she still had to look good.

When Marlon had first told her he wanted to be a chef, she thought he was joking. When she realized he was serious, she supported him 100 percent. When others tried to belittle him because of his career choice, she was right there to defend him. When he graduated from culinary school, received a job at Pavoli's, and then made executive chef, he was too modest to say, *I told you so*. Therefore, Meme said it for him. Before she had ruined his trust, she ate at his restaurant at least once a week, was on a first name basis with the front house staff, and had tasted just about everything on the menu. On her first visit, Marlon had personally walked her around, introducing her to everyone except the chefs. He never explained why she wasn't allowed in the kitchen and she never asked. She just accepted it as some ritual that only chefs knew about.

Stepping inside of Pavoli's, Meme inhaled the familiar aroma of rich Italian food. Her stomach growled, reminding her that she'd burned off her breakfast and probably everything she'd eaten that week while working out with April. She reigned in her appetite and looked around for someone who could direct her to Cole.

No matter how many times she ate at the restaurant, she always marveled at how the deep-chocolate wood finishing of the hardwood floors and chairs made the white tablecloths pop out. Each table looked like a fluffy marshmallow floating in chocolate syrup. It was perfect elegance. Combined with the reception she always received, the ambiance made her feel like a celebrity. Today was no different. Vanessa, a hostess, greeted her with hugs and smiles, gushing about how beautiful she looked.

"I know Marlon is out of town, but will you be dining at the chef's table?"

Meme had planned to give Cole the message and leave, but now she was here and the aromas were so enticing she thought, *What the heck? I might as well eat. Lord knows I deserve it.* The wait staff smiled and nodded in her direction as she was escorted to her seat. Vanessa passed her a menu, informed her of who her server would be, and then turned to head back to the front.

"Vanessa…" Meme was so excited about eating some good food she'd almost forgotten the reason she came in the first place. "I need to see Cole. Can you have him come see me?" Meme asked as she perused the menu.

"Why?" Meme was so into the menu that she hadn't noticed the awkward silence that developed after her request. She actually thought Vanessa had walked away, but the tone of her voice and the deep-set furrow of her brow were obvious signs that there was a problem. Her face softened and she cleared her throat, offering more of an explanation. "I don't mean to question you. It's just that with Marlon gone, it puts more pressure on Cole. He may not have the time to step away. I could give him a message if you want."

Not wanting to read too much into Vanessa's initial reaction, Meme accepted her explanation, but refused her offer to give Cole a message. She wasn't taking any chances. If Cole missed the delivery tomorrow, it wouldn't be because he didn't receive the message. The message would travel from her lips to his ears and what he decided to do with the information was up to him. She'd never met him, but from the way Marlon talked about him, he seemed like a decent guy. She was pretty sure he'd do the right thing.

Meme ordered her favorite dish of Ricotta and Spinach Ravioli in a Buttery Sage Sauce. She sat back, sipping her wine as she waited for her Stuffed Mushrooms appetizer to arrive. Her stomach growled at just the thought of all the rich flavors she was about to enjoy. She didn't know why Marlon had chosen Italian cuisine, but she was glad he did.

That first mushroom touched her tongue and she was in heaven. Meme didn't care that she was dining alone, or that people might be watching her lick her fingers. Each bite was better than the one before, and when her entrée arrived, she was so caught up in the flavors that she didn't notice the man watching her across the room. She sipped wine and ate, and sipped and ate some more until every last bit was gone. Afterward, she sat back and belched out her gratitude to the chef. Sitting up straight and covering her mouth, she looked around, hoping no one heard. She giggled in embarrassment. She had no idea how much wine she'd ingested. All she knew was her glass had gotten topped off all night; now she felt real nice.

He was still watching from across the restaurant. It was that same tipsy giggle that had gotten him caught up a few days ago. She was truly the most beautiful woman he'd ever seen, yet she was totally off limits. As he approached, he prepared his mind for the battle ahead. She was going to go ballistic when she saw him, but he couldn't avoid it any longer.

"You know you are very beautiful when you eat."

She giggled as her eyes traveled up his body. They landed on his face her smile faded. "What are you doing here?" Startled by his appearance, she shouted, causing several people at tables nearby to stare.

"You asked to see me. Now lower your voice before you cause a scene." He took a seat at her table, hoping she would take heed to his warning.

"Mike, I didn't ask to see you. If I never saw you again in my life I'd be happy." *I can't take seeing you in my dreams, let alone in person.* Images of their encounter in the bathroom at the reception hall danced across her mind. Meme guzzled the rest of her wine, trying to drown those thoughts and images. Her eyes raked over him taking in his attire and then it dawned on her. "Wait. You're Cole?" He'd given her a fake name the night they met. She couldn't even be upset, because she gave out fake names often.

"In the flesh." He smiled, taking the time to give her the same perusal that she'd given him.

That lazy smile and deep timbre in his voice made her mouth dry. She reached for her empty glass, and right on cue, someone was there to fill it. She sipped wine as a pretext to get her thoughts together. How could she not know that he worked with her brother? One thing was certain; he was off limits. Then again, that wasn't a problem, because she didn't do men.

Finding her resolve to get as far away from this man as soon as possible, Meme pushed back from the table and stood to leave, but all the wine she'd drank had a different plan. She stumbled backward and Cole grabbed her waist to steady her. Stepping closer as he stood, Cole gently stroked his thumbs up and down her stomach as he clutched her small waist.

"Are you all right?" When she didn't answer, he stooped to her eye level and asked again.

She couldn't get her brain to function with him touching her. That gentle caress burned through her clothes as if he'd snubbed out his cigarette on her skin. Her eyes dropped to watch the source of such sweet torture and his hands stopped. One moved to her chin and he lifted her face to his searching gaze.

"Are you all right?" His eyes roamed her face.

The concern she saw in his eyes and heard in his voice helped her find her voice. She collapsed in the chair, her body still reeling from his touch. "I'm fine, I'm fine," she proclaimed as she fumbled for her glass of wine.

"How much have you had to drink?" He kneeled in front of her, searching her eyes for signs that she was drunk. "I'm driving you home."

Before she could protest, Cole grabbed her purse off the table, took her by the elbow, and led her out of the restaurant.

"I'm not drunk," she yelled, once they were outside. She violently snatched her arm away, stumbled, and hit the ground before Cole could grab her. Her heart knocked against her rib cage as he bent down to pick her up. He scooped her into his arms with little effort. "Put me down," she protested, but the breathless whisper only made him smile. His smile made her even more breathless.

Assisting her into his car, Cole buckled her seatbelt, shut the door, and then jogged around to the driver side. Once inside, he turned to her and apologized. "I'm sorry for the way I treated you on Saturday. If it's any consolation, I've been kicking myself in the butt for not taking what you offered. Once I found out you were Marlon's sister, I was glad I hadn't." He let the conversation die with that statement. Never in his adult life had he apologized to a woman for anything. They were expendable to him. If one started trippin', requesting things he was unwilling to give, he'd move on to the next. Seeing that the list of things he was unwilling to give was pretty long, most of his relationships didn't last any longer than the few hours it took him to get in and out of a woman's bed. He didn't do cuddling or overnights, and at that revelation, most women cursed him out as he got dressed and fled out of their front doors.

The ride was quiet besides the sporadic direction from Meme as to an exit to take or what street to turn on. When they arrived at her apartment, Cole had come to the conclusion that the only reason he felt the need to apologize was because she was his friend's sister. If she decided to tell Marlon what went down, he wanted to at least be able to say that he apologized. Meme spent the ride going over her game plan. There was to be no more touching. She couldn't think straight when he touched her, and by no means was he getting inside her apartment.

"Do you think you can make it by yourself?" Cole asked as he parked in front of her apartment. Cole shouldn't have taken off in the middle of dinner rush, but he couldn't just let her drive drunk. Of course, he could've just called a cab, but she was his friend's sister and it was his duty to make sure she got home safely, at least that's what he told himself. Well he'd seen her home safely, and now it was time to get the hell out of dodge.

"Yeah." Meme cleared her throat, trying to understand her momentary disappointment. His not wanting to walk her to the door was a good thing. *Isn't it?* "I told you I wasn't drunk." She managed a smile as she climbed out of the car. *This is what I wanted, so why am I so upset? I'm not upset; am I?* She talked to herself as she walked to her apartment. She stopped to shoo Cole away, but he stuck his hand out of the car window and gave her the same hand flailing motion she'd given him.

Once inside, she took a moment to think and calm her racing heart. No man had ever been able to invoke such emotion in her. Fear, yes; pain, yes; anger, plenty; but passion, never. At the reception, she felt it. From the moment their eyes connected in the restaurant to the second she stepped inside of her apartment, she felt it again. This was a passion so strong it took her breath away and stirred a yearning within her to just be in his arms. She needed to shake away this obsession with a stick, because he was off limits.

She took a few deep breaths to calm her racing heart, only to have it excited again by the ringing doorbell. Her breathing stopped as she

24

looked through the peephole. She slowly opened the door and asked, "Is everything all right?"

"You forgot to tell me why you came to see me."

"Oh God, I can't believe I forgot."

"Why don't you make some coffee, so we can talk." Before she could protest, he had slipped past her into the apartment.

*Don't let him inside your apartment—fail.*

She nervously beelined toward the kitchen, hoping to put some distance between them, but he followed her.

"Did you enjoy your meal tonight?" Cole asked, taking a seat at the kitchen table.

"I did. I've had that dish several times. It's my favorite, and tonight it was off the chain. It tasted better than ever." She pulled out the coffee and placed two scoops of grinds into the machine.

"Thank you." He smiled and her traitorous heart skipped again. "I know Marlon personally cooks your meals. So when they told me you were in the restaurant, I had them bring your order to me and I made it myself. I'll be sure to tell Marlon you think I'm a better cook than him," he laughed. The ricotta and spinach ravioli was his creation. It was the one item on the menu that Marlon had given him complete control over and it was her favorite. Cole tried to disregard how that affected him.

Meme tried to ignore the effects that knowing he cooked for her had on her heart. "Does he cook for me every time I come?" Her hands shook as she heard him get up from the table and then felt his heat behind her.

"He does." His breath danced across the back of her neck as his hard chest connected with her back. His hands clutched the counter on both sides of her locking her in place.

*No more touching—fail.*

"But I think I'm going to fight him for the honor. Watching you eat the food I prepared excited me." Further proving his point, he pressed into her, and when the unmistakable bulge in his pants grazed her backside, she almost buckled at the knees. "Would you like for me to cook for you again?"

She tried stepping to the side to get away from him, but he tightened his hands on the counter. "Please let me go." Her trembling voice was barely above a whisper and totally contradicted what her body wanted. Her voice pleaded for freedom, but her body leaned back against him, molding itself into the contours of his chest.

Meme freely offered her lips to Cole and he more than willingly accepted. The timid kissing and touching was cute, but Cole was tired of playing. He turned her completely toward him and aggressively took full possession of her mouth. Her full submission was only deepening his thirst for her. He had to get away. As soon as he could pull his lips away, he would back up, let her say why she came to see him, and he would leave. He couldn't pull away. The kiss they had shared at the reception was spectacular; now, he wanted more. Normally, he wouldn't kiss a woman this deeply. He probably wouldn't have kissed Meme at all; however, when he followed her into the restroom, she had slammed her lips against his. The soft flesh of her lips and the sweet taste of her tongue invaded his mouth swiftly, and he was hooked before he could protest. This kiss was simply about feeding his hunger. The deeper he took the kiss, the hungrier he became. When she whimpered into his mouth, his hands began wandering. He ventured into territory deemed off limits.

"Damn," he grumbled, pulling his lips from hers as he spun away. They stood at opposite ends of the kitchen staring each other down, both trying to get their breathing under control. Meme tried to build the courage to kick him out; Cole tried to find the strength to leave. If he didn't leave soon, he would be forced to break his cardinal rule of dating. The very rule that made him put an end to their encounter in the restroom. Meme was off limits for more than one reason. Although he might've been able to overlook the fact that she's his friend's sister, he couldn't forget the cardinal rule. "I have to go," he finally said as he made his way toward the door. Each step strengthened his resolution to stay away from her.

"Marlon," Meme blurted out, finally finding her voice. "He called. That's why I came to see you." She followed behind him and waited for him to respond. It wasn't until he opened the door and was standing on the front porch that he turned to acknowledge her. "He'd been trying to call you, but you weren't answering. He said there is a delivery tomorrow and you need to be down at the restaurant to receive it."

"He told me about the delivery last week," Cole said, shaking his head. "Latrice is doing something to your brother's mind." He still didn't understand how Marlon could get burned so badly by his first wife and then jump right into another relationship. Marlon claimed there was a connection between him and Latrice that hadn't been there with his first wife. He claimed she was the most beautiful, kindest, and sweetest woman he knew. Cole had experienced the pain of betrayal at a young age. He didn't trust any woman, no matter how sweet she was, even if she was as sweet as the woman standing in front of him.

Meme made her way to the door and Cole stuck his hands in his pockets to keep from touching her. "I'm sorry for wasting your time. I'll be sure to tell Marlon he is losing it." The light shaking of her head as she contemplated her brother's absentmindedness allowed loose strands of hair to fall into her face. Cole balled his hands in his pockets to keep from brushing them away.

"I can pick you up in the morning on my way to the restaurant, so you can get your car." Cole started backing away. The look on Meme's face seemed to be begging him to stay. If he stayed, he'd touch her again. If he touched her again, he wouldn't be able to stop.

"No, that won't be necessary. I've taken up enough of your time. I'll get a friend to take me."

Cole said goodbye and walked to his car as quickly as possible. He had to get out of there before he changed his mind about leaving. *Marlon isn't the only one losing his mind.* His attraction to women rarely went beyond the superficial lusting over a curvy body and a pretty face. Rarely would he notice more, but always immediately found her flawed in some way or another. With Meme, he noticed too many positive qualities. Trying to do right by her had caused him to pick up on aspects of her personality that totally contradicted his personal beliefs about women. When he came on to her at the reception, her response wasn't one of a woman used to playing the field. That fact was proven in the restroom when her innocence was revealed. And even this time, he noticed her compassion as she'd driven all the way to the restaurant just to deliver a message for Marlon. What put him on edge was the fact that she seemed just as drawn to him as he was to her. He could tell she was shocked and afraid of her own response to his advances. Her hands slightly trembled when he spoke to her, and when they touched, her entire body quaked. Although she tried to avoid eye contact, her eyes told a story her mouth refused to utter. Meme wanted him so bad it was terrorizing.

## 3

The next day, Meme picked up her car, only to find the word *slut* scratched into the hood. Three days later, she was just as clueless as to who would do such a thing and just as pissed as when she first saw it. She'd driven around with the derogatory comment on display for the world to see while she searched for a body shop that could fix it within her budget. She dropped it off that particular morning and rented a little Hyundai Accent to drive to work. This compact car was nothing compared to the sleek Nissan Maxima she drove. That car was her baby. She worked hard every month to pay the note. Livid couldn't even begin to define how she felt when she saw the scratches on her car. Immediately, she pulled out her phone to call Cole. She wanted to curse him out. Cole was the only explanation she could come up with. Maybe one of his exes had spotted him carrying her to his car and took revenge on her car. She would have given him an earful, but realized she didn't have his number.

Now that she had taken some time to think about it, she realized that it wasn't very likely anyone would've known which car was hers. One of Cole's women couldn't have seen what kind of car she drove. That thought scared her. She couldn't think of anyone who had a motive to vandalize her car, except for maybe her brother. Even he wouldn't stoop that low; plus, he was out of town.

Meme walked into the salon and blew a kiss to Wayne, the owner. Then, she went to the staff lounge to put her lunch in the refrigerator. She made a fresh pot of coffee to go with the donuts she brought in, put on her smock, and made her way out to her station to prep for her first client of the day. As usual, a copy of today's appointment schedule along with a brief note on the services each client would be receiving was at her station.

Euphoria, a full-service salon, offered everything you could want in a spa experience: facials, massage therapy, body treatments, waxing, nails, hair, and makeup. Although they serviced women of all nationalities, they specialized in the hair and skin care of African-Americans. People mocked Wayne because of his feminine appearance, but under all the wigs, makeup, and dainty clothes, Wayne was a businessman. Having been disowned at seventeen-years-old by his father for his lifestyle, Wayne moved in with his grandma. She was a God-fearing woman, but loved her grandson regardless of his choices. She died shortly after he graduated from high school, leaving him her house and what she considered a small fortune. He used his inheritance to pay for cosmetology school. When he finished and received his license, he did hair out of his grandma's house until he built up enough clientele to afford booth rent. In ten years, he went from doing hair in the kitchen to owning one of the hottest spas in the city, simply because he had a vision and had refused to let anyone or anything stand in his way. He held a license to perform every service that Euphoria offered and encouraged Meme to do the same. He had taken her under his wing, showing her several techniques no longer taught in cosmetology school.

They became quick friends and he was there for her during one of the roughest times of her life. She'd had her heart broken and was attacked by the man who claimed to love her. She couldn't turn to her family. They had told her he was wrong for her, but she continued to date him behind their backs. It was Wayne's friendship that had kept her from losing her mind. He introduced her to the lifestyle she was currently living. The days following her ordeal, she had come into work looking pitiful, trying to hide behind scarves and sunglasses, but Wayne wasn't fooled. He saw the bruises and her inner-pain. He became her shoulder to cry on. When she wanted to lock herself away from the world, he dragged her out, showing her there was life after heartbreak.

Meme liked Euphoria over all the other salons she'd worked at. There was no loud music playing or equally loud, graphic, men-bashing conversations. Her clients weren't paying with bad checks or trying to get a hook-up. In fact, her clients didn't even have her personal number. They scheduled all appointments through the receptionist, and when they arrived for their appointments, they paid up front with the receptionist. When she arrived at the front to escort her clients back, she was always given a complete list of services to be rendered. Stylists wore matching smocks and had to dress presentably. No half-combed hairstyles or weaves to be finished on breaks. There was no over-scheduling where one stylist had three clients under the dryer and one at their station. First and foremost, tardiness wasn't tolerated. If your client had to wait more than ten minutes and you didn't have a viable excuse, you'd be fined. If you refused to pay your fine, termination was inevitable. Since Euphoria charged more for their services than the neighborhood salons, which meant more money in the stylist's pocket, no one wanted to be dismissed.

The first client of the day was Ms. O'Neil, a sixty-five-year-old, retired high school principal who only wore wigs, but came religiously into the salon every Friday morning to have her hair washed and braided. She was a single mother who had raised three boys. Every Friday, she some way or another managed to mention how good looking and single they were. Meme wanted to tell her that they were not born with the right equipment to satisfy her, but didn't want to give the poor lady a heart attack. Instead, she would smile and politely change the subject.

"Good morning, Ms. O'Neil." Meme extended her hand. Most of her clients insisted on hugging when they came in and when they left. Ms. O'Neil was not one of them. "I see you are here for your usual. Can I interest you in any of our other services? Maybe a manicure and pedicure for the weekend?"

"Not today." Ms. O'Neil led the way back to Meme's station, her lips pursed in a no-nonsense disposition.

*This woman needs to relax. I hope I'm not this tense when I retire.* Meme had to bite her lip to keep from laughing at that uppity sashay and death grip on her purse. Meme shook her head, covered Ms. O'Neil with a cape, and proceeded to take her braids down.

Whatever Ms. O'Neil ate for breakfast had her mouth running a mile a minute. She talked and talked about nothing in particular. It seemed like she just wanted to hear her own voice. Meme was so tired of her mouth that she let her mind wander to things she'd avoided since Monday

33

night. She made sure she nodded and gave the occasional *mhmm* to Ms. O'Neil, but her mind was somewhere else. In the days since their encounter at her apartment, she'd forced her mind to refocus every time Cole popped into it. She was determined to stop allowing her emotions to control her. That's what she'd done in past relationships, and they all ended disastrously. She was not in the right frame of mind for a relationship, or whatever it was Cole was after.

Those kisses were hard to ignore, hard to forget, and would be even harder to turn down. Cole could kiss a woman back to life. The heart monitor could've flat-lined, body could've turned cold, but one kiss from Cole would raise her from the dead. He was aggressive but passionate, rough but tender. He demanded all of her mouth and gave his in return. Just thinking about it made her lips tingle with desire.

Ms. O'Neil jumped up squealing with excitement, startling Meme out of her daydream. "Oh, thank you. Let me call him, so you can give him your address."

"Wait, what?" Meme's brows rose in confusion as this woman bounced around and punched numbers into her cell phone. Meme tried to recount what Ms. O'Neil had been saying, but couldn't recall anything that would have gotten her so excited. When she overheard the phone conversation, she almost broke her neck trying to get the phone from Ms. O'Neil.

"Scott, do you remember the young lady I was telling you about? She has agreed to go out with you tonight."

Meme tried to come around the chair and grab the phone, but tripped over Ms. O'Neil's handbag that she always refused to lock up.

"I know you don't need my help, but I really want you to meet a nice girl and settle down."

Meme took deep breaths to calm her nerves as she silently cheered for Scott to win the battle of wills against his mother. A smirk tipped the corners of Ms. O'Neil's mouth and she knew the battle was now hers. Meme plopped down in the chair Ms. O'Neil should've been sitting in and tried to hide her frustration. In defeat, she accepted the phone her client was almost shoving into her hand.

"Hello." Meme tried her best to sound polite.

"Meme, I want to start off by apologizing for my mother. Once she gets an idea in her head there is no stopping her. I know this is probably just as awkward for you as it is for me, but this is what I propose. My mom is relentless and will keep badgering both of us until we go out. So, let's have dinner tonight and a little fun, as friends of course. We can tell her we had a horrible time and she will let us live our lives…well, let you live your life. I, on the other hand, will never be free of her nagging."

Meme chuckled and could see the elation on Ms. O'Neil's face. No doubt she was hearing wedding bells. What options did she have? If Meme declined, she could possibly lose a client. If she went out with him, had a horrible time, or maybe even a fantastic time, she'd be done with all the pestering from his momma. She definitely wanted Ms. O'Neil to back up, but did she really want to be bothered tonight?

At her silence, he pressed on. "So, can I pick you up at seven?"

"No, but name the place and I will meet you there."

Ms. O'Neil grumbled and snatched the phone away. "You independent young women have a lot to learn. He will pick you up. Now, what's your address?"

Meme recited her address. It was either that or curse Ms. O'Neil out. She was working her last nerve. In a minute, she was going to be all in her clients face telling her where she could go. Then she'd definitely lose the client and possibly her job. They ended the call and Meme finished braiding her hair. She braided it as tight as possible, getting satisfaction every time Ms. O'Neil squirmed in the chair.

The rest of the day went on without incident. When all her clients were gone, Meme strolled around the salon finding insignificant tasks to occupy her time, hoping it would fly by and she could use working late as an excuse to miss her date. Time was not on her side. The hands on the clock ticked by at a snail's pace, and when five thirty rolled around, there was nothing left to do but go home and get ready for her date.

The outfit for the evening had been chosen carefully. Last thing she wanted was for Scott to like what he saw and change the game plan. She had a certain standard of dress, but tried to tone it down as much as possible. Meme donned her black, strapless, knee-length BCBG cocktail dress that flowed with the curves of her body. She pulled her hair back into a ponytail and wrapped the ends in a tight bun, not a strand was out of place. She went a little paler on the foundation to make the red lipstick stand out. Last but not least, her feet were clad in black Louboutin pumps with studded heels. Everything about her look said, *I am not a woman to be messed with.*

The doorbell rang. Meme dabbed the excessive gloss off her lips and went to answer. Heels sinking into the carpet, she had to tiptoe to the door. When she answered it, she was pleasantly surprised. Scott was a good-looking brother. The obvious comparison popped up, but she pushed

Cole out of her mind, grabbed her purse, and accepted Scott's extended elbow as he escorted her to his car.

Joining her in the car, Scott turned to her with a devilish grin on his face. "I have to say you are stunning. My mother tends to look at the inside instead of the outside, but you are a pleasant surprise."

*Was that supposed to be a compliment?* Meme tried to hide her distaste. "A woman is only as beautiful on the outside as she is on the inside."

Scott laughed. "What world are you living in? The beautiful people are in the spotlight. Everyone else wants to be just like them. Save all that, 'beauty is on the inside' crap for someone else. A woman can give you the shirt off her back, but if she's a dog, she's a dog. There isn't any amount of charity that can fix that."

*Jerk!*

Biting her lip to avoid the impending argument, Meme stared out the window, wondering if karma was ever going to swing back in her favor or if the bad choices she'd made would forever keep her dealing with idiots. She could see him out the corner of her eye occasionally stealing glances, and she cringed when he opened his mouth to speak.

"Don't tell me you are one of those sensitive females who gets all worked up when a brother speaks his mind?"

Meme's hands fisted in her lap and she clamped down on her retort. To her, calling a woman a female in that tone of voice was just like calling her out of her name.

"All I'm saying is, if an ugly brother tries to get at you, you'll tell him to step without giving his inner-beauty the time of day."

"All I'm saying is," she paused, taking a deep breath to formulate her thought. "If you were an ugly brother, you'd want someone to see your inner beauty."

The corners of his mouth tilted up and the timbre of his voice dropped. Most women would have found it sexy, but it made Meme's stomach turn. "So you think I'm good looking?"

Rolling her eyes, she turned back toward the window. *This is going to be a long night.* Arrogance, another reason she'd given up on men. Looking out the window, she could've screamed. Of all the restaurants in this city, he would decide to bring her to Pavoli's. Before ordering her appetizer, the news of her being on a date would reach her brother in whatever part of the world his honeymoon had taken him. Or even worse, Cole would see her. Ignoring why she didn't want Cole to see her, Meme hopped out of the car. She didn't wait for Scott to open her door.

As Meme stepped through the front door, Vanessa, the hostess, scowled in her direction. That was the coldest greeting she'd ever received in this restaurant. Before she could comment, Scott stepped next to her and placed his hand on the small of her back. Just like that, the bubbly little Vanessa was back, but Meme had turned as rigid as a board.

*He better get his hands off me.*

If this were a real date, his comments in the car would have been strike one and putting his hands on her strike two.

They were seated at their table. Meme pretended to look over the menu to avoid conversation while Scott eyed her like she was the special on tonight's menu. She knew exactly what she wanted to order the moment she walked through the door, but she also knew that if they had another conversation like they had in the car, she was going to turn this restaurant out trying to get to him. She kept up the pretense of looking through the menu until the waiter arrived.

The waiter arrived and Meme almost drew blood from her own lip biting down on it so hard. She opened her mouth to order, and Scott snatched her menu, shushed her, and then proceeded to order for her.

*Strike number three, time to go.* Leaning back in her seat with arms folded across her chest, Meme's eyes blazed with contempt.

"Relax." That arrogant smirk flashed across his lips and Meme wanted to slap him. "You'll enjoy it."

"Do you think I don't have a brain to figure out for myself what I'll like? It is the twenty-first century. What man still does that, ordering for a woman like she can't speak up for herself?"

He sipped his wine, chuckled, and changed the subject like she hadn't just posed a question. "So, how long have you been a stylist?"

Meme exhaled deeply and tried to go with the flow of conversation. There was no point arguing with him. It was obvious that he was a jerk, and after today she would never see him again.

Cole was in the kitchen finishing up a plate when one of the wait staff came up to him with a piece of paper. "Meme is here. Do you want to make her order, or do you want me to put it in with everyone else's?"

"I'll make it." Cole feigned indifference, but just the mention of her name sent his libido into overdrive. "Just set it right there."

"She has a date, want his too?"

Cole almost dropped the plate he was working on, but quickly recovered. "Yes, just set it right there." He kept working as if unaffected by Meme having a date, but brewing inside him was an emotion he couldn't quite put his finger on.

Looking over the slip of paper with Meme's order, Cole rolled his eyes. Veal Chops Milanese and Prime Beef Tenderloin. *The tenderloin had to be her date's order, but the veal chop was not her at all. She must be trying to make a good impression.* Watching her the other day as she rubbed her breadstick around in the sauce, eating every last drop, he could tell she loved rich, filling food. The veal was good, but would not satisfy her taste buds. He'd prepare her veal, but he would also prepare what she really wanted.

The veal and tenderloin were delivered first and after she'd taken a few bites, her favorite dish was delivered just for her. Cole thought about delivering it himself, but decided to have it sent instead. He then picked a nice quiet spot out of sight where he could watch her eat. Her face lit up when she saw the dish and the waiter explained where it came from. She pushed the veal to the side, only taking an occasional bite from it, but devoured the spinach and ricotta ravioli.

Patrons were dining all around. The soft chatter of conversation hummed as the wait staff busied themselves taking and delivering orders. There was some commotion going on behind him between the manager and one of the waiters, but Cole was in his own world. The restaurant could've collapsed around him and he wouldn't have noticed. His eyes zeroed in on one thing: the beautiful woman in the room who had managed to take something as simple as eating and make it an erotic dance of seduction. The two other times he'd seen Meme, her hair was down, hiding portions of her face. Tonight it was pulled back. Her delicate features intensified her beguiling innocence. The red lipstick against her caramel skin made her lips stand out. Every time she opened her mouth to take another bite, his chest tightened.

Her innocence was painstakingly alluring, but it was that same innocence that was making him fight to stay away. The cardinal rule was, innocent ones are clingy and they want forever. Forever was on that long list of things he couldn't give. With that thought, he tore his eyes away from Meme and marched back into the kitchen.

## 4

On Saturday afternoons, the salon was always in full swing; it was Meme's sensible shoe day. She'd made the mistake of trying to be sexy on a Saturday, and by the end of the day her toes were numb, ankles swollen, and she limped barefoot to her car after her shift was over. This particular day, she had a full schedule. By nine o'clock, she was already on her third client. Her only scheduled break was at noon for a mere thirty minutes.

With a glob of base crème on the back of her hand, Meme parted small sections and applied it to her client's scalp. She had the kind of hair you couldn't really wear natural unless you were into afros or locks, but would relax into being silky straight if done properly.

Halfway through the relaxing process, the receptionist came toward Meme carrying a beautiful vase of flowers. "Look what just came for you," she sang, grinning from ear to ear. She handed Meme the card and took the vase to the lounge.

Meme rolled her eyes, tossed the card on the shelf, and continued working. There was no doubt that the flowers were from Scott. Their date gave her a much needed reminder of why she was through with men. Arrogant, aggressive, domineering, self-centered, and controlling, Scott was all of the above and then some. Keeping Ms. O'Neil as a client was not worth the hassle, and if she tried to hook her up with another son, she'd be looking for a new stylist.

Their date ended with Scott pressing her up against her apartment door, trying to kiss her good night. She didn't know what signal made him think a good night kiss was warranted. She quickly kneed him in the balls to let him know he was way off base. While he kneeled on her porch moaning and calling her out of her name, she unlocked the door, went inside, and made a large bowl of butter pecan ice cream. If Ms. O'Neil's other sons were as big of jerks as Scott, they'd all be single for a very long time.

She finished up her client's relaxer, washed and conditioned her hair, and then placed her under the hair dryer. Before getting her next client from the reception area, Meme took a few seconds to read the card from the flowers. She took one look at it and wanted to scream. Marching into the lounge she tossed the flowers into the trash vase and all. There was only one word on that card: *Slut!* She tossed the card in the trash along with the flowers and tried to bite down the panic that was starting to rise.

*It's just a card. No need to panic. Someone is just playing games.*

Meme had convinced herself that her car was vandalized because it was parked at the restaurant all night and some idiot with nothing better to do thought it would be funny. The flowers proved that she was being targeted. Whoever it was must've followed her to the restaurant, which means they had to know where she lived since she came from her apartment. Most likely they now knew where she worked. Suddenly, beads of sweat formed on her brow and her stomach twisted in knots. Memories of being attacked and the hopelessness she felt flooded her mind.

Wayne walked into the lounge and Meme was in the middle of a full-fledged panic attack. Her back was to the door when he came in, so he couldn't see her distress. He walked to the refrigerator, jabbering about a gathering at his house after work. Meme didn't respond to his inquiry on whether she was attending and he turned to look at her face. Immediately, he rushed to her side. Helping her into a chair, Wayne grabbed a bottle of water and forced her to take small sips. There were napkins on the counter. He wet a few and patted them across her face.

Finally, her breathing became normal again and her eyes focused. She didn't know if she passed out or not, but she hadn't realized Wayne was in the room. Meme smiled awkwardly and reached for the bottle of water with unsteady hands. Wayne watched her every move. Even when she averted her eyes to avoid the questions in his, he studied her. When he tossed the wet napkins in the trash, he saw the flowers.

"Aren't these the flowers that were just delivered for you?"

She nodded.

"Who sent them?"

She shrugged and he pursed his lips together in disbelief. At her silence, Wayne dug into the trash and read the card. Gasping in shock, Wayne sat next to Meme grabbing her hand in comfort.

*Oh great, here comes the melodramatic musings of Ms. Wayne the drama queen.*

He had told her to call the police about her car, and she refused. Now, she wished she had. At least she'd taken pictures like he told her, but what good would they do? She had no clue as to who was targeting her.

Wayne held her hand while cupping her cheek and with more bass than she had ever heard in his voice, he said, "Call the police." Then, he got up and walked out. About halfway down the hall, Wayne yelled out, with his feminine tone returned, "Margaritas at my house at eight o'clock tonight. Be there or I will come find you."

Thank God he left the dramatics at home. When he'd first seen her car he was more emotional than she was. He had cried, cursed, and threw a fit, all things she had didn't even do. Perhaps if she had, that little panic attack might not have happened. Meme eventually made her way back out to the reception area to greet her next client. Thanks to her little episode, she would have to work through her break to get back on schedule.

By the end of the day, Meme was so tense that she decided a few margaritas would do her some good. Wayne's little gatherings were always a blast. Whatever the drink was for the night, it was made just right. Be it margaritas, martinis, daiquiris, or pink panties, Wayne knew how to mix them right. Meme planned on drowning her sorrows in the bottom of the blender tonight. She stopped at the gas station to buy two more bags of ice just in case Wayne was running low.

Kevin, Wayne's boyfriend, answered the door. Meme kissed his cheek and strutted in with her bags of ice. Kevin was a nice guy, but he was so deep in the closet that he and Wayne hardly ever went anywhere. It was a surprise to see him answering the door. Whenever there was a gathering, Kevin always disappeared. The love between them was obvious, but it couldn't grow and flourish until Kevin was ready to reveal who he really was.

"Did I ask you to bring something?" Wayne huffed as Meme entered the kitchen.

"Please." She waved him off and tossed the bags of ice into the sink. "After the day I've had, you might have to send Kevin out to get more ice."

"Kevin is going in the room to watch a movie," Kevin mumbled as he walked past the kitchen.

"Come on, baby; just hang with us for a little while," Wayne whined and pouted, but Kevin wasn't changing his mind. He was a six-foot-two, exquisitely sculpted, Timberland, baggy-pants wearing, hat-cocked-to-the-side drill instructor for the United States Army. The hardcore exterior made him intimidating. If anyone ever found out that he was gay, it would ruin his image and his effectiveness as a drill instructor. Therefore, he kept his sexuality under lock and key. None of Wayne's whining could persuade him to do otherwise.

His demand for secrecy was actually how Meme had met him. She was the only one of Wayne's friends who had the privilege of knowing Kevin. They'd had a pretty bad argument and Wayne showed up on her door step more distraught than she'd ever seen him. He was crying and rambling incoherently as if something had happened to one of his immediate family members. She had no idea he had a boyfriend. Wayne was always solo when they went out.

Once she calmed him down, he started spilling his guts. He was in love with a man who was ashamed of whom he was. All he wanted was to love his man openly, not just behind closed doors. Wayne, who had never been in the closet, had a hard time understanding those who were. So, after he fell asleep, Meme used his cell phone to call his house phone, knowing that Kevin would recognize the number and answer.

Of course, Kevin was a little leery and didn't want to talk to her, but once she reassured him that she wouldn't run his business in the street, he opened up a little. At the time, she was still in the closet and shared how she feared her Christian family's reaction. He sympathized and confided that he wasn't ashamed of being gay. It was just difficult to be an openly gay man, especially in the military. The military and its code of justice, in his eyes, were twisted. He could train soldiers, go to war, and risk his life for his country, but the moment they find out he liked men, that somehow made him incompetent to do his job. He'd sat around with superior officers listening to their gay-bashing conversations, not able to say a word for fear of being dishonorably discharged from his job. They weren't even half the man he was in skill, intelligence, fitness, and probably even the bedroom. They all knew it and were looking for a way to knock him down a few pegs. That's why he demanded secrecy in his relationship with Wayne.

Before the conversation was over, they had exchanged numbers and both felt like they'd made a new friend. A few times, they went to the movies as a threesome. Kevin and Meme would walk in holding hands, looking like a happy couple, with Wayne looking like the third wheel. As soon as they were seated in the dark theater with Kevin in the middle he would kiss Meme's cheek, thank her, and then clasp hands with Wayne.

Wayne should've known better than to ask Kevin to hang out with them tonight, but he had and now they were in a standoff. "If this is going to be a problem, I can stay at my place tonight." For Kevin to even be in

47

Wayne's house when he was having company was a miracle. Wayne should've left it at that.

"I am tired of you always threatening to leave."

"And I'm tired of you always trying to get me to kick it with your friends. This is who I am and this is the way our relationship is going to be. If you can't accept it, then move the hell on."

*Whoa!* Meme looked back and forth between Wayne and Kevin like she was watching a tennis match. Wayne's arms folded across his chest. Kevin's hands fisted at his sides. The tension was thick like standoffs in western movies; any minute a tumble weed would roll by.

"I think I'm ready to move the hell on. Get out of my house," Wayne mumbled as he marched out of the kitchen.

"Wayne, you don't mean that." Meme tried to stop him as he walked by, but he didn't want to hear a word she had to say. Cutting her eyes at Kevin she picked up a hand full of ice out of the bowl on the counter and threw it at him. "Go fix this."

"It can't be fixed. He wants something I can't give him. He is miserable and it frustrates me to know that I'm the cause. Maybe it's best that I leave. He can find someone to give him what he wants."

"Yeah, but will that person love him like you do?"

"No one will love him like I do."

"Then go fix this."

Taking a few seconds to think it over, Kevin shook his head. "I can't expect him to keep living a lie. All his neighbors think I'm his brother. His friends don't even know he has a man. Sometimes loving someone means you have to set them free, so they can find happiness."

With that said, Kevin took his keys out of his pocket, removed the key for Wayne's house, and walked out the front door.

Meme watched the door shut, wondering how in the world this happened. A simple request just ended a twelve-month relationship. She was unsure of what to say to rectify the situation, but what she could do is make some margaritas, because when Wayne came back into the kitchen and saw that Kevin actually left, the hysterics were going to fly. It would take a good strong drink to calm him down.

Right on cue, Wayne marched back into the kitchen. "And you know what else Kevin…" Wayne looked around, and Meme held her breath as she loaded ice into the blender. "Where is he?"

"He left." She cringed as she waited for those words to sink in.

"He left?"

"Yes, he said he is setting you free so you can be happy." She passed him the key Kevin left and he almost hit the floor. Meme was at his side trying to comfort him the best she could, but at this point he was inconsolable. His wails echoed off the walls, his tears soaked the sleeve of Meme's shirt, and she stared at the blender, wishing a batch of margaritas would magically appear.

The doorbell rang, Wayne froze, and Meme asked, "Do you want me to send everyone home?"

"No, a good drink and hearing someone else's problems will do me some good right now. Let them in and make the margaritas. I'll be out in a few." Wayne dragged himself toward his room with a defeated slump in his shoulders. "Make them heavy on the tequila; the faster I get drunk the better," was his departing request before he slammed his bedroom door shut.

Meme let the guests in, turned on some music, placed the trays of finger foods out on the table, and hooked up a toxic batch of margaritas. Forty-five minutes had passed, all the guests had arrived, and they were eating and sipping their drinks before Wayne came out of the room. His eyes were puffy and everyone knew he'd been crying, but no one said anything.

As soon as he sat down, Meme passed him his drink. He took a sip and almost choked. "Did you pour the whole bottle of tequila in here?"

Meme tried to stifle her tipsy giggle. "You said heavy on the tequila."

Wayne grabbed her glass out of her hand, "Give me this. You know you can't hold your liquor, and you know too much of my business to be up in here drunk and spilling your guts."

The room erupted with laughter and Meme snatched her drink back. "I can hold my liquor just fine." She went to sit on the arm of the sofa and completely missed it. Tumbling to the floor, her drink flew into the air, and laughter erupted again. Meme had to laugh at herself. Maybe she was more than a little tipsy. The doorbell chimed and she trotted off to answer it.

"Make yourself a pot of coffee and a pitcher of virgin margaritas before you come back in here," Wayne joked. They laughed at her again, and she gave them the finger.

Meme glanced through the peephole and snatched the door open ready to go off. "What are you doing here?"

"Wow, is that how you greet everybody?"

"I just wasn't aware that you and Wayne were friends."

"I wouldn't call us friends, but like I told you the other day, we party in the same circle. Kanani invited me. Is she here?"

"Yes, follow me." Halfway back to the living room, Meme stopped to clear the air between them. "Sahara, I want to apologize for how I just hopped out of your car the other day. You were nice enough to take me to my car. I was rude. It was uncalled for and the only explanation I can offer is that it had been a long, emotional day. I'm sorry." Extending her hand and a smile Meme asked, "Friends?"

"I'd like that." They shook hands and then joined everyone else in the living room.

They walked in and Wayne was collecting car keys. "I can see already where this night is headed and I'm not in the mood for a funeral." Everyone gave up their keys without complaint while Wayne went to the kitchen to make round two.

"Guess who I saw the other day?" Kanani downed the rest of her drink and smiled. "Brandy."

Sahara, along with everyone else, shook her head and sighed. "Please don't tell me you guys are getting back together." Brandy was Kanani's on-and-off girlfriend. They were perfectly in love as long as they were in bed. Outside of the bed, they stayed at each others' throats, annoying everyone around them. Everyone was glad when they called it quits for good.

"No, but we did manage to go back to my place for a little fun."

"You are so nasty." Meme threw a sofa pillow and hit Kanani in the face.

"Come over here. I'll show you how nasty I can be."

Meme rolled her eyes and gave Kanani the finger. She was the only stud in the group and it was her life goal to get the draws of every woman she met. Meme had yet to give in to her advances and didn't plan on it. Kanani was more man than she was woman. That just didn't do it for Meme. She felt a man should be a man and a woman should be a woman. She didn't knock anybody for the lifestyle they chose to live, but for her, a woman had to be soft and feminine—the way a woman was meant to be. Besides Meme, Kanani had probably slept with every woman in the house. Meme assumed she was working on Sahara, but with her open advances perhaps she wasn't.

Endless pitchers of margarita were passed around, and besides Meme, everyone was well past drunk. Between Kanani and Sahara's sexual glares, she thought it best to remain level-headed. She didn't want to get drunk and wake up in bed with the wrong person. When she was sure everyone was asleep, she grabbed her keys and went home.

<u>5</u>

Cole had been sitting idly for over ten minutes trying to figure out what he was doing. He had gotten up early to work out. He needed to burn off the anger, frustration, and confusion he'd been dealing with since Friday. Deciding against the gym, he went to the Pancake House instead. He ordered to-go breakfast for two and was now sitting outside her apartment. She affected him in ways he couldn't explain. Seeing her at the restaurant on a date had sent his mind into a whirlwind. He was angry that she had a date and frustrated that he couldn't get her off his mind.

Cole gathered the bags of food and made his way to her apartment. Had he sat there too much longer, someone would probably call the police on him. His heart thumped as he approached her door. He had no clue what he was doing or how she'd react. If he left now, she'd never know he was there, but once he knocked he would have to own up to the fact that she was on his mind—to the point where he couldn't sleep without dreaming of her.

Cole went to press the doorbell and his entire being froze. *What am I doing?* His hands dropped to his sides as he berated himself for acting like he was new to the game. He'd been in this game for a minute and had mastered his technique of pursuing a woman. *This one is different though.*

There was an undeniable fire that burned between them whenever they touched. He wanted her in a way he'd never wanted another woman, but she was off limits. Coming to her house was a mistake—one he didn't mind making. With that thought, he pushed the doorbell and nervously waited.

Meme tumbled out of bed to answer the door; she was still half-asleep. She had no idea who it could be. Whoever it was, would wish they'd came a little later after Meme finished with them. She yanked the door open with enough strength to snatch it off the hinges. "What the—" The words died on her lips when her eyes met his and that sexy smile greeted her. Holding his eyes, she returned the smile until she realized she must look a hot mess. She excused herself to brush her wayward strands into a ponytail.

When she returned, Meme found that Cole had made himself at home. He'd found the plates, utensils, and cups, and then set the table. He noticed her watching him from the doorway and invited her to sit at the table. Her slender legs taunted him as she slid into the offered seat. His hungry eyes roamed every inch of leg exposed through her skimpy boxer shorts. Her tussled hair was sexy and he was pissed that she'd combed it. If she hadn't run off when she did, he wouldn't have been able to keep his hands to himself. Now that he was over the shock of how sexy she was, he was able to think rationally.

Cole cut his pancakes, poured the syrup on, and dug in. He could feel her eyes on him from across the table, but he pretended not to notice. He figured she was trying to piece together what he was up to. A few minutes had passed before she stopped watching him and accepted it for what it was, breakfast. She took her first bite of eggs and Cole hid his smile behind a forkful of country potatoes.

They ate in silence, cleared the table in silence, and when they were done, Cole marched into the living room with Meme behind him. The couch was his destination. Cole grabbed the remote and turned on the Chargers game. Meme stood with her hands on her hips; she was confused. *What is he doing?*

The game was just getting started and Cole leaned back against the sofa, kicking his feet up onto the coffee table. Meme took a seat on the opposite end of the sofa, gnawing away in uncertainty.

She stole several glances at his long, massive frame lounging in her apartment. He looked perfect, like he belonged there. His almond-colored skin, dark eyes, and strong jaw line accentuated his succulent lips. Those same lips had beckoned her at the reception and kissed her into a simultaneous state of peace and war. Her mind and body had melted into a mass of hormones incapable of thoughts and movement only capable at his request. He removed his hooded sweatshirt, his t-shirt pulling tight across his chest. His chest was so glorious, it suppressed her sexual preference. Her heart thumped hard, but it must not have been pumping blood to her brain, because she was about to do something foolish.

Her mouth ran dry as she contemplated her next move. She weighed the pros and cons of seduction. No doubt, he would give her hours of pleasure, but where would they be after that? Then, there was still her little 'situation' that he'd made clear he couldn't get past. He may just out right reject her. Was she even ready to be with a man after years of being with women?

*He is gorgeous though, and came all the way over here with breakfast.*

Her silly emotions were talking again. Those were thoughts of the old Meme: selfish, shallow, and led by her emotion, but not anymore. She straightened her backbone and gathered her strength, shifting her focus to the game.

His size thirteen shoes propped up on the table were racking her nerves. Without permission, she reached over, untied his shoes, and took them off. As she returned to the couch, his hand caressed her cheek. The warmth radiating from his hand was enticing. She needed to escape soon before she yielded total control. Meme kept her eyes down. If she looked at him, her resolve to not be led by her emotions would crumble. Cole slid his fingers underneath her chin, trying to lift her head to look into her eyes, but she pulled her head away and returned to her spot on the couch.

The contact was brief, but potent. The blood in his veins heated at an alarming rate. If her gaze rose to meet his, he'd take her, right there, mid-game. Even now as he watched her cower away from him, his heart pulsed harder, yearning for her to be closer. He turned his eyes back to the game, but his mind was on those creamy thighs protruding from those tiny shorts. Every time she moved, folded, or unfolded her legs, those mouth-watering thighs taunted him. Before he could stop himself, he reached over and ran his hand down her thigh. Its smooth, silky texture was a vast contrast to his rough hand. An electric current sizzled between them. The pulse at the base of her throat thumped out of control and he knew she also felt it. Her eyes were closed and he watched her throat constrict as she nervously swallowed. He wanted to feel how soft the rest of her was, but before he got carried away, he pulled his hand back.

Neither one of them knew if the Chargers were winning or losing. Their eyes were glued to the television, but their minds were on each other. Meme was recalculating her whole lesbian equation. It wasn't like she was born that way. Most of her friends recalled having homosexual tendencies at a young age, but not her. She loved men at one point, but the fear of them had led her into this life. So maybe it was normal to be affected by him, and maybe it was okay to spend time with him. Cole had drawn a conclusion. His mind was made up. Rules be damned, he wanted this woman and he was going to have her. He just had to figure out how to get what he wanted and avoid all of the clinginess that was sure to follow. He'd worry about that later; as for right now, he just needed to touch her.

Reaching across the couch, he placed one hand beneath her knees and the other around her waist. Cole lifted her up towards himself, adjusting his body, so she could sit between his legs. Objection sat on her lips and he kissed it away. With one leg on the couch, the other on the ground, and Meme resting between them, Cole let his kiss explain what he couldn't find the words to say. He kissed her until her body relaxed, signifying her understanding and acceptance. He then wrapped his arms around her and pulled her as close as possible. When she rested her head on his chest, he leaned back to enjoy what was left of the game.

Taking slow, deep breaths was the only explanation she could give for not passing out. Her heart fluttered and danced around so much she thought she was going into cardiac arrest. Her mind argued with itself. One side saying, *Get a grip. Get away from him.* The other side protested, *Oh my God, this gorgeous man has his hands all over me.* The cradle of his arms squeezed tighter around her. Rational thinking went out the window. Meme made a mental note to work on not giving in to her emotions tomorrow. But right now, she was just going to enjoy the sensation his touch sent coursing through her body.

The peace and completion he felt with her in his arms flooded his senses. He couldn't believe he was actually cuddling this woman—they hadn't even had sex—and he was enjoying it. Her heartbeat against his stomach, the smell of whatever she used in her hair, the sound of her breathing, and the warmth of her body calmed him. She had taken over his mind to the point where his natural reaction to flee was the furthest thing from his mind. Instead, he scooted lower and deeper into the couch, pulled her closer to him, and stroked the column of her spine.

The rhythmic strokes down her back were heavenly. With each stroke, she was lulled to sleep. Her body sank into his, her eyes fluttered closed, and she was out like a light. There was no need to dream about him since she finally had the reality lying beneath her. For the first time in a week, her dreams were Cole-free.

Cole felt the heaviness of her body and knew she'd fallen asleep. He kissed her forehead and settled in to enjoy the rest of the game. Before long, the game was watching him. A week of sleepless nights and a heavy breakfast combined with having the source of his frustration finally in his arms sent him to dream land.

Hours later, Meme stirred in his arms, stretching and yawning as she sat up. Cole's eyes blinked opened. It took him a second to remember where he was. Their eyes connected and they smiled. Both realized that they'd spent the entire afternoon together and hadn't said a word to each other. Meme whispered through her smile, "Good morning."

Cole caressed her cheek. "Indeed it is good, but more like afternoon."

"Do you need anything? Are you hungry or thirsty?"

His eyes left her face and roamed down her body. There was definitely something he needed. His mouth watered and he licked his lips as his eyes made their way back to hers. Meme shuddered at the desire she saw in them.

*Slow deep breaths, slow deep breaths.* The thumping of her heart rattled her rib cage as she waited for his reply. She wanted him to say *her*. She wanted him to need and want her as much as she wanted him. She hoped he had forgotten about why he had stopped their sexcapade at Marlon's reception. She wanted him to give her what her body craved more than anything. Finally admitting she wanted him unleashed a flood of desire that her denial had been holding back. The flood was so thick, she had to squeeze her thighs together to quell the fire. She couldn't blame this desire on the emotional atmosphere of a wedding, being drunk, or being vulnerable. She wanted this man and wanted him to want her.

"For right now, I'll take some water."

Hiding her disappointment, Meme stood to get his water, only to have him grab her from behind. Pressing his body into her, there was no mistaking his desire. Molding her back against his chest, Cole whispered in her ear, "Think carefully before you ask me that question again, because next time I won't play nice." Need thickened his voice as he pressed further into her.

Feeling bold, Meme turned to meet his lips and whispered into his mouth. "The next time I ask, feel free to get what you really want." She sucked his bottom lip and then rushed off into the kitchen, almost not believing her shamelessness.

Not trusting himself to speak or move, Cole watched her walk away. If Marlon wasn't his friend, he'd have his little sister pressed up against the wall calling on God. Since they were friends, he most definitely had to feel him out before moving any further. Cole slipped his shoes back on and moved toward the front door.

Meme returned with his glass of water as he leaned against the wall. He looked beautifully carved like a sculpted masterpiece. She handed him his water, trying to conceal all traces of disappointment in of her voice. "Are you leaving?"

"Yeah, I should have been at the restaurant thirty minutes ago." He flashed his cell phone at her, so she could see the time. She grabbed it.

Cole watched as she dialed her number from his phone. He wanted to ask for her number, but wasn't too keen on her having his. He took the phone back and went to the placed calls list and saved her number to his contact list. He pulled her close and planted kisses on her cheeks and neck. He didn't trust himself to kiss her lips again.

His tenderness was so unexpected, totally contradicting his six-feet-four muscular physique. Even when being aggressive, his touch was softer than she ever thought a man could give.

Cole grabbed the doorknob and huffed, "Tell that fool you brought to the restaurant the other night that it's over."

Meme shook her head. *That's what this was all about? He's jealous.* "I'm sorry, but I'm a grown woman and am very capable of deciding who to spend time with." She squared her shoulders, crossed her arms over her chest, and matched the intensity in his eyes. "Last I checked, I was a single woman and—"

"Not anymore you're not." Cole couldn't believe what had just spewed out of his mouth, but he didn't back down from it. He could tell it shocked her just as well.

"Well," she stuttered, searching for a comeback, "Whatever you require of me, I require of you. I deserve all of you." That got him to back down. He had never given a woman all of him and wasn't about to start now, no matter how bad he wanted all of her.

"I thought so," Meme's voice cracked as she choked on her disappointment. "Don't ask for anything that you aren't willing to give." She opened the door, silently asking him to leave.

Cole noticed a note taped to her door. He read the brief note. Anger now removed the awkwardness that had developed between them.

"Who wrote that?"

Meme read the single-word note and fear crept up her spine. First her car, then the flowers at her job, and now this. Wayne was right. She needed to call the police. Ignoring Cole's suspicious gaze, she stepped out onto her porch to see if anyone was around, but they were probably long gone. The note could've been left at any time since Cole arrived that morning. Cole asked one more time. This time his voice was more demanding, erasing any possibility of ignoring him.

"Meme, who wrote that?" Meme relayed the events of the two previous incidents. Coles jaw twitched as he spoke.

As his rage rose to surface, his fists clenched so tight that his knuckles cracked. If she hadn't just spent the morning in the soft caress of his arms, she would've been terrified. His expression was lethal; the tone of his two-word response let her know it was not up for discussion.

"Get dressed."

<u>6</u>

**B**y the time they arrived at the restaurant, Meme was pouting. She begged and pleaded for Cole to drop her off at one of her friends' houses, but he outright refused. The car rolled to a stop in front of the restaurant. Meme hopped out and started walking in the opposite direction. She was all for not sitting alone in her apartment all night, but she wasn't going to sit in a restaurant all night either. She didn't make it far before his long strides caught up with her. He grabbed her arm to stop her and she turned on him so fast he barely had time to think. She turned around, ready to give him a piece of her mind. The look on his face smothered her anger. His brows were knitted together and his jaw tight. His hand smoothed over the stubble of his beard as his eyes pleaded for her to stay.

"Just stay for a little while. We can call the police and file a report. I will feel much better about you being alone once the police are notified."

"I won't be alone. I will be with friends."

"You won't be with me, and no one will protect you the way I will."

The sincerity in his voice and his protectiveness touched her deeply. Even the edge of possessiveness in his tone affected her. Meme exhaled and marched into the restaurant with Cole on her heels. Neither of them thought of what their walking into the restaurant together would implicate, but as soon as they ran into Vanessa, the look on her face said it all. First, she looked confused; then, tears welled in her eyes as she looked to Cole for an explanation. Once she put two and two together, her eyes cut toward Meme. If looks killed, Meme would've dropped dead on the spot. Vanessa stomped past them, not even giving them a chance to explain. Why Meme felt the need to apologize, she didn't know. Vanessa clearly had issues, but Meme was unwilling to be on the receiving end of drama.

Once inside Marlon's office, Cole tried to wrap his arms around Meme, but she stepped out of his reach. "Call the police, so I can leave."

*Why in the world is she being so difficult and why do I care?* Cole thought, questioning his reasoning for putting up with her attitude. He was trying to keep her safe, and it seemed the more he tried, the harder she fought. He should've let her leave, but the thought of her out there by herself being stalked by some lunatic didn't sit well with him. He needed her to stay with him for his sanity's sake. He'd lose his mind worrying about where she was. How could he get her to stay without revealing his inherent need to keep her safe? He didn't understand the need himself, so he couldn't expect her to understand it either.

"Look, I know you don't want to be here." He tried touching her again, but once again, she pulled away. Not one for being rejected, Cole slipped his hands into his pocket and allowed his slow, easy stride to carry him across the room. "Marlon will kill me if something happens to you and I knew you were in danger. So please just stay here."

Meme knew she was being difficult, but she needed some distance from him. All the mixed emotions floating around her head needed to be sorted. He was sweet for bringing breakfast, tender when he held her, a jerk for demanding exclusion when he wasn't willing to give it, domineering when he commanded her to get dressed, frustrating for not taking her to a friend's house, and possessive in wanting her to stay with him for protection. Then, the passion in his kiss confused her even more. But, he'd hit the nail on the head. Marlon was her weakness and she didn't want to do anything else to upset him. She tossed her purse onto the couch, plopped down next to it, and slung her feet onto the adjoining pillows.

Two hours later, the police finally dragged themselves into the restaurant and spent all of ten minutes taking Meme's statement. When they were done, she looked at Cole and rolled her eyes. She was even more pissed with him than before.

"Come on, Meme; give me a break. I have absolutely nothing to do with those lazy cops." The only response he received was a stern glare and another eye roll. Cole knew exactly what to do to get through that attitude. She loved to eat and he loved to feed her. *She must do some serious working out in order to eat like that and have a body like that.*

Meme's cell phone rang as she scowled at Cole's retreating back. "Hello?" She answered the phone with all the attitude and frustration she was feeling at the moment.

"Dang girl, what's wrong with you?" April chuckled.

"Nothing. What's up with you?" Meme sat up in a vain attempt to sound friendlier.

"Well, we haven't talked in a while. I was thinking we could work out in the morning."

Meme laughed. "You have got to be kidding me. I could barely walk up the stairs to my apartment the last time."

"I promise to take it easy on you. Besides, Candice is coming and she'll curse me out if I work her too hard."

"What time?"

"6:30."

"You expect me to get up that early on my day off?"

"Well, we have to be at work later." April heard her sigh and knew she was about to decline the offer. "Look, I will bring a DVD. We can work out in your apartment, and then you can go back to sleep."

April held her breath while she waited for Meme to respond. When she grumbled, "all right," April cheered and giggled with excitement.

"Don't get too excited. If you come into my apartment tripping the way you did the other day, I won't be as nice." Meme noticed Cole standing in the doorway with his shoulder leaning against the frame, legs crossed at the ankles, two glasses of wine in his hands. He looked as sexy as ever. Her mouth dried up and her heart skipped a beat. "April, I have to go." Meme sat up on the couch and fumbled with the phone as she tried to end the call.

She almost stopped breathing as he walked toward her. The overwhelming virility of his stride, the heat that radiated from his body when he sat next to her, and the timbre of his voice when he beckoned her to come to him made her dizzy with desire. Meme forced herself to stay put, clutching onto the couch to leverage herself. Giving in to him would be a mistake, but she could feel him sliding toward her. She didn't know how long she could hold out.

"Are you hungry? I made you something to eat, but first, have a glass of wine with me."

He was so close that his heat scorched the right side of her body, but Meme refused to look at him.

"You don't want to be mad at me anymore. I can tell by the pulse in your neck. In fact, it lets me know that you want to be here with me." Cole got up and kneeled in front of her. He filled his mouth with wine and placed his lips on hers to share it with her. Her lips parted and the cool liquid pooled into her mouth, followed by his warm tongue. The sensations were more intoxicating than the wine. She swallowed every drop and suckled his lips for the remnants.

"I much rather have wine with you like this," Cole groaned once she released his lips.

The kiss was the most erotic thing she had ever experienced. She grabbed the glass from his hand and returned the favor. They finished both glasses in the same manner. When the wine was gone, they were both heady with lust. The moans pressed into his mouth were fuel to the fire surging through his veins. His hands sought out the buttons on her shirt.

Meme caught his wrist before he could go too far. "I am still the same woman you turned down last week. You sure you want to do this?"

"You make me forget about all my rules," Cole said, shocked by the little truth that had rolled out of his mouth. He slowly backed up. He ran his hand over his face, trying to wipe away the sexual haze that was making him crazy.

"I'm going to get your food." Not even looking in her direction, he left the room and sent someone else back with her entree.

~

The next morning, Cole was awakened by the sound of Meme's doorbell. The crook in his neck was a culmination to an uncomfortable, restless night on her couch. He was terrified to step a foot back into that office. He had left her alone all night. Cole barely spoke to her on the ride to her apartment, because he knew he couldn't leave her in that apartment alone. But, he didn't think he could maintain the man he was if he stayed the night. When he told her he was staying the night, she put her foot down and all but cursed him out. Her disapproval fell on deaf ears. He stood in her doorway and kissed her until she caved in, and then promised to sleep on the couch.

He had lain on the couch berating himself for putting his hands on her again. He had to be the dumbest man in the world for putting himself in this situation. The decision to take her the next time she offered had already been made. However, when the opportunity arose, he backed down, chickened out, and ran. He was in her apartment. Her scent wafted up his nose, the soft jazz CD she'd put on permeated the atmosphere, and thoughts of her scantily clad body sleeping in the next room ignited his libido. Torture was the only word to describe the night. Karma had finally found him and was using this one woman as vengeance for every woman he'd scorned.

With the doorbell ringing out of control, he cursed with frustration and answered the door. Cole snatched the door open, and growled. "It is way too early for you to be ringing the doorbell like that."

April and Candice jumped at the sight of his muscular frame towering in the doorway. "I'm sorry. Is Meme here?" April stammered as her eyes raked over the gorgeous bare chest in front of her.

Meme must've heard the doorbell or Cole's angry voice, because she appeared behind him. "Come in, you guys." Seeing the suggestive little grin April gave as she passed Cole stirred an emotion Meme didn't have time to analyze. Meme stepped in front of April and gave her a look that said, *Don't even think about it.* Then, she turned to Cole, whispering low enough to be intimate, but loud enough for everyone to hear. "Get in my bed. I will join you when I'm done."

His eyebrows rose in shock, but he didn't question her. He'd seen a woman defending her territory and knew that's exactly what she was doing. He ran his lips down the column of her neck to help drive her point home and to let her know what would be waiting on her when she joined him in bed.

April waited until Cole was in the bedroom and blurted out, "Damn a work out, you need to explain."

Feigning innocence, Meme asked, "Explain what?" She turned away from two sets of interrogating eyes.

"Don't play dumb." April followed behind her demanding answers. "Explain the caramel treat waiting for you in bed. You know and I know that you don't get down like that, so explain."

Meme wanted to bury her face into the pillows and scream. How could she explain what she didn't understand herself? She paused and shrugged her shoulders, speaking the only answer she possessed. "I have no clue what's going on." Meme prepared to give them a short summary of her long week.

"Last Saturday when I ran into you guys outside of Marlon's reception, you had assumed I was leaving because of the tension between me and Marlon. I was running from him." Meme pointed toward the bedroom door, shook her head, and then proceeded to give them the rundown of her scandalous behavior.

*After three glasses of champagne, the tension eased out and the giggles eased in. Meme didn't become loud and obnoxious when drunk; she became giggly and playful. Anything remotely funny would send her into a fit of the giggles, and the man staring at her from across the table was doing exactly that. Meme tried to focus on the best man's toast, but she could feel the man's gaze burning through her. She giggled out loud and was shushed by people at the surrounding tables. Meme grabbed another glass of champagne and tried to drown her laughing out with the bubbly liquid.*

*Meme stole another glance at her admirer, and although she'd just guzzled a glass of champagne, her mouth instantly went dry. His gaze went from flirty to flat-out lust. Meme saw him get up and come toward her, never taking his eyes off her. She racked her brain trying to figure out how to respond, but was still confused by her body's reaction to him. Her eyes bulged as she watched him walk toward her. His six-foot-four muscular body towered over the seated guests at their table. As he approached, Meme tried to swallow the lump in her throat.*

*Meme shook his hand as he introduced himself and quickly turned back to her food, thinking about just ignoring him altogether in the hopes that he would go away. No such luck. Kneeling next to her, he placed his hand on her bare thigh and her traitorous body shook. His hand boldly crept up her thigh, and powerlessly, she allowed him.*

*"You are the most beautiful woman in here."*

*She giggled.*

*His hand crept.*

*She giggled.*

*"I am feeling you and I know you're feeling me."*

*She giggled.*

*"When you're ready to do something about it, I will be sitting right over there."* *His hand caressed the fullness of her lips.*

*She stopped giggling and he walked away.*

*Before he made it to his seat, Meme was up from the table and running from the room. After five minutes, she reappeared in the doorway and locked eyes with him; then, shockingly signaled for him to come. She made her way to the bathroom and checked all the stalls to ensure they had complete privacy.*

*She'd walked slowly, hoping he saw where she went, and when he knocked, her heart almost exploded. Slowly, she opened the door and smiled seductively. "The coast is clear," she purred, stepping aside and allowing him to enter. She immediately locked the door behind him. He turned around and Meme slammed her lips on his as if her life depended on it. Their tongues greeted each other and he moaned hello.*

*Lifting her onto the counter, he nuzzled her neck while unzipping her dress. The spaghetti straps slid off her shoulders and the dress fell around her hips. He feasted on her body as if she belonged to him while she moaned in appreciation.*

*Meme saw the foil packet the moment he took it out of his pocket. What she was doing became all too real and she choked.*

*Sensing her apprehension, he asked, "What's wrong?"*

*"I have never done this before."*

*He laughed, but seeing the sincerity in her eyes shocked him.*
*"You're a..."*

Meme *nodded before he could get the word out. "No, don't stop." She felt*
*his retreat and didn't want this newfound passion to end.*

*"I can't do this."*

*"It's okay. I want you too."*

*"I don't do virgins." He adjusted himself and fled the scene.*

"Now, I didn't know who he was until Marlon called on Monday
and asked me to go down to the restaurant."

"Wait a minute. Wait a minute," Candice interrupted. "You're still
a virgin?"

"In the medical sense of the word, yes I'm a virgin. My hymen is
still intact."

"That fine man slept here last night and it's still intact." April
chuckled in disbelief and started collecting her things. "Well, don't let us
stand in your way."

"Wait! It is not that simple." Meme grabbed April's wrist and
forced her to sit. "Like he said, he doesn't do virgins, and I don't do men."

"The simple fact that he is here proves both of you wrong. Now
stop tripping and go get what you know you want." April pulled Meme up
off the couch and pushed her toward the bedroom.

Fighting her off, Meme reclaimed her seat on the couch. "I'm
scared. I think I'm starting to like him." Meme told them about their
interactions since the reception, ending with the wonderful afternoon
they'd spent together before he turned into a jerk.

"That's the problem with women. They always allow their emotions to trip them up. Stop thinking with your heart and sex him out of your system. Then kick him out." That's the philosophy April lived by. It had never steered her wrong.

Candice waved off April's foolish rambling. "You never know what will happen unless you give it a try. Yeah, living like April keeps your heart from being broken, but it also keeps you from finding love. If he says he doesn't do virgins, he knows that hasn't changed about you. But, he keeps coming around. Maybe he likes you, too."

That got Meme's mind to thinking. Seeing the distant look in her eyes was Candice and April's cue to leave. They hugged her goodbye, promised to call later, and then let themselves out.

## 7

**M**eme froze in front of her bedroom door as her emotions waged war with her conscience. The hurt from men in her past battled with the desire for the man in her present. Weighing Candice and April's advice, Meme was confused to the point of tears. Was it fair to make all men pay for what one idiot had done? In doing so, wasn't she actually punishing herself? She'd been having meaningless relationships with women because they were safe. The one woman who had meant something to her should've been the one she avoided at all costs, but she hadn't. Her life was now suffering because of it. She wanted to find love, didn't want to ignore her emotions and sex a man out of her system. How could she find the balance between letting her emotions dominate her life and shutting them out completely?

She was certain about her feelings for Cole. There was only one way to find out if he liked her, too; she was going to outright ask him. Meme inhaled, seeking deep within to find the courage to move forward with Cole or end it all. Meme slowly opened her bedroom door. She stepped inside and Cole stepped out of her adjoined bathroom with a towel wrapped around his waist. His bare chest glistened with water from the shower he'd just taken. A cloud of steam hovered behind his head and her toothbrush hung out of his mouth.

Meme marched up to him and snatched her toothbrush. "We need to talk." She disregarded the apprehension that flashed across his face as she sat on the bed.

Silence enveloped the room as Meme collected her thoughts. No matter what his response, she would accept it and they would move forward—together or separately. "I am having a hard time figuring out what you want from me. If it was sex you could've already had that." She giggled awkwardly and continued. "Yesterday was sweet. You held me and it felt good. Then, you demand I see no one but you, yet you aren't willing to do the same. So my question is: what is going on with us?"

As that million-dollar question rolled off her tongue, Cole wanted to retreat to safety. He couldn't even look at her, let alone answer. *Be honest*, he told himself, but couldn't get the words to formulate. The silence lingered on and there was nothing he could do about it. His tongue refused to form words.

"Look, I'm not asking for your hand in marriage, not asking you to move in, not even asking for us to be a couple. I just want a little honesty, so that we can be on the same page."

"I thought…," he stammered as he chose his words carefully. "We were getting to know each other."

"I can accept that. Just so you know, what I see so far, I like." Meme ran her hand down the side of his face trying to get him to make eye contact.

With the slightest glance in her direction, Cole replied, "Me too." He held his breath, hoping the conversation was over. He was all for sexing a woman senseless, but when it came to having feelings for one and admitting those feelings, he was inexperienced. He exhaled when Meme stood and walked around to the other side of the bed.

Meme laughed as she watched his tense shoulders relax. "Oh God, was it that hard for you?"

"What?" He asked, tensing up again.

"Discussing your feelings," Meme laughed. "Oh forget it, for now. Come over here and hold me while I go to sleep."

She climbed under the covers and Cole sat at the edge of the bed staring at her. Cuddling on the couch while watching TV was one thing, but getting into the bed with her and spooning was another. "I don't do the cuddling thing." Cole stood to return to the bathroom and get dressed, but Meme's sexy little voice halted him.

"Just like you don't do virgins?" Meme slinked across the bed on her hands and knees. Gripping his shoulders she turned him around. "Well, I hate to inform you that one day real soon you're going to do this virgin. Just like you're going to get in this bed and hold me." She took his hand and placed it over her heart and covered his hand with hers. "What I feel in here is new and unlike anything I've ever felt. If you don't feel this chemistry, let me know and I'll back off." She searched his eyes to gauge his true feelings.

Cole's throat was thick with an emotion he couldn't describe. No longer trusting his voice, he simply lowered his forehead to hers.

Meme smiled. *Progress.* "Let's not treat each other the way we have treated relationships in the past. I don't know what woman hurt you to make you have all these rules, but don't make me pay for her mistakes."

Cole watched her crawl back across the bed and get back under the cover. She scooted over, leaving a spot for him and patted the mattress for him to come to her. Step by step, he inched his way over to her. When he was close enough she grabbed his hand and pulled him toward her. She exhaled when his warm muscular frame melded against her backside.

There were at least ten things he wanted to do to her, but for the life of him, he couldn't make the first move.

"How is it that you're still a virgin?" He heard himself say. He rolled his eyes at his idiocy.

That subject was off limits. Meme stiffened and tried to move away from him, but he stopped her.

"Don't push me away. Remember, we're not repeating past mistakes. Now talk to me."

The compassion in his voice made her open up like never before, telling him things she'd only shared with a few people. "Like my brother, I used to be really into the church. I was saving myself for marriage. After high school, I started dating this guy from our church. He was a few years older than me, but that didn't matter to me. He had just begun the minister training classes. Everybody said he was so anointed that he must be called to be a pastor. I thought he was gorgeous and didn't care about some ridiculous call upon his life. Every girl at the church wanted him and he was mine."

Cole jealously rolled his eyes and Meme managed a smile.

"Marlon didn't like him. He wouldn't tell me why, but forbade me to see him, so I hid my relationship and engagement from him and everyone else. To this day, Marlon and my parents don't know anything. Long story short, our relationship was perfect, we dated for a few years, were engaged to be married, and we were going to live happily ever after, or so I thought.

"A week before we were going to tie the knot at the courthouse, he gave me a key to start moving my things into his apartment. I often wonder how things would have played out if I had called first or even knocked before using the key, but I didn't. When I walked into that bedroom and saw my fiancé banging a sister from the church, I almost passed out. My stomach flipped and the room started to spin. But that wasn't even the worst of what happened.

"As I tried to get my bearings, I must have knocked something off the dresser because they finally noticed me standing there. He walked over to me like everything was okay. He acted like they'd been caught baking cookies instead of having sex. He said, 'Don't worry. I am done with her once we get married. You had your principles and I had my manly needs, but once we start making love I'll have no need for her.' He tried to kiss me and I lost it. I told him to get his hands off of me and to never touch me again. I broke up with him and tried to march out." Meme's voice cracked as she recalled the events that happened next.

"He grabbed a fist full of my hair and pulled me back to him. I looked into his eyes to beg him to let me go, but I didn't see the man I loved. I saw a monster. His face was so close to mine that I could feel his lips move when he talked. 'This is your fault,' he told me. 'You have been holding out on me for years and when I find someone to take care of my needs, you want to get upset and leave. You aren't leaving, at least not until I get what I've been waiting for all these years.' He threw me on the ground and started ripping off my clothes.

"I fought him off. Maybe I should have laid there and let him get what he wanted, but I fought back. He fought me like I was a man. Then out of the blue, the woman he was banging jumped in to save me. She grabbed him by the face, pulling him off of me, and then she sprayed him with mace. I ran out of there and never looked back. It took a while for me to get over it and when I did, I swore off men for good."

Meme looked into Cole's eyes. "For the past few years I've been a lesbian."

Cole's eyes widened as his mind replayed what she said. His grip on her loosened and the hand that stroked her back stopped. He wiped the tears from her cheeks as he continued to study her face. No matter how much she claimed to be over it, he could see the pain that still lingered. "You dated women because you thought they were safe?"

Meme cried even harder. *Is it possible that he understands and is not judging me?* "Yes, I didn't want to be alone and was terrified of being hurt, physically or emotionally."

"What's his name?"

"I can't tell you."

"Why?"

"The look in your eyes is the same reason I never told Marlon. I don't want you going to jail trying to defend me."

"Do you think he might be the one who put the note on the door?"

That had never crossed her mind. Why would he even bother? He'd gotten away scot-free with assault and fornication. Last she heard, he was still ministering at her old church. Why would he risk everything just to mess with her? "I don't think he would bother."

"What's his name and where can I find him?"

"Cole..."

"It's not up for discussion. What is his name and where can I find him?"

After making him promise not to tell Marlon, she gave him the information he requested. She then relaxed in the warmth and healing that his arms offered.

Cole held her tight. His body was a tornado of emotions. This woman evoked feelings that were foreign to him. The tears flowing down her cheeks as she told her story had tugged at his heart. Hearing about her emotional pain made him want to protect her from the world. Hearing about her physical assault angered him. That anger was now the driving force behind the whirlwind that was raging within him. Damien Henderson would definitely be hearing from Cole Monroe.

"Promise me you won't hurt him," Meme pleaded.

Cole looked into her eyes and kissed her deeply, but never responded. His kiss spoke his thoughts. She was his. Whether it was past or future, anyone would pay for hurting her. He didn't understand it and couldn't begin to explain, but she brought out the innate protector in him. She melted beneath his touch and they bathed in their chemistry for a moment before he pulled back. He had to be careful. He could so easily get caught up in her. Her aura of innocence could prove to be deadly.

They'd had a late night, and thanks to April and Candice, an early morning. Falling back to sleep took little effort, especially entangled in each other's arms. They slept well into the afternoon. The heat and light of the midday sun beamed through the window. Cole knew he needed to head home and get ready for work, but it was the hardest thing he'd ever had to do. For the life of him, he couldn't remember the last time he'd ever slept so soundly. Slim limbs and soft skin brushed across his bare chest. It was the best feeling in the world. If he'd known having a woman sleep in his bed would've been this comfortable, he would've done it a long time ago. He highly doubted that any other woman would do though. He opened his eyes, rolled over, and caressed Meme's sleeping face. *It has to be her.*

Meme's eyes fluttered open, and her first sight was the gorgeous face of this Adonis whose gentleness and presence in her bed were equal shockers. She smiled sheepishly and lowered her eyes to avoid his intense gaze. Cole tipped her head back with a slight press of his fingers to her chin. He brushed his lips across hers, partly out of need, but mainly in thanks for helping him get some much needed rest.

"I have to go to work," he finally spoke after moments of simply staring into her eyes and stroking her cheek. "I don't feel comfortable leaving you alone."

Meme could've stayed there all day and hid the pout threatening to mar her face. "I can go to a friend's."

"Good, get dressed."

Meme showered and dressed in no time. She was tempted to throw some jeans and a t-shirt on, but she wanted to make Cole drool. When she stepped out of the room, he did just that. She didn't know if the sound that came out of his mouth was a word, grunt, growl, or a moan. Meme smiled, satisfied. She strutted around her living room collecting her purse and car keys, seemingly oblivious to his eyes traipsing across her body, but she felt every glance. His gaze was so intense that it burned through her clothes, almost searing her flesh. Every sound he made in appreciation of her body made the hairs on the back of her neck stand on end.

"Okay, grab your stuff." She paused to clear the wispiness from her voice, "So I can lock up behind you."

Cole arose from the couch and stalked toward her. He grabbed the keys from her hand as he slid his lips down her neck and back up. His mouth opened and her knees buckled in anticipation of what he was going to do. The words that came out of his mouth heated her, but it was a different type of heat all together.

"I hope you don't think I'm letting you drive to your friends."

Meme snapped out of his embrace so quickly that she stepped on his foot in the process. Cole groaned and bit down on his lower lip to hold back the explicative on the tip of his tongue. They weren't little girl heels. They were made for seduction and Meme knew he had to be in pain, but she couldn't care less. "What do you mean let me drive?"

"I'm dropping you off and picking you up, end of discussion. Let's go." He turned his back her and marched to the door as if she was going to follow like a good little girl. He was sadly mistaken. He opened the front door and Meme snuck up behind him so quickly he didn't see her coming. She squeezed passed him, snatched the key out of his hand, and ran to her car as fast as her heels would carry her.

Cole locked her apartment up and chased after her. If he wasn't so pissed, he would've laughed. Her dainty little steps were no match for his long strides and he caught her in seconds. She squealed and tried to increase her pace as she heard him approaching. She clutched her keys tighter, assuming that was what he was coming after. Cole was pissed. He didn't have time for the games. He grabbed her by the waist, spun her around, and lifted her over his shoulder. She squirmed, yelled, tried to buck off his shoulder, and called him everything but a child of God. He was relentless.

By the time they arrived at the car, he'd had enough. He placed her on her feet and kissed some sense into her. "Now get into the car." He growled through panting breaths that had nothing to do with the exertion from carrying her and everything to do with his lust for her. "If you even think about getting out when I walk away, I will not be this nice." He kissed her with all his frustration, and when she melted against him, he knew she'd behave.

*This woman is going to drive me crazy,* Cole thought as he pulled away from Meme's friend's house. He refused to entertain the thought that he was being irrational. Hearing about Damien had made him even more worried about her safety. Hopefully, whoever was sending the notes was just trying to scare her, but he wasn't taking any chances.

~

Meme could feel the depression as she walked into Wayne's house. The melancholy music, the bottle and glass of Jack Daniels on the coffee table, and Wayne's red puffy eyes created the atmosphere. Wayne grabbed his glass, swirled the brown liquid around, and downed it in one gulp.

"Oh honey, have you talked to him?" Meme pulled him down to the sofa and wrapped her arms around him.

"Nope."

"Did you at least call him?"

"He didn't answer. I am trying to move on, but this hurts."

Meme laid his head in her lap and let him cry his heart out. She stroked his head, giving him the physical comfort he needed. "I don't think you should move on. I think you should give him time. That man loves you. I bet he is just as miserable as you." To prove her point, Meme pulled out her cell phone and called him.

The voice that answered was rough, raspy, and so unfamiliar that Meme had to check the phone to make sure she dialed the right number. "Kevin?" She felt Wayne stiffen at the sound of that name.

"Yeah, what's up Meme?"

"Why are you torturing yourself?" She could hear the pain in his voice and pictured him in the same state as Wayne. "This is pain neither of you have to experience if you'd just get over here."

"I can't." His words slurred. She knew he'd had a bit more to drink than Wayne. "I can't give him what he wants and deserves. He will find someone who will love him the way I couldn't."

"You don't believe that and neither do I. The chemistry you guys have isn't something you find every day. If you don't come to your senses, you will hurt him more than not being able to go public with your relationship ever did."

"I hear you, but think about this. We will never be able to go anywhere together without you pretending to be my girl. We can never move in together. Wayne wants us to adopt a child. How can I be in a child's life when I am pretending not to be in love with its father? We can't take family trips or go to the zoo. Our relationship can't go any further than the four walls of his house. Is that the life you want for your friend?"

*Dang, he has a point.*

"In the end, he will just wind up resenting me for causing him to miss out on life."

The volume on Meme's phone was loud enough for Wayne to hear every word. Reaching between her ear and the phone, Wayne pressed the end button. "It's over. Just help me get past the pain."

Meme went into the kitchen and brought back a gallon of ice cream and two spoons. "This has gotten me through some of the roughest times of my life."

"Unless you plan on mixing that ice cream with this bottle of Jack, it ain't going to work for me."

Meme stared at the ice cream and then at the bottle on the table. Smiling, she took them both into the kitchen and proceeded to make a Jack Daniels float.

Hours later, Wayne had gone from a depressed heartbroken man to Wanda, a drag queen and lounge singer. That Jack was surging through his veins as he stood in his living room decked out from head to toe in full diva mode. Meme could barely stand on her feet as they performed for their imaginary audience. The sad music from before was gone. They were now giving a concert from the radio station's greatest hits. With boas around their necks, wigs on their heads, and make-up caked on so thick you could peel it off, they sang their hearts out. Meme stumbled over her own feet as she tried to dance. She did more giggling and stumbling than she did singing.

Her phone rang. She fumbled in her purse to get it, and answered with a giggle.

With that laugh, Cole knew exactly what was up. She was drunk. "Are you ready to go home?"

Meme smiled. "Hi baby, are you working hard?"

His heart thumped at the endearment she used and warning sirens blared in his head. "I am outside are you ready to go?"

"Hold on a second. Wayne?" Meme tried to yell over the music

*Wayne? Who the hell is Wayne?* Cole could hear her talking to someone in the room. She said it was a friend's house when he dropped her off, but he didn't bother to ask what type of friend. Cole was all set to get out the car and wreck shop when the music in the background turned off. He could hear her sexy sweet intoxicated voice clearly and he smiled at her words.

"My baby is here to pick me up. Are you going to be okay?"

A few minutes later, she came stumbling out of the house, dragging her purse on the ground. Those shoes that had accentuated every curve of her body and left Cole in the car drooling when he dropped her off were now tripping her up with each step. Finally tired of stumbling, Meme tossed her purse in the grass and sat down next to it. She was fumbling with the buckle on her shoe when Cole decided to stop laughing and come to her rescue.

"Hi baby." Meme smiled so brightly that it lit up every dark place in his heart.

Cole effortlessly stooped and lifted her one-hundred-twenty-five-pound frame off the ground. He carried her to the car and buckled her in. She laughed the entire time. The interior light of the car illuminated her face. Cole saw the excessive make-up and wondered what in the world she and Wayne had been up to.

By the time he'd driven down the street, Meme was asleep. He carried her to her apartment, took her into the bathroom to wash her face, took off her shoes and pants, and helped her into bed. He had already planned to spend the night with her and was headed back down to the car to get the bag he had packed earlier. She whispered and he went back to the side of the bed. He should have kept going, but he didn't. What she said to him next almost stopped his heart.

"I love you," she snickered and then said it again.

Cole slowly backed away, trying to convince himself that she was drunk and not thinking straight. How on earth could those words even be in her vocabulary? He reflected over the past few days, searching for something he might've done to make her think that love was what he wanted. He'd done a lot, starting with the night he brought her home from the restaurant, to the day he brought her breakfast, and spending the night last night. They had promised not to make the same mistakes they'd made with past relationships. She was still in danger, but self-preservation was a hard thing to beat. Instead of getting his bag out the car, Cole started the engine and drove home.

## <u>8</u>

**M**eme woke up the next morning in her own bed, but couldn't remember how she got there. She assumed Cole had brought her home since that was the plan, but couldn't remember a thing. She called him to thank him, but he didn't answer. She waited all day for him to call back, but he didn't. She worked through her hangover, trying not to read too much into his silence.

The next day, again, he didn't respond. By the morning of the third day, she told herself she was done. The ball was in his court. She worked through her clients, went home, and waited. He didn't come by, call, text, or anything. By the time Saturday arrived, she was ready to end the week in the same drunken stupor in which it'd started. She'd gotten another note that had scared her to death. *Where is your boy toy, slut?* She took it down to the police station and they pretty much blew her off again. Now, all she wanted to do was forget.

It was a well-known fact that Meme couldn't hold her liquor well. That's why she never drank when she went out with Wayne or her girls. Normally, she was the designated driver, but this night she let it be known that she needed to drown her sorrows in a bottle; someone else would have to drive. By the time they arrived at Golden Stone, the club was already jumping. She had a couple glasses of wine before leaving the house and was feeling real nice. Meme wasted no time. She bought the first round of drinks and downed them so fast her throat almost caught fire. Wincing from the burn, she grabbed Sahara's hand and led her to the dance floor. She had promised her a dance for agreeing to be the designated driver.

Sahara didn't waste a second of finally having Meme in her arms. Her lips found Meme's and kissed her like she'd been doing it all her life. Meme started to protest, but changed her mind. *If you can't be with the one you want, then be with the one who wants you.* Trying to ignore the lack of heated yearning that rose when her lips met Cole's, Meme relaxed, allowing Sahara to get what she needed. Sahara felt way more from the kiss than Meme had. Her eyes were glossed with desire and her chest heaved with each inhale and exhale as she tried to regulate her breathing. Meme simply started swaying her body to the music. Sahara's kiss had nothing on Cole's, but it would have to do for now.

Kanani walked in and saw Sahara and Meme all hugged up on the dance floor. She almost lost her mind. "What's up with that?" She yelled over the music to their group of friends sitting around the table.

"Relax, Meme is drunk. It doesn't mean anything," one of them replied.

"Really?" Kanani's eyes widened in shock and her mind started plotting. She'd wanted to get Meme into bed for a while now and this might just be her opportunity. Wayne wasn't there to protect her and she'd actually gotten drunk.

Apparently sensing where Kanani's mind was headed, someone else pleaded, "Please don't take advantage of her."

"Why not? Sahara is going to. If anybody gets her tonight, it should be me."

"Listen to you. She is not an object or possession. She's our friend. And if you really want her, don't you want her sober? If you get her tonight, she won't remember a thing in the morning. She'll wake up with you in her bed, and she will hate you for taking advantage of her."

Conceding her point, Kanani plopped down at the table. It was going to be a long night if she had to sit around and watch Sahara pawing all over Meme across the dance floor. Kanani wasn't one to dwell on one woman for too long, so she moved on to the next piece. It wasn't like she had feelings for Meme. She just wanted to tap it and keep it moving. She looked around the table for someone to warm her bed. At each face she thought, *been there, done that, and bought the t-shirt*. She wanted something new, hence her fixation with getting Meme into bed.

Kanani watched Meme and Sahara dance for all of five minutes and made up her mind. If she couldn't have Meme, Sahara couldn't either. She was out of her seat and on the dance floor before anyone could stop her. Forget protocol, tapping on the shoulder and saying excuse me. Kanani wedged her way in between Meme and Sahara without so much as a look in Sahara's direction.

"Hey, when did you get here?" Meme smiled, hugging her tighter than she ever had. Kanani took advantage of the hug by wrapping her arms around Meme's waist, lifting her off the ground, carrying her to another

90

part of the dance floor, and leaving Sahara standing there with her mouth hanging open.

The aggressive roughness of Kanani's touch was a pleasant change. Get that soft, caressing mess that Sahara was offering out of here. If it had been a week ago, softness would've been right up Meme's alley, but after Cole, a rough caress was what she craved. Kanani wasn't close to the real deal, but she was a better substitute.

Sahara was livid. She guzzled a drink sitting on the table that wasn't even hers. She sat back and watched Meme. Kanani was going to pay for messing up her chance to be with the woman she'd been pining after for months. She slammed the empty glass down on the table so hard it shattered. The fragments of glass pierced her hand. Blood was dripping on the table, but she didn't notice. Nor did she notice the stunned faces watching her homicidal expression. Adrenaline and the fire of vengeance pumped through her veins, blocking out the pain.

The only reason Sahara had agreed to be the designated driver was it meant, for once, Meme would be drunk and out of control; her defenses would be down and her over-protective, wannabe daddy, Wayne, would be out of the picture.

"You all right?" Someone at the table tried to caress Sahara's shoulder and help her calm down, but she swatted the hand away. The table erupted in laughter which only heightened her volatility. "Look at you all pissed because Kanani outplayed you. You shouldn't have been trying to take advantage of that girl while she's drunk anyway."

"That's funny, because you sure don't have a problem with Kanani doing it." Sahara's fist clenched as she turned back toward the dance floor, her eyes searching for Meme.

"That's not going to happen. Kanani likes to put notches in her belt, but she also wants the woman to remember how good she is. Meaning, as long as Meme is drunk, Kanani won't go there. You, on the other hand, are obsessed with Meme and will take her any way you can get her."

That pushed Sahara over the edge. Grabbing a shard of broken glass off the table, she jumped up into the woman's face, holding the glass to her neck. Everyone at the table moved quickly. Sahara was quicker. They tried to grab her, but she had already kicked the woman's feet from under her and was taking her down to the ground before they could get a good grip on her. The group was finally able to grab Sahara before she could do any damage. She squirmed for freedom, but even with adrenaline pumping, she was no match for the four women holding her.

Seeing the commotion, Kanani and Meme ran over. "What happened?" Meme looked around at all the sweaty faces, her friend getting up off the floor, Sahara being restrained, and drew her own conclusion.

"This heifer done lost it," someone announced while prying the glass from Sahara's hand. "Get out of here before you get hurt." They released her, pushing her toward the exit.

Sahara desperately looked back at Meme as she headed for the exit. The group huddled around the woman Sahara was about to cut, comforting and caressing her. Not once did Meme look Sahara's way. As the pain in Sahara's hand increased, she grabbed it and exited the club like a sad dog with her tail tucked between her legs.

~

Cole was relieved to leave Pavoli's on Saturday after his night shift. Marlon would be back tomorrow from his two-week honeymoon. At the beginning of the two weeks, Cole was all for Marlon getting a break and enjoying his lady. They had both been through so much over the past nine months that they needed to get away, but toward the end he wanted to kick himself for insisting Marlon take two weeks. Who needed a two-week honeymoon anyway?

It had already been agreed that Cole was taking Sunday off. From beginning to end, he planned to spend it in bed. He didn't even plan on getting out the bed to eat.

He wanted Meme to be in bed with him, but he trampled that need under his feet like he'd been doing all week. Ignoring her phone calls and deleting her messages hadn't worked to get her out of his system. Hitting the gym hard didn't expunge her, neither did hitting the bottle. Cold showers couldn't douse his yearning for her. Never before had a woman become so entrenched in his mind that it caused him to lose sleep. That body, her laugh, her voice, her touch, her walk, the way she dressed, and her scent; they all were driving him insane.

Relationships and love just didn't work out for men, except for Marlon and maybe Marlon's cousin, Jaleel. There was also Paul and Tim who were also related to Marlon some kind of way. They all played basketball together once a month. Even though they had a good time, it always seemed like they couldn't wait to get home to their wives. He'd met Marlon's wife, Latrice, and she seemed nice enough. She wasn't controlling and let Marlon live his life. Most importantly, she seemed faithful. Instead of complaining about Marlon's long hours at the restaurant, she'd come down some nights and help out. Not always cooking, but organizing his office, doing inventory, or helping him with paperwork. She was beautiful, and Cole had seen the other chefs checking her out. He'd even checked her out a few times, but she only had eyes for Marlon.

That life seemed fine for Marlon and the others, but most of the men he knew were either being controlled by a woman, played by a woman, or driven crazy by a woman. He wanted no part of it. He'd played nice with Meme because she was his friend's sister—at least that's what he tried to tell himself—and look where it had gotten him. He was getting crazier and crazier by the day. If he didn't do something soon, he was going to be in a padded cell with a jacket making him hug himself.

Cole guzzled down a cold beer, hoping the cold liquid would soothe everything that was ailing him. He planned to get so drunk tonight that he'd have no choice but to sleep. Hopefully, he'd pass out and not wake up until Monday evening in time for work.

He'd downed half the beer in one gulp and seeing that it was the last one, Cole went for the hard stuff. A couple of shots were guaranteed to lay him on his back. Pulling out the crystal bottle, he ran his fingers across the letters etched on the front. Gran Patron Platinum silver tequila; it cost over two hundred bucks a bottle and was worth every penny. Smooth, silky, and would quickly mess you up if you weren't careful. Its taste was so refined that it made you forget you were drinking the hard stuff. Cole knew his limit. He knew exactly how much to pour into the glass to tilt him on his axis. He filled it up to his limit and then gave the bottle another quick dip to his glass for good measure.

Cole's cell phone rang. The name flashing on the caller ID made his stomach turn: *Vanessa.* Any other time, he would've ignored her call like he'd been doing for the past year. Since Marlon was out of town and he was technically in charge, he had to answer to make sure it wasn't restaurant-related.

A year ago, against his better judgment, he'd accepted Vanessa's invite back to her apartment. She was an attractive woman and had caught his eye when she was first hired, but not being one to date coworkers, he left her alone. He'd been doing a good job avoiding her advances, but lost the fight when she cornered him in the pantry at work, unbuckled his pants, and dropped to her knees.

They heard someone coming toward them before they could finish, but the girl had skills. He had to see what else she was working with. She waited for him to finish up at the restaurant and he followed her to her apartment. Not one for playing games or reading more into a situation than there was, Cole was all over her as soon as she shut the door. It was a booty call and nothing more. He thought bending her over her kitchen counter, pleasuring them both, and then walking out would've driven the point home, but apparently it didn't.

The clingy, desperately obsessive phone calls would come at all hours of the day and night. Each time, Cole wanted to kick himself for being so stupid. Despite of his threats to have her fired for harassment, the calls continued. Every call was sent to voicemail. In hindsight, maybe he should've answered and explained that he wasn't feeling her, but he was never one to explain his actions. Her voicemail messages angered him. She whined and ranted about the unspoken promise that intimacy infers, that not answering her calls was breaking that promise, and begged him to give her a chance to make him happy.

Coming to work had become awkward. He avoided her like the plague, but she managed to find him at least once a night. What she couldn't say with words was conveyed in her eyes, and with his eyes, he'd shoot her down. He should've gone to Marlon when the calls first started, but he would've had to admit that he'd crossed the line with her. Although he and Marlon were friends now, they weren't as tight a year ago. Cole feared that in the process of getting Vanessa fired, he'd lose his own job. Therefore, he kept quiet, enduring weeks of harassment, until one day she cornered him in the pantry again. She fumbled with his buckle and he knew if he allowed her to put her mouth on him, her skills would render him unable to resist her. Before she could get the belt unbuckled, he swatted her hands away and pushed her back. He used a little more force than he intended and she tumbled to the ground and hit her hand on one of the racks. Vanessa cradled her hand to her chest, moaning in pain. Cole tried to help her up, but the look she gave him was lethal. The quiet voice in the back of his head that he'd ignored when he went to her house was screaming. He knew it was time to talk to Marlon. There was no doubt she'd have put a spin on the incident and would've had him looking like the bad guy.

Marlon listened to both sides of the story and reprimanded them both for inappropriate conduct in the workplace. He couldn't do anything about how they behaved before and after work. He insisted that if their involvement outside of the restaurant affected their performance inside, they'd both lose their jobs. Hearing the threat of termination come from the person who had authority to do so must've been enough to slap some sense into Vanessa. The phone calls and harassment stopped.

Occasionally, Cole would catch her looking at him with longing in her eyes, but he'd go on about his business.

Days after everything was over with, Marlon called Cole into his office for a little man-to-man conversation. Apparently, an hour after he had left Marlon's office, Vanessa stumbled in crying hysterically, claiming sexual assault. He warned Cole to slow his roll, and that the next time he might be sitting inside a jail cell. The only thing that kept Marlon from involving the police was that he had already noticed Vanessa pushing up on him, recognizing the same tactics she used on him when he first started. Only he wasn't stupid enough to give in to her. Once Marlon calmed her down, he was able to get her to listen to reason. Informing her that Cole had saved the messages she'd left and calling the cops on him might land her in jail as well. She quickly changed her mind. She apologized for wasting his time and promptly left his office.

Plopping down on the couch, Cole answered his phone, "What's up, Vanessa?"

"I just wanted to check on you. You weren't yourself tonight. Are you all right?"

"Yeah, I'm good." Was he that obvious? Could she really tell something was bothering him?

"It's her, isn't it?" Vanessa asked as if she heard his thoughts. "It's Meme. She's the one that has you moping around." She sighed. "Let me ask you this. What does she have that I don't?"

He didn't have an answer, so he hung up the phone. He didn't understand it himself. Even if he did, he wouldn't bother explaining it to Vanessa. Determined to unwind, Cole guzzled his drink.

The Patron had its desired affect and Cole didn't wake up until two o'clock the next day. The sun was shining, the birds were chirping, his head was pounding, and the chaotic turmoil of emotions he was trying to escape was right there to greet him when he rolled over and opened his eyes.

## 2

Staring up at the ceiling, willing his hangover to go away, Cole swore he was throwing that bottle of Patron out. The word headache was an understatement. The throbbing swelling pain made it feel like his head would rupture if he moved it. His parched cotton mouth begged for some fluid, but the heaviness of his head prevented him from getting up. The sweat-slicked clothes he slept in clung to his body. He had one shoe on, one off, and for the life of him, he couldn't remember how he'd gotten in bed.

He was by no means a punk. He could hold his liquor with the best of them. But for some reason, last night's dose was hitting him harder than usual. Maybe it was fermented or something. It had been sitting in the cabinet for a few months, but it tasted fine. *Maybe I got up and took another shot.* That was a possibility, seeing as he couldn't remember something as simple as climbing into bed.

Cole managed to roll the rest of his body over and the movement made his stomach lurch. There was an uneaten hamburger on the nightstand and the sight of it made his stomach tilt a little more. *Where did that come from?* The smell of onions sent him scrambling out of bed for the toilet. Making it to the bathroom just in time, Cole hugged the toilet bowl while his stomach released what seemed like everything he'd eaten for a week.

As soon as he was able to stand, Cole searched for the Tylenol. He swallowed two capsules with a handful of water from the bathroom sink. With slow, measured steps he made his way to the kitchen. What he saw churned his stomach and almost sent him back to the bathroom. Raw, ground beef was smeared all over the counter. Chopped onions were strewn about, sliced tomatoes were on the floor, and just about every seasoning and spice he owned was lined up on the counter. If he put all that into his burger, it's a good thing he didn't eat it. In addition to the normal burger seasonings, there was cinnamon, oregano, sage, and the weirdest of all, sugar. *Who gets drunk and decides to cook?* Fortunately, he had sense enough not to drive to get some food.

Walking further into the kitchen to clean his mess, Cole stopped mid-stride. Suddenly everything made sense. Sitting right next to the stove was the empty bottle of Patron. When he brought it out the cabinet last night, it wasn't full. After he poured his glass, it sure wasn't empty either. He must've been cooking and sipping. That empty bottle explained why his head felt like someone blew a hole in it. It explained why he slept until two in the afternoon, and it also explained the half-naked woman that just walked out of the bathroom.

"Janine?"

"Good morning," she laughed as she planted a kiss on his cheek. "From the look on your face I can tell you don't remember inviting me over last night."

"Sorry." He held up the bottle of Patron and tried to explain, but she stopped him.

"It's okay. When you called, I kind of figured you were a little toasted. But a girl can hope, can't she?"

Cole wanted to kick himself. He didn't like misleading women, especially this one. Janine was the closest he'd ever come to a real relationship. He didn't love her, and she knew that, but he cared about her. They'd helped each other through one of the worst times of their lives. The first time they'd slept together it was for comfort, but it was good, so they did it a few more times until she decided she wanted more. "Did we—"

Her finger to his lips silenced him. "It was obvious that I wasn't the one you wanted. I would've loved to make love to you, but you kept calling me Meme. As much as I want to be with you, I'm not down for being a substitute. She must really be something to have you twisted in knots. If she is the one your heart wants, don't try to replace her with meaningless sex."

Cole started to interject that sex with her wasn't meaningless, but thought better of it. He had never lied to her about where she stood with him and wasn't about to start now. Sure he enjoyed her company, but when it came down to it, sex with her was just that.

"Stop being scared and just be with her. I know you're scared to get your heart broken, but if it happens, hearts do mend." Caressing his cheek, Janine softly kissed his lips and then turned to the mess in the kitchen. "Now, help me clean this mess you made."

They laughed and talked as they cleaned the kitchen. Janine did most of the cleaning, because Cole's head started pounding every time he moved. She also did most of the laughing as she explained why the kitchen was a mess. Apparently, he was trying to be the gracious host and make her something to eat. When she saw everything he put into it, she refused to eat. He, on the other hand, ate every last bit of his burger. As for the bottle of Patron, they had a couple of shots together, and the rest was poured into that crazy concoction he called the tonic burger. She laughed at how he was all in chef mode explaining his every step like he was doing a cooking show. She was laughing so hard by the time she was done telling the story that he was laughing too.

Janine dressed, they said their goodbyes, she admonished him again to follow his heart, and she left. Cole was alone in his apartment with Janine's words echoing in his mind. Was Meme what his heart wanted? Was that why he couldn't forget about her? How could his heart want someone he barely knew? Yes, he was attracted to her. He could even admit that the attraction was a little more than sexual. He was too old not to know the difference between lust and adoration. Up until this point, Meme had just been a woman he wanted to have sex with. But because of his foolish, self-imposed rules, he couldn't. Plus, she was a friend's sister. At least that's what he'd been telling himself since he left her apartment last week. Truth be told, he liked Meme. Images of her smiling at him and her intoxicated giggle flashed across his mind. He liked her a lot and was clueless as to what to do about it. He didn't want love or a relationship, but he wanted to spend time with her. Was that fair to her, for him to occupy her time and not give her what she wanted? No it wasn't. So regardless of what Janine said, Meme was still off limits.

The alarm on his phone went off, reminding him that he had an appointment to meet with Damien Henderson at two o'clock. Cole had dodged the man's invitation to church and requested to meet him after service. They agreed to meet at a family-owned fish joint that was right up the street from the church in Spring Valley. He hadn't been to church since he was a child and wasn't about to start now. The brother probably thought he was a lost soul seeking redemption and was ready and willing to lead him to Christ. Unbeknownst to Damien, one wrong answer to Cole's questions would immediately put his life in danger.

When he set up the meeting, he tried not to overanalyze why he still felt the need to protect Meme. The notes she'd received had been on his mind every day. The messages she'd left him said nothing about more notes. That gave him a sense of peace, but he was still a little uneasy. A man who could assault a woman once would more than likely do it again. That thought alone made Cole want to choke Damien just for good measure. If he wasn't after Meme, then he was more than likely putting his hands on whatever woman he was seeing.

In spite of his headache, Cole showered and headed to the restaurant. Walking in, Cole approached the only other diners. His massive frame donned in low-hung jeans, a black, hooded sweatshirt, and a black San Diego Padres hat tilted to the side was intimidating. Combined with the slow pimp in his stride, he looked like a prime candidate for criminal activity instead of the gourmet chef that he was.

A man and woman sat off to the left side near the window. They noticed him as he approached and stood to shake his hand. "Are you Cole?"

"Yeah," Cole nodded trying to decide if he was going to accept the offered hand or punch Damien in the mouth. The desire to do such had been building up the whole ride over. Since they were in public, Cole shook his hand and took a seat. Sliding his hands into the front pocket on his sweatshirt to ensure things didn't get physical, Cole took a moment to size Damien up. In the height department, he had Damien by at least a good five inches. They both looked as if they hit the gym on the regular, but Cole surmised that underneath that muscular physique was a pretty boy punk who liked to emasculate women and couldn't hold his own against a real man. That revelation put a smile on Cole's face as he proceeded with the conversation.

"We have a mutual acquaintance that I want to discuss. You might want to excuse your lady friend, so we can talk man to man."

Damien declined the offer. Clearly, the pissing contest had begun and he wasn't going to take another man's advice on what to do with his woman. Cole's little perusal set the tone for the meeting. It wasn't a friendly social call or request for spiritual counsel. He didn't care how tall or ruthless looking Cole was, he was going to stand his ground.

"Suit yourself. Do you remember a woman named Meme?"

That cocky smirk slid off Damien's face and the color drained from his cheeks as he nodded.

"Well, the other day she told me the most interesting story." Cole watched him nervously swallow. Surely, Damien wanted to excuse his lady now, but he couldn't back down. "She tells me that you were her

104

fiancé and just weeks before the wedding she caught you getting your rocks off with another woman."

Before he could finish the sentence, Damien was shaking his head in denial. "That bit—"

Cole had Damien by the collar and was dragging him out of the restaurant before he could finish the word. "Go ahead and disrespect her. It will be the last coherent word you utter for the rest of your life." Cole sneered into the man's face. The pissing contest was over and Damien might have pissed in his pants.

"Look man," Damien stuttered, tossing his hands up and pleading for understanding. "I was under a lot of pressure back then. I was trying to live up to everyone's expectations. Melanie was my heart, but I needed to relieve a little stress. She refused to give me what I needed."

"Please spare me the details on why you broke her heart." Cole tightened his grip on Damien's collar. "What I'm interested in is why you put your hands on her when she caught you." His grip was so tight, tiny beads of sweat lined Damien's brow. His eyes bulged as he gasped for air, his knees buckled, and the woman they left sitting at the table came running out. The fear in her eyes caused Cole to loosen his grip.

Coughing and gagging as he attempted to get his breathing under control, Damien begged for mercy. "I'm sorry, but like I said I was under a lot of pressure. When I turned around and saw her standing in the room, I didn't know what to do. I tried to explain. I tried to comfort her, but she was hysterical. Then, she called the wedding off and I snapped. All the pressure tumbled down and I lost it."

Cole had no sympathy, "Well, maybe the pressure is building again because someone has been sending her harassing notes. And you know what? I think it's you." The bulging vein on his temple throbbed as he readjusted his hands on Damien's collar.

"Why would I do that?" Damien was stuttering and shaking so bad it looked like he was on the verge of passing out. "I should be in jail right now for what I did to her. Why would I risk that?"

He did have a point, but Cole wasn't giving in that easily. "Like I said, maybe the pressure is building up again or maybe you're just plain crazy."

"My life is finally on the right track. I just got married, and for once I am living for me, not to please others. I don't know who is harassing Melanie, but it is not me," Damien pleaded one more time and Cole let him go. He dropped to the ground and immediately his wife was at his side. He'd definitely be spending the night explaining that story to his wife.

Hovering over him, Cole suppressed the urge to kick him in the gut. He could hear sirens in the distance. Surely someone in the restaurant called the cops. That's probably what took his wife so long to come outside. "I hope we are not going to have a problem with the cops."

Damien shook his head and Cole turned to leave.

"And stop calling her Melanie." Cole didn't know what bothered him more, Damien saying her name like it was his own personal name for her or the fact that he hadn't known what her real name was.

Cole walked to his car. He wasn't worried about the cops. Damien wasn't crazy. He knew what he'd done to Meme outweighed what Cole had done to him, and if he talked to the cops, Cole would have his own story to tell. That jail time he'd feared over the past few years would become reality. Once inside his car, Cole exhaled deeply, drove out of the parking lot, and pulled out his cell phone.

~

Looking down at the caller ID, the name glaring back at Meme clogged her throat. When she answered, all she could manage to say was, "Hi." She would've loved for her voice to not sound so wispy and awestruck, but she did her best.

That one word washed over him like the morning rays of sun and instantly, he knew he should have sent a text instead of called. "I just met with Damien Henderson."

That put a smile on her face. All week she had feared that what they shared last weekend was only special to her. She thought once he left her apartment he had forgotten all about her. But, he was still trying to figure out who was harassing her. As he continued to talk, the deep timbre of his voice melted over her like butter over hot pancakes. It oozed all down her sides and seeped inside her. She almost moaned out loud, but caught it before it parted her lips. She then forced herself to focus.

Cole relayed everything that went down, and by the time he finished, Meme was almost in tears. After all these years, Damien had finally been confronted on what he'd done. Questions regarding his true feelings for her and the person he really was had been answered. A huge weight was lifted. After she reprimanded Cole for putting himself at risk for arrest, she thanked him.

After a brief pause, Cole asked, "When were you going to tell me that your name is Melanie? He kept saying your name like…" He growled out his frustration and refused to finish his thought.

"Did you give us enough time to find out all there is to know about each other?" She let that question hang out there.

Silence settled in on their conversation and she knew he was getting ready to end the call. She finally had him on the phone and was not about to let him off the hook that easy. "Cole, what happened? I thought we were trying to get to know each other. If you decided you were no longer interested, that's your decision to make, but I think I at least deserve an explanation."

"I'm sorry. I just can't give you what you want. You deserve more than what I can give."

"Please," Meme huffed so heavily into the phone he practically felt it through the receiver. "Spare me your version of the, *it's not you it's me* speech."

"I can't love you the way you need to be loved." His tone pleaded for understanding.

"I didn't ask you to love me." Her voice cracked under the weight of his words. Why couldn't she just let it go? Why did she have to continue torturing herself?

"Yes you did," Cole sighed once again, berating himself for making this phone call. If he had sent a text message, they probably would've still had this conversation. He just wouldn't have had to listen to the anger and frustration in her voice. "The night I picked you up from Wayne's house, I took you home and put you to bed. As I was leaving the room, you told me you loved me. I knew you were drunk and it was probably the alcohol talking, but it helped me to see that for you, love was a possibility. For me, love is a hardship. It's best for us to part ways now, while it's still easy."

*Speak for yourself.* Meme sat silently on the phone, daring a tear to fall from her eye. She would not cry. Not today she wouldn't. Not over some man she barely knew. She harnessed that sorrow into anger and liquid fire surged through her veins and out her mouth. "Save that sorry excuse for someone who'll believe it. You're feeling me stronger than you've ever felt a woman and you're scared as hell. Instead of owning up to those feelings, you are running and it's a shame. We could have been great together." Meme hung up the phone before she lost her nerve and started retracting everything she'd said.

She sat on the couch for ten minutes getting her emotions under control. Deep breaths soothed the storm that had begun to brew. Hadn't she told herself to stop following her out-of-whack emotions? Now, she had turned around and did just that with Cole. When would she learn her lesson? Satisfied the storm wasn't going to hit land, Meme got up from the couch, trying to continue her day without thoughts of Cole.

## 10

The phone ringing on the night stand woke Meme out of a deep sleep. Instantly, she checked the time and her heart slid into her stomach. Phone calls at three in the morning were one of two things, booty calls or bad news. Seeing as she didn't have any candidates for the former, she feared the latter. Jumping up out of bed, she answered the phone without checking the display.

"Goodbye," the intoxicated voice droned through the receiver. "I just wanted to say goodbye."

"Wayne?" She couldn't make out the voice so she checked the screen to be sure. "Where are you going this time?" She giggled, because this wasn't the first time he'd called her drunk. The conversation was always hilarious and she'd have a blast teasing him about it when he was sober.

"Of all the people I know, you're the only one I don't want to leave behind."

Meme's smile faded. Something in his voice terrified her.

"I hope you are not mad at me, but I couldn't take it anymore."

The sobs that followed had Meme out of bed and scrambling for her house phone. She dialed the paramedics, informed them of her suspicions, grabbed her car keys, and ran out of the house with Wayne still rambling into the cell phone nestled between her shoulder and ear.

"Oh my God," Meme repeated, trying to keep the hysterics under control, but it was harder and harder with each passing second. Of all the nights it chose to rain in Southern California, why would tonight be one of them? She was soaking wet before making it to the car, but didn't let the rain slow her down.

"I know you're upset, but I just couldn't take living in a world that hates me because of who I am. My parents won't speak to me and they threatened to disown my siblings if they do. My man is embarrassed to be seen with me. Why does it have to be like this?" His words were garbled and slow with long pauses in between.

A few times, Meme thought he'd fallen asleep and yelled out his name.

"You are the only one who loves me completely. That is why I left everything I own to you. Euphoria, my house, the cars; everything is yours."

"Wayne, don't talk like that. Everything is going to be fine. I'm on my way over and I will make everything better."

*Silence.*

Meme called his name and this time he didn't answer. She checked the phone display to make sure the call was still connected and it was.

Yelling his name over and over again, Meme pressed harder on the gas pedal and floored it to Wayne's house.

About a block from his house, Meme blew through a light and hit a dip at the intersection. The slick roads caused her car to hydroplane. That three thousand pound car glided weightlessly through the air. Terror filled shrieks filled the car as Meme tried to gain control of it. For the life of her, she couldn't remember what she was supposed to do in the situation. Turn into the curve or turn out of it. She tried them both and neither seemed to make the situation better. Meme thought for sure this was her last night on earth. She was going to die in the car, not be able to make it to Wayne, and they both were going to meet their maker. Someone must've been praying for her. The car made contact with the ground and she was able to regain control.

When she pulled up in front of Wayne's house, she was thankful for her life being spared, but a dark heaviness settled upon her. She feared she was too late to save Wayne. The cops pulled up just as she picked up a rock and busted the glass panel on the front door. They rushed up the walkway and into the house behind her. Wayne was laid across his bed with his eyes closed, looking as peaceful as can be—an empty prescription bottle lying next to him.

Meme's heart raced out of control as she watched the cops check for a pulse. The EMTs came barging in and time seemed to move in slow motion. Wayne's body lay limp and motionless as they checked for vital signs. Finding a pulse, they decided to transport him immediately. The police questioned her as she watched Wayne being loaded onto the gurney, but their voices couldn't penetrate her grief-stricken distress.

Trying to get her attention, they shook her shoulders, but her eyes and thoughts never strayed from her friend.

~

Having no idea who to call, Meme called Kevin. As far as Wayne was concerned, he had no family. Although his parents and siblings lived in San Diego, it had been years since he'd seen them and months since they talked on the phone. They probably wouldn't care one way or the other if Wayne survived or not. Kevin needed to be there. This whole situation was his fault anyway. If he had just manned up and loved Wayne the way he deserved to be loved, none of this would have happened. Security had better be present when he showed up, because she was going to wrap her fingers around his neck.

It was taking forever for the doctor to come out with a report on Wayne's condition, Kevin still hadn't arrived, and Meme felt like she was losing her mind. She called the only person who would be able to comfort her at a time like this. Despite their broken relationship, her brother got out of his bed and was on his way to sit with her. She had only hoped for some comforting words or a quick prayer, but that wasn't like Marlon. He always went out of his way for everyone.

Marlon rushed into the hospital, and like the supportive woman she was, Latrice was right behind him. Pregnant belly, duck walk, and all, Latrice would follow him to the end of the world. As they walked toward her, Meme couldn't help but smile. After all her brother had been through, after all she'd put him through, he had found the kind of love you only see in movies. This was the love most people dreamed of and spent a lifetime searching for.

Wiping her tears, Meme stood to greet her brother. Marlon wrapped his arms around her, and it felt like they were back to the times when things were simpler. She hadn't screwed up, and he hadn't disowned her. He was her only sibling. The love and the bond they once shared seemed to have rekindled in the midst of that hug. Latrice watched with tears in her eyes. The woman once threatened Meme's life if she hurt Marlon again and was very capable of following through. Now, she was cheering on their reconciliation. When they parted, Latrice stepped up to hug Meme as well.

Meme looked around the waiting room of the ER as she leaned on her brother. There was a woman with a bucket who looked as though any second now her stomach was going to unleash it contents. By her pale complexion, you could tell her stomach no longer contained much. There was also a man with his hand wrapped in a blood-spotted towel. The anguish on his face said it all; he was going to need stitches. Those two were the only people there with outward signs of discomfort. Everyone else laughed and talked as if everything in their life was fine.

No one in the waiting area seemed to be battling the same distress as Meme. Her eyes filled up with tears again as Marlon asked her what happened. She incoherently wailed through the phone when she called him and all he could make out was that she was at the hospital with a friend. Even now, as she explained Wayne's phone call and his condition when she arrived at his house, emotion distorted her voice.

Marlon silently prayed as Meme spoke. He asked God to intervene on Wayne's behalf, but feared the worst. Those pills had been in his system for a long time. That was just calculating from the time he called Meme to the time he arrived at the hospital. No telling how much time had elapsed between him ingesting the pills and the phone call. One could only assume, since he was alert enough to make the phone call. From what he knew about overdosing, if you could get the victim to vomit before the pills dissolved into the blood stream, there was still hope. They could only hope for the best.

Meme's spine stiffened as Marlon caressed her back. Kevin had arrived and she spotted him as soon as he stepped through the double doors. They locked eyes and he made his way toward her.

"This is your fault!" Meme yelled out, lunging toward Kevin as soon as he stepped in front of her. With natural instinct, Kevin deflected her charging body, knocking her to the floor.

Marlon's nostrils flared as he watched his sister tumble to the floor. Latrice felt his body tense and gripped his arm trying to hold him in place. He rose to his feet with heat blazing in his eyes, and instantly, Kevin started apologizing. Marlon was a good Christian brother. He wasn't perfect, but tried his best. Putting your hands on his sister was a sure way to get him to step out of character. That incessant apologizing was raking his nerves and Marlon was ready to put an end to it. Latrice pushed her way in between them and her protruding belly brushing up against his arm was enough to bring him to his senses.

Smirking as he shook his head, Marlon turned to Meme and asked, "Who is this?"

"Wayne's boyfriend," Meme said, rubbing the elbow that had banged on a chair on her way to the ground.

Latrice's jaw dropped as she eyed him up and down. Kevin was definitely someone she would've been interested in if she hadn't already found the man of her dreams. From what Meme had said about his and

Wayne's relationship, it was too bad such a fine specimen of man was hiding, too afraid to live his life. "That's a shame."

"What is that supposed to mean?" Kevin asked defensively.

"Don't you dare," Meme forgot about her hurting elbow and rushed into Kevin's face. "Don't act like a gay brother down for the cause now. If you were down for the cause, you would've loved Wayne the way he needed to be loved and we wouldn't even be here right now."

Sensing her emotions spiraling out of control, Marlon wrapped his arms around Meme just as she started to lunge toward Kevin again. He lifted her off the ground and carried her outside, leaving Kevin alone with Latrice.

"So, you think I am a waste of a good, fine brother?" Kevin laughed as he plopped down in a seat.

"Please spare me that line. I have had that insensitive comment spoken about others directly to my face by people who didn't know I was gay. So, if you think it's a shame that a good looking brother is gay, get over yourself."

"What I really think is a shame is," Latrice sat next him placing her hands on each of his cheeks and turning his face toward her.

"Because of an image you insist on portraying, you've caused a lot of hurt." He tried to turn away, but she held firm.

"I have my own religious beliefs about homosexuality, but this life is filled with so much hatred and horrible things. If in the midst of the coldhearted world, you find love, you shouldn't allow the opinions of others to keep you from it. Now, if you decide you don't want to live this lifestyle then let that decision be based solely on your beliefs, not the opinions of others."

116

"With my job, it's next to impossible to be my true self, but my co-workers are the least of my concern. I see how Wayne's family disowned him, what if mine does the same? I don't think I can live with that."

"Do you have that little faith in them? If they mean that much to you, it's safe to assume you mean that much to them. If they can't accept who you are then you are better off without them instead of having to live a lie for the rest of your life."

Kevin's head dropped into her hands as tears filled his eyes. Latrice pulled him as far into her arms as her pregnant belly would allow and was still embracing him when Marlon and Meme walked up to them.

"Sorry Kevin, this is not the time to be playing the blame game." Meme tried for sincerity, but fell a little short. Marlon had taken her outside and told her to calm down before she got arrested. He also made her promise to apologize. She only agreed because that's what she always did when he was busy being her daddy instead of her brother.

"No, you were right. I should have loved him the way he needed me to." The dam of his emotions broke and Meme couldn't help but embrace him. She sat in his lap wrapping her arms around his broad shoulders and pressed his head to her chest. As they rocked back and forth, they whispered encouraging words of comfort. To anyone watching from a distance, they looked like a loving couple comforting each other.

Sliding onto the seat next to Latrice, Marlon whispered into her ear. "I never would have guessed he was gay."

"I know," Latrice whispered in return as she turned her back to Meme and rested her stomach on Marlon. "I guess there isn't really a gay look. Some men choose to be flamboyant, some women choose to be butch, but the majority of them are like Kevin and Meme."

Looking over Latrice's shoulder at Meme and Kevin all hugged up, Marlon shook his head. "The way his hands are all over her, you would think they were together."

"Oh please," Latrice playfully pushed his shoulder. "Stop trying to act like the over-protective brother. If they were a couple, that would be your dream come true."

Marlon tried to suppress a smile, but failed. Latrice leaned in closer so Meme wouldn't overhear.

"Your hope that this gay thing is just a phase for your sister is the reason why you swore something was going on between her and Cole at our reception. You sent her down to the restaurant to talk to him, hoping something would spark and it didn't. So promise me you will stop interfering in her life."

He opened his mouth to once again explain that he saw Cole walk back into the reception hall trying to keep his cool, but doing a horrible job at it. Then just seconds later, Meme came from the same direction looking just as flustered, but Latrice stopped him.

"Promise me you will stop."

"Okay, I promise." Marlon pouted like a two-year-old, and Latrice thought it was the cutest thing he'd ever done. She leaned in to kiss him, but her belly got in the way and she had to adjust her position.

Another two hours passed and there still was no word on Wayne's condition. Marlon was ready to call it a night. He needed to get his wife and unborn child to bed. Saying his goodbyes and making Meme promise to call as soon as she heard something, he and Latrice headed out the door.

After a while, Meme began to relax. She figured if Wayne was dead they would've already notified her. So in her book, no news was good news. She and Kevin talked, sharing stories about crazy things Wayne had done. She convinced Kevin to call his sister and tell her about his life. When he agreed, she insisted he do it right then and there before he lost his nerve. The conversation was short and when he hung up all he could do was laugh. They all thought he was gay anyway. His sister cursed him out for waking her up, saying, "No man can be as fine as you and never have a woman around unless he's gay." She told him to call back after nine and then hung up.

That little bit of honesty made Kevin feel so free that when the doctor came out to update them on Wayne's condition and asked their relationship to him, Kevin proudly told the doctor he was Wayne's man. All these years he'd been hiding were for nothing. He wasn't going to waste any more time.

"Well," the doctor said once he got over his initial shock. "Your man is very lucky. He regained consciousness once he arrived and we were able to pump his stomach. He should make a full recovery, but we are putting him on a seventy-two-hour hold. It is very clear he intended to kill himself. If he'd taken more pills, he might have succeeded."

"Can we see him?" They asked in unison.

"Make it quick. We are in the process of admitting him." They followed the doctor back to Wayne's bed and the sight of him with IV tubes in his arm, heart monitor cords dangling from his chest, and a tube in his nose brought them to tears.

The guilt Kevin felt lodged in his throat rendered him speechless. Because of his stupid hang-ups, someone he really cared about tried to take their life. If Wayne had succeeded... Well, Kevin didn't want to think about that. Wayne didn't succeed at taking his own life and that's what

Kevin would focus on. Wayne's eyes blinked open and Kevin made his way to the side of the bed. Meme blew Wayne a kiss and told Kevin she'd be waiting for him in the lobby. They had some things to work out and she gave them some privacy to do so.

Thinking about them getting another chance at love made Meme think of Cole. Pulling out her phone, she ran her fingers across the screen as she debated whether or not to call him. Her last relationship, although it should've never been, was emotionally intense, and the sex was great, but in hindsight, it was one-sided. Meme was there for her, putting her life on hold for an empty promise of a future together. The intense chemistry she felt with Cole was far from physical. It was so emotionally deep that it was almost spiritual. When in his presence, his soul seemed to speak to hers, crying out, "Where have you been all my life," and her soul responded, "Searching for you."

Against her better judgment, Meme dialed Cole's number and after one ring it went to voicemail. A call going to voicemail that quick meant only one thing, he sent the call there. *I guess soul connecting will have to wait until someone stops being scared.*

## 11

Fumbling for his cell phone on the nightstand, Cole accidentally sent Meme's call to voicemail. He stared at the screen, contemplating whether or not to call her back, but thought better of it. He had tamped down his desire for her. Hearing her voice would only ramp it back up. Adjusting his pillows, he rolled over and tried to go back to sleep. After several attempts to find a comfortable position, he gave up and flopped over onto his back, staring up at the ceiling. It was a little after three in the morning and he had just barely fallen asleep when the phone rang again. As tired as he was, going back to sleep should've been easy, but that one little phone call made him fall apart. Since he'd last spoken to Meme, he avoided all thoughts of her. Whenever one crept in, he quickly found something else to occupy his mind. He was finally starting to feel like his old self. His reasons for rejecting Meme were solidified, his resolve to avoid her intact, and now, with one simple phone call, he was back on edge again. He hadn't even talked to her and she had him falling apart.

"Why is she calling this early in the morning?" He groaned in frustration, partly from being awakened from a good sleep, but mostly because of the heat that flooded him with just the thought of her. "Only calls at this hour are booty calls or…" With that thought, he sat up straight in the bed and grabbed his phone. Although he wouldn't give in to her, he preferred the booty call over the other possibility. Without a second thought, he called her back. It wasn't until her voice came across the line that he allowed himself to breathe freely.

"Hey."

"What's up? You called?" Cole tried to keep his voice mellow and not reveal how the wispy purr of her voice affected him. Its soft caress soothed him and eased an ache for her that he refused to acknowledge existed. In the still, quiet darkness of his room—just for a moment—he allowed that ache to be stroked. Quintessentially, he'd taken a step backward and would have to restart the process of trying to forget about her, but he'd deal with that later. That single word she'd spoken had brought light to his darkness. Every day since meeting her, he tried to figure out why this woman could get him to feel things and desire things no other woman could. He'd let his guard down somewhere along the way. It would do him good to remember his stance on relationships before he wound up like his father.

"I'm at the hospital and just needed—"

"What's wrong? What hospital?" He was up, on his feet, and finding clothes to put on before she could formulate her response.

"Calm down. I'm fine." *Wow, what a reaction from the man who claims to not want me.* The urgency she heard in his voice put a smile on

122

her face. There may still be a chance to have the man she wanted. "I'm here with my friend, Wayne. He tried to kill himself."

"Oh baby, I'm sorry to hear that. Is he going to be all right?" He cringed at the little slip of the tongue, but the sorrow in her voice tugged at his heart. All he wanted to do was comfort her.

"Yeah, we got to him in time."

"We? You found him?"

"Yes, he called me as the pills were starting to take effect. Listening to him say goodbye was one of the most horrific experiences of my life." Her voice quivered as she relayed everything that had taken place. Every time her voice cracked with emotion, Cole soothed her, reminding her that it was all over and that Wayne was going to be all right.

"Cole, he tried to take his life because the person he wanted didn't want him. I don't want to end up like that." Wayne had made himself physically and mentally ill by obsessing over what could have been if he hadn't pushed Kevin to the limit. She didn't want to spend months obsessing over what could have been with Cole. "By no means am I comparing our situation to Wayne's. I just want to explore the possibility of us. Do you think we can meet for breakfast tomorrow and just talk?"

As his rejection rattled through the phone, Kevin approached. Meme had to stave off the torrent of emotion that was starting to swell. Cry, tell him off, cuss him out, or simply hang up on him all were possibilities, but instead she took a few deep breaths, smiled at Kevin as he sat down, and tried to prepare a sugary sweet response.

Her response was on her lips until Kevin spoke up. "All right, baby, you ready to go?"

"Who is that?"

Meme shook her head in confusion. "It's Kevin." *Mr. I'm-not-the-right-man-for-you has some nerve questioning me.*

"Who is Kevin?" The accusatory tone of Cole's voice left no question as to where his thoughts were headed.

"You forfeited your right to ask me that question." With that, she hung up the phone, shaking her head.

The silence on the other end caused his jaw to clench together so tightly that if he didn't ease up soon, he would grind his teeth down a layer. Minutes after the phone called ended, Cole was still up pacing around his room. He was trying to talk himself off the ledge, trying to convince himself not to drive over to Meme's house and see exactly what was going on. *She doesn't belong to you,* echoed over and over in his mind. He was losing it. All his effort to avoid relationships had been for nothing. Without even being in a relationship, this woman was causing him to lose his mind, just as his mother had caused his father to lose his. Awake in the wee hours of the morning, pacing and talking to himself just like his father used to. Cole was pretty young when his mother left, so his father's early behavior was a little fuzzy, but the things he did and said once Cole got older stuck with him for the rest of his life.

*"She played you all these years. Everything you've done for her, and she played you. Had you sitting around braggin' to the fellas about how your woman is, and she played you."*

*Cole heard his father's voice, snuck out of bed, and peered around the corner into the living room. His father marched around in circles with a beer in one hand and a cigarette dangling from his lips. Occasionally, he paused to take a long drag on his cigarette and then chased the smoke down with a swig of beer. Cole watched quietly, wondering why his*

124

mother had to be a whore. He had no idea what a whore was, but he'd heard his father say it plenty of times. It had to be pretty bad if it made his father act like that. It had to be pretty bad to make her leave her son.

"Ain't ever gon' get caught slippin' like that again." He finished his beer and stumbled into the kitchen for another. "Have to make sure my son doesn't get caught up either. These hoes ain't ready yet. They want to play games, let's play."

He rambled and jumped from topic to topic so much that Cole had a hard time understanding. As he stood there trying to decipher the code in which his dad spoke, he forgot he was supposed to be silently watching and laughed out loud when his dad stumbled over the coffee table.

"Boy, what you doing out of bed? Come here."

Cole walked at a snail's pace over to his father, hoping to delay his butt whooping as long as possible.

His father grabbed him by the shoulders and looked him square in the eyes. "Hear me and hear me good son, women ain't nothin' and neither are these little girls you runnin' behind at school. They're good for one thing. Use them for what they're worth then move on."

Cole had no idea what his father was talking about. He didn't run behind girls. They always chased him on the playground. He'd run as fast as he could, so that he wouldn't get caught. Instead of commenting or asking questions, he just nodded his head and continued holding his breath to avoid the stench of beer and cigarettes coming out of his father's mouth.

It had been three years since his mother left, and it wasn't the first time his father had said such things. Cole had yet to figure out what he was talking about. All he knew was he missed his mother. Whenever he

125

*asked about her, his father would go into another spiel like the one he just had, so eventually Cole stopped asking. All traces of her had been removed from the house and thoughts of her were fewer and fewer. The one clear thing from all of his father's rants that took root was that his mother didn't want him. There were plenty of kids in his class who didn't have fathers, but everyone had a mother...everyone except him.*

Cole shook off the memory and grabbed his gym bag. There was no way he was going over Meme's, so he did the only drama-free thing he could to relieve stress that early in the morning.

~

Weight machines clanked together as other insomniacs completed their workouts. The sound alone helped to ease Cole's frazzled nerves. He slid his headphones over his ears, pulled on his weightlifting gloves, and straddled the nautilus machine. With a head nod to a few familiar faces and a tight pull on his arms to loosen up the muscles, Cole gripped the handles of the bench press machine. He failed to check the weight and could tell from the first push it was more than he was used to, but the challenge was what he needed.

*You Gots to Chill* by EPMD blared in his ears; he took the words to heart and tried to chill out. The suction of the headphones and the sound quality drowned out all background noise. It was just him and the machine. With slow, steady breaths, he relaxed his body and focused all his energy on completing each rep. Adrenaline surged and tension flowed. Repeatedly, he pumped his arms, pushing himself to the limit. He pushed until thoughts of his dad were gone, until images of his mother faded, and until his sudden fascination with Meme no longer plagued his conscious mind.

Cole went from machine to machine, attacking each piece of equipment as if it had personally caused him harm. He was determined to leave all anger and frustration in the gym. He was a grown man and it was time to come to terms with his demons. His mother was gone and he couldn't go back in time and change that. His father did the best he could, no sense in trying to correct his mistakes. He and Meme wouldn't be together, so no sense fretting over what could've been.

Arms, legs, back, and abs, he wore out every muscle he had except his heart. It was still pumping, pushing adrenaline and endorphins through his veins. He was exhausted, but he felt good. Mind successfully purged of all tumultuous thoughts, Cole grabbed his gym bag and headed to his car. The roar of his Dodge Charger revving to life put a smile on his face. He made himself comfortable on the buttery smooth leather seat, put the car in reverse, and prepared to back out. Before he could move, his cell phone chimed, signaling a new text message. He checked the display and wanted to throw the phone out the window.

*You want me. Stop running!*

His jaw clenched and he squeezed the phone until the hard plastic of the protective case dug into the palm of his hand. Just that quick, he was back to square one. He worked out beyond his limit to get rid of the tension and with five little words, it came surging back. The man in him wanted to drive over there and make her eat her words. Normally, his self-imposed rules kept his life at peace, but not this time. His body was rebelling against his practiced disciplines, demanding he set her straight and prove the man he was by taking what he wanted. What's the worst that could happen? She could want forever. Hell, the way she made is heart thump, he could want forever. Then, he'd be in the same boat his father was. No thanks! He just had to keep repeating: too clingy, friend's sister, off limits.

## 12

**M**eme hung up the phone and jumped off the sofa. *All that drama with Wayne and now this.* The situation with Wayne nearly scared her to death. Her heart rate and nerves were finally settling back to normal. She should have known that normalcy in her life was too good to be true. She hadn't heard from Cole since she called him from the hospital the other night. Now, he calls out of the blue, telling her to meet him at the hospital. When she asked why, all he said was, "Your brother needs you." Her pulse skyrocketed as her mind conjured up horrific images of her brother being ill, maimed, or even worse, dead. *I can't lose my brother,* her mind chanted as she bolted out the front door.

The drive was a blur and she stomped into the hospital in full panic mode. Frantically, her eyes scanned the ER, searching for Marlon or Cole. Her heart threatened to jump out of her chest. There was no sign of either of them. She ignored all the inquiring glances in her direction and turned toward the nurse's station. Surely everyone saw the look of panic on her face and wondered what tragedy had brought her to the ER. She had no answer for them and was out of her mind with worry. She stepped up to the nurse's desk and as she opened her mouth to speak, the nurse held up one finger and silenced her while she finished a phone call. Meme's lips were poised for a good cursing out. The nurse was saved by the chiming of Meme's cell.

*Come to the fifth floor,* was the message from Cole, and without question, Meme complied. She pivoted away from the nurse's station and headed toward the bank of elevators. The slow torturous ride to the fifth floor was her undoing. Tears that had been collecting behind her eyes since Cole called now trickled down her cheeks. Her nerves rattled and she anxiously paced around. The elevator doors had barely opened when she stumbled out of them. She was in a terror-driven, emotional frenzy and tripped over her own feet in her haste to get to her brother. She threw her arms out to break her fall and before she hit the ground, two strong arms wrapped around her and steadied her on her feet.

Meme lifted her eyes to say thank you and the eyes that met hers intensified her sorrow. "Where is he?" Meme wailed, releasing her bottled up emotions into Cole's chest.

Although he warned himself to say away, Cole cradled her into his chest. Her tears affected him like nothing ever had before, and in that moment, all his reasons for staying away vanished and she seeped a little further into his heart. Holding her was as natural as sleeping. No matter what you do to prevent it or put it off, your body will eventually succumb to sleep. Caffeine can surge through the veins to keep you awake, but as soon as that drowsy head hits the pillow, it's lights out; so was it with his desire for Meme. Countless times, he admonished himself to keep his distance, but as soon as he touched her to keep her from falling, his good sense flew out the window. Before long he was holding, caressing, and enjoying.

"Shh," he whispered as he planted his lips on the top of her head. "He is fine. It's Latrice and the baby."

Meme jumped out of his arms. "Oh my God, what happened?"

"She called him at work and said she had a really bad headache and drove herself to the hospital just to be on the safe side. Her blood pressure is out of control, and if it doesn't go down soon they are going to take the baby."

"Oh my God, why?"

Cole pulled her back into his arms to ease her trembling. "I don't know. Marlon went searching for her and I've been waiting for you."

"Okay, let's go find them," she choked out as she tried to pull away from him.

"Hold on." He tightened his grip. "Whatever is going on, Marlon needs you to be strong." He wiped her tears with the pads of his thumbs, and she attempted to pull herself together. Seeing her efforts unsuccessful, Cole covered her lips with his. He tried to tell himself it was just to comfort her, but the moment their lips connected, he could no longer entertain that lie. This was for him just as much as it was for her.

The deep, heady kiss silenced Meme's sobs. She gripped the lapels of Cole's jacket and leaned into him as he molded their bodies together. He lifted her off the ground for better access and her hands slid up his neck, gripping the back of his head to lock him in place. His taste buds were overwhelmed with the sweetness of her mouth. His body came to life with the feel of her flush against him.

*How can he kiss me like this and not feel the chemistry we have,* Meme thought, but he trailed his lips down her neck, grazing them along her clavicle and scattering her thoughts in the process.

Cole realized he was getting carried away and abruptly let her go. He succeeded in settling her, but now he was the one rattled. Ensuring she was steady, he stepped away and broke their connection. He was seconds away from pinning her against the wall and reenacting every dream he'd had about her. "Are you ready?"

"Yes." Meme gazed into his eyes and responded to the sexual current flowing between them, not to what he was referring.

Seeing the desire in her eyes, Cole knew to what she was agreeing to and wanted to kick himself for getting carried away. For a few tense moments, they stood eyeing each other warily. Cole wanted her lips again, but commanded himself to stay put. Meme, wanting to break down the walls around his heart, reached for him, but he backed away.

Dropping her head in defeat, Meme stared at the floor as she nodded her head to his original question. The combination of rejection and desire in his eyes was too much to handle right then. If this was how he wanted things to be between them, she had no choice but to accept it. Timidly, she stepped past him, trying to refocus her mind on finding her brother.

Cole knew he had hurt and confused her once again, and that wasn't how he operated. He had enjoyed his share of women, but he never led them on or gave them a false hope for a future with him. This woman in particular was driving him crazy. As long as she wasn't in his presence, he could find things to occupy his mind and chase thoughts of her away. When she was near him, it was an entirely different story. He was drawn to her like metal to a magnet, and when they touched, he'd lose control. Being with her would be stimulating, but she wanted things and could feel things that he wasn't capable of. Therefore, he had to keep his distance. Her drunken confession of love wafted across his mind, further solidifying his stance to stay away.

Fetal heart sounds greeted them as they walked into the labor and delivery ward. A few wails of agony from women in various stages of labor echoed down the hall. Doctors scurried about preparing to bring new lives into the world, but Meme and Cole didn't pay attention to any of that. Meme tried to get her mind off the man standing behind her and refocus it on Latrice and the baby. Cole tried to get his eyes off Meme's curves. The sway of her hips and the lingering taste of her on his lips had his heart working overtime trying to compensate for the blood rushing below his waist.

They checked in at the desk and followed the nurse's directions to Latrice's room. Inside the room, Meme expected to find Latrice crying hysterically and Marlon doing all he could to calm her, but what they actually walked into was serenity. Latrice lie on her side in the bed with Marlon snuggled up behind her. The lights were dimmed and the only sound was the whooshing from the fetal monitor. Marlon caressed smooth circles across Latrice's abdomen. His lips moved as he whispered in her ear, but his voice was drowned out by the sound of their baby's heartbeat through the monitor.

"Hey," Meme spoke softly as she approached the bed. "How are you feeling? What did the doctor say?"

"Trying not to focus on that. We're expecting a miracle. Whether God chooses to lower Latrice's blood pressure so she can carry the baby to term, or have the baby born tonight, we want both of them healthy and all risks eliminated." Although Marlon tried to hide it, Meme saw the worry etched on his face.

Cole stood in the doorway watching Meme timidly approach Marlon and didn't understand. From what he knew, Marlon was a good a guy who loved his family. Meme's wariness toward him made no sense. The fidgety, unsure of herself woman she'd morphed into was a stranger to him. From the day he'd met her, she challenged him, made him feel and do things he'd never experienced. This passive woman was not his Meme. Something was definitely wrong. Come to think of it, her apprehension around Marlon made seating arrangements at the reception more understandable. If she had been seated with the family, she wouldn't have been sitting across from him, tempting him. Had she been seated with her family, he would've known she was related to his friend. He would've left her alone, never tasted her sweetness, nor developed an addiction to her. *If only I'd known.*

"Well, I am here for you. If you need anything, don't hesitate to ask."

"We really need your prayers," was Latrice's whispered reply.

"You got it." Meme leaned over the bed, kissing her brother's cheek and then Latrice's. "I'll be in the waiting room praying harder than I have in years." On the brief walk back to the waiting room, Meme contemplated her relationship with the Lord. It was pretty much nonexistent. Communication is a main component of any relationship, but theirs was nonexistent. She hoped He overlooked all of her indiscretions and how she had turned her back on Him, because she really needed Him to hear her heart. Marlon had already experienced heartache, losing his wife or child would destroy him.

~

Cole and Meme had no idea how long they'd been sitting in the waiting room. Chairs that were once full of excited relatives anxiously awaiting the arrival of a new family member were now empty. Those families received their joyous announcements, celebrated, and went home, but Cole and Meme were still rooted to their seats. Meme pulled her cell phone out of her pocket and checked the display. She couldn't believe what time it was. She impatiently rose to her feet, pacing back and forth.

Hours had gone by while she and Cole sat in the waiting room. They sat several chairs apart, neither speaking nor making eye contact. She wanted to go to him and find comfort in his arms, but was afraid she'd find rejection instead. He was the most frustrating person she'd ever met, and she wanted him badly. Her desire for him was beyond reason and she didn't want to accept the fact that they wouldn't be together. She tried to remind herself of the drama she'd gotten herself into the last time she followed her desires, but once again her emotions outweighed commonsense. She stared at him, willing him to look up, so she could look into his eyes and see what his heart was feeling, but he didn't. Well, she hoped he was at least praying. If he wasn't, there wasn't any point in him hanging around.

Just as she started to ask him why he hadn't left, Marlon walked through the door. His shoulders slumped and a cloud of dejection hung over him. Instantly, Meme feared the worst. She threw her shoulders back in an effort to remain strong for her brother. As he approached, she extended her arms to embrace him.

"She's getting worse and they are taking the baby." Marlon sucked in a lung full of air, trying to restrain his emotions. As he exhaled, he released his frustrations and fears. Meme absorbed them all.

"Don't worry. God's in control. They're both going to be okay."

Marlon nodded as they released each other. "They are preparing her for a C-section, so I better get going. Just wanted to let you know what was up." He walked a few steps then turned back. "I'm glad you stayed."

He walked out, and as soon as he disappeared, Meme collapsed into a chair, no longer able to contain her emotions. Tears flowed down her cheeks, tearing at Cole's heart, and before he could stop, he was making his way toward her. He lifted her onto his lap and wiped her tears with the pads of his thumbs.

"Baby, don't cry." He guided her head to his chest and stroked his hand up and down the column of her spine.

The beat of his heart against her cheek was soothing. Tears subsided and she relished the feeling of his arms around her. With a slight lift of her chin, Meme brushed her lips across his neck. His hand stilled and his pulse accelerated, but he did not pull away. Taking that as encouragement, her tongue joined her lips and danced a slow rhythm up his neck to his jaw. She placed her hand over his racing heart.

"This," she patted his chest, "tells me you feel the connection between us. It tells me you want me as bad as I want you. Why are you running?"

"I have to go." He motioned to remove her from his lap and she held onto him.

"No." She attacked his mouth, giving him no opportunity to reject her. The kiss was deep and demanding. It was aggressive, as if the kiss was the long awaited argument they were due to have. Each aggressive stroke of the tongue spoke their heart's sentiment.

*Why are you running?*

*I can't give you what you need.*

*All I need is you.*

*I am not enough for you.*

*You're more than enough.*

He pulled away abruptly, ending their kiss, which spoke his final reply. *You need to move on.*

Cole stood as he placed her onto the seat next to him. Tears swelled in her eyes and he had to leave before they fell. Before walking out of the room, he chanced a look back at her. She was the most beautiful woman he'd ever laid eyes on. She made his heart pump stronger and sent blood surging through his veins like no woman ever had, but she was better off without him. That thought was all the motivation he needed to walk out the door.

## 13

**A**s Cole walked to his car, he fought the greatest battle of his life. Everything within him wanted to run back to Meme and take away that pained look that he'd placed on her face. She was sweet, innocent, and wanted love. He couldn't taint that with his issues. She'd have to find love elsewhere. Shaking his head, he folded his brawny body into his car. He should've never kissed her, should've left when she arrived, but he didn't. Now he was suffering. This woman had his body contradicting his mind. It was next to impossible to keep his hands to himself when she was around.

The night wind blowing through the window helped to calm Cole's nerves. The tension in his neck eased and the intoxicating allure of Meme's presence lifted. By the time he arrived at the restaurant, he had given himself several pep talks to avoid Meme. Deep down, he knew it was a lost cause. If she kissed him again with the fire she had at the hospital, kissing would be the least of their worries. Distance was the best solution, but even that was becoming unbearable.

Even now, as he walked through the restaurant making sure everything had been closed out and cleaned properly, he couldn't help but wonder if Meme had eaten. Images of her eating his food the night she came to talk to him and the night of her date flashed across his mind. His heart thudded as he remembered her puckered red lips blowing her food and how kissable those lips looked as they parted, making room for the food to enter her mouth. That mouth. He had firsthand knowledge of its sweetness. Every time he got a taste, it diminished him to an out of control addict who couldn't refrain from taking a hit, even though he knew it could be the one that killed him.

Cole groaned in frustration as he clicked on the kitchen lights and made his way to the pantry. He needed to cook something to take his mind off of Meme. He gathered a few ingredients and stood in front of the stove shaking his head, more frustrated than he was before. He'd collected the ingredients to make Meme's dish. A stupid desire to protect his friend's sister—at least that's what he told himself was the start of it all—had him losing his mind. Yes, he almost sexed her at the reception, kissed her when he drove her home a few days later, and then showed up at her house with breakfast, holding her for hours. That was all before he ever knew she needed protecting. That was the excuse he was using at the moment, and he was sticking to it. Cole slammed the skillet down on the stove. He was in deeper than he thought. Helpless to do anything else, he flipped on the stove and cooked her food.

~

Meme did all she could to keep her mind off Cole. She marched around in circles, praying for Latrice and the baby. As time ticked by, she became more and more concerned. She was tired, hungry, and on the verge of setting it off in the hospital if she didn't get some answers soon.

She scooted a small table in front of the mounted TV and stood on it. Maybe watching a little television would settle her nerves. As she flipped through the stations, she heard someone clear their throat behind her. She froze, hating how much she hoped it was Cole, and slowly turned her head. Seeing the nurse standing in the doorway, she practically jumped off the table and ran to her.

"How are Latrice Wright and the baby?"

"I'm sorry. I don't have a status update. I came to bring you this." She held up a paper bag with the Pavoli's logo on it. "The man that was here with you earlier brought this a few minutes ago. He asked me to wait a while before bringing it in. These last five minutes have been the worst torture of my life. Whatever it is smells great, enjoy. I will check on Latrice for you." Meme accepted the bag and thanked the nurse as she walked out.

In spite of the stab of rejection she felt from knowing Cole didn't want to see her, Meme smiled. He cared enough to make sure she ate, and even prepared her favorite meal. They were just barely getting to know each other when those three little words slipped out of her mouth. *I was drunk for goodness sake.* She couldn't understand why he was taking her literally. He was running from the prospect of love when she was nowhere near in love with him. *Why do I even want to be with somebody that has crazy issues like that?*

As she pulled the tray of food out of the bag, her mind flashed to the brief but wonderful moments they'd spent together. Her body hummed with the unquenchable fire that burned between them and she knew exactly why she wanted to be with him. Being with him reminded her that she was a woman and made her hope for things she hadn't thought of in years. Marriage, two-and-a-half children, a dog, and a house with a white picket fence; she could have that. Maybe not with Cole since he was tripping, but she could have it. Those desires dwindled with Damien's attack. Now they were back and she refused to ignore them. She couldn't help but think of what those things would be like with Cole. With that in mind, she sent him a quick text.

*Wish you were here to eat with me. Thanks for thinking of me…miss u.*

Cole typed *miss u 2* into his phone, but quickly deleted it. "No mixed signals," he scolded himself. Instead he sent, *You're welcome. Have Marlon call me when he gets a chance.*

Shaking her head, Meme slid her cell phone back into her pocket. She didn't know what she was hoping he'd say, but that certainly wasn't it.

The aroma of her food wafted up her nose, intensifying her stomach's growl and silencing her thoughts of Cole. Each bite of the pasta with its creamy, rich sauce was heavenly. For a moment, she was lost in the food, devouring it as if it was her first meal in years. She knew she had to be an embarrassing sight, smacking and slurping like she didn't have table manners. The waiting room was empty and she couldn't care less. Some people might call her greedy, but she just loved good food. This was so good she scraped the bowl to get every last drop. *He may have issues, but the boy can cook.* Meme giggled as she placed the empty Styrofoam container back into the Pavoli's bag and walked it to the trash.

Meme was settling into her seat, feeling full and ready to take a nap when the nurse reappeared. "I checked on Latrice. She's in recovery and doing fine."

"What about the baby?"

"We've been ordered not to release the status of the baby's health."

"Oh God." The room spun and Meme gripped the arm of the chair to steady herself. This could not be happening. The only reason Marlon would give that order was if something terrible happened.

"Latrice wants you to go to her room." The nurse gave her the new room number and pointed her in the right direction. Meme was off and running before the nurse could finish her sentence.

Emotions surged through Meme as her heart fiercely knocked against her chest. By the time she reached the room, her heart felt as if it was on the verge of rupturing. Whether it was from fear or exertion, her pulsed hammered out of control. She took a minute to calm herself and nearly passed out when she walked into the room.

Latrice was lying in the bed gazing at her little bundle of joy. Marlon sat at her bedside with utter elation plastered on his face. God had answered his prayers. His wife and baby were healthy. For hours, doctors ran every test they could think of to prove this three-month-premature baby had a health problem, from underdeveloped lungs to an irregular heartbeat to jaundice. If it was a condition of premature birth, they tested for it. The baby was given a clean bill of health.

Tears uncontrollably ran down Meme's cheeks as she stood in the doorway watching her brother and his family. She was overwhelmed by how happy they looked. Her gut clenched at the longing she felt. Marlon gazed up at Latrice and caressed her cheek. He brushed wayward strands of hair off her face and tucked them behind her ear. Meme watched with envy and realized that's what was missing and causing her to make poor decisions. She wanted someone to truly care about her, put her needs before his, and look at her the way Marlon was looking at Latrice. You'd never have to question whether he loved her. It was all over his face.

"Stop crying and come meet your nephew."

Meme laughed as she wiped her cheeks. "I thought..." She didn't want to verbalize what she'd thought. She was just grateful it wasn't true.

"I'm as amazed as you are. I think the doctors are too. Now they are trying to say Latrice's due date must have been wrong. They are trying to come up with an explanation for him being so healthy instead of acknowledging that God performed a miracle."

"Yes he did." Meme paused, taking a moment to silently thank God. She smiled down at her brother and the blissful look on his face. She was happy that he was happy. "Wait a minute." The smile slowly faded off her face. "Did you say my nephew?"

Marlon laughed. "Yes I did. After all these months of thinking we're having a girl, out pops a son, Michael Anthony Wright."

"Try not to smile too hard, honey." Latrice laughed as she motioned for Marlon to pass the baby to Meme.

"You hold him, so he can get to know the wonderful daddy God blessed him with. You deserve this happiness." Her eyes misted up again, but she held the tears back.

"Well, you know what?" Ignoring her objection, Marlon placed his baby in her arms. "God has blessed him with a pretty awesome auntie too. Michael, meet your Auntie Meme." He kissed the crown of her head before reclaiming his seat.

For a moment, Meme allowed herself to forget. She forgot about her betrayal and how she destroyed Marlon's life. At that moment, all she felt was her brother's love. There was a time where he would have given his life for her and she'd have done the same for him. Things were much different now. Although she would still try to move heaven and earth for him, she seriously doubted he'd do the same for her. In spite of that, it still felt good to feel that brotherly love.

Meme smiled at Marlon and then down at his son. "You sure you don't want to name him after you? You still have time to think about it. All these no-good dads jump at the opportunity to have a namesake, but give the child nothing to look up to. You are a good man and this little boy," she nodded toward her sleeping nephew, "would be proud to have your name."

"I agree." Latrice smiled at Marlon's shocked expression.

"You do? Why didn't you say so?"

"I know, and I should have. Sorry." She caressed his cheek. "But you said you hated being named after your father, so I just left it alone. I want my son to be named after a remarkable man. There is no man more noteworthy than you."

Meme watched Marlon melt into Latrice's arms and sighed with envy. She looked down at her nephew. He was sound asleep with a smile on his face. She smiled back. "Yeah, looks like you're getting a name change." She looked toward Marlon to comment on the baby's smile and he and Latrice were joined in a fierce lip lock. She turned her back on them and whispered to the baby. "Looks like you're gonna get a little brother or sister too."

"I heard that," Marlon mumbled as he pulled his lips away.

"Yeah, and the doctor said there is to be none of that for at least six weeks." Latrice playfully tapped his cheek to drive her point home.

"Six weeks!"

The look on Marlon's face was priceless. Latrice and Meme shared a good laugh as they teased Marlon. Twice Marlon had to tell Latrice to calm down. When she laughed too hard she gripped her stomach in pain.

"I am gonna go before you bust something." Meme tried to pass the baby back, but they just stared at her.

"Aww, don't leave. We're going to call everyone." Latrice finally accepted the baby.

"I'm sure it will be a much happier occasion if I'm not here." She saw the look of chastisement on their faces and proceeded to plead her case. "And besides, you guys need time to bond."

"Meme," Marlon spoke up in that fatherly tone he'd take with her at times, which let her know the conversation was over and she wasn't going anywhere. "Today, no one else's happiness matters, but ours."

Without any further discussion, Meme took a seat. She caught Latrice smiling at her. Like a two year old who'd just been put on time out, she stuck her tongue out. Latrice cracked up laughing and quickly gripped her stomach. Marlon shot Latrice the same look of chastisement he'd given Meme. Meme smiled with vindication and waited quietly while Marlon called all their close friends and immediate family.

After he finished his phone calls, Meme got up and took a few pictures on her cell phone. She knew once everyone else arrived, she would fade into the background. That's exactly what happened. Marlon kept trying to engage her in conversation, but she just wanted to disappear. The judgmental, disapproving eyes of her mother were more than she could bear. Eventually, she caught Marlon's eye and waved good bye. He nodded his approval and she slipped out the door without anyone else noticing.

In spite of how Meme felt about her mother at the moment, she still felt grateful to God for answering her prayers. She made some serious promises to God as she marched around that waiting room. He'd upheld His end of the bargain, now it was time for her to follow through on her end. She took a deep breath and sighed. *This is not going to be easy.*

## 14

After weeks of worrying about the people she loved, Meme was ready for some fun. Wayne was home with Kevin, Latrice and the baby were at home, and the stress was finally starting to subside. A night out with friends was exactly what she needed. She would've preferred to hang with her friends at the Golden Stone, but didn't want to risk someone asking her about Wayne. He wanted to keep his ordeal on the low, and the best way to avoid spreading his business in the streets was to avoid those who would ask. So she called up April and Candice; they were meeting at one of their spots. Whether dancing with a man, woman, or by herself, Meme was determined to have a good time.

Putting on her strapless denim jumpsuit that hugged every curve and propped her assets up in perfect position and her strappy stilettos that magnified the sexy in her walk, Meme was almost ready to go. With a few quick flips of her head to give her hair that tussled, after-sex look and light application of lip gloss to make her already sensual lips pop, Meme grabbed her black clutch and headed out the door.

It was dark, and those who had to work in the morning were probably heading to bed, which is what she should've been doing. Going out on a week night wasn't usually her thing, but she'd have Wayne duty this weekend, so her need to let loose overrode common sense. The path to the parking lot of her apartment complex seemed darker than usual. Looking around, she noticed a few of the lights were busted. The more she thought about it, it seemed really dark outside her apartment too. That thought made the hairs on the back of her neck rise. It had been a while since she received any anonymous notes and she had let her guard down, but the eerie feeling that rolled over her had her picking up the pace until she was practically running to her car.

Once inside the safety of her locked car, Meme had to laugh at how ridiculous and scary she was being. She turned up the radio to shake off the eeriness and to get her mind back on her night out. Party hard was her theme for the night, minus the drinking of course. April and Candice seemed cool, but they were still pretty early in their friendship for her to trust them to have her back while she was drunk.

Pulling up in front of the club, Meme's jaw dropped. If it wasn't for the loud music and the people standing around outside, she would have driven right past it. The little hole in the wall establishment looked like it used to be a house. Before she let the complaints start rolling out of her mouth, Meme shook off the negative, parked her car, and headed inside. The music really wasn't her preference either, but hey, all you need is a good beat when you're on the dance floor.

Stepping up on the curb, Meme stood in what she assumed was some form of line. She had barely been standing there for five seconds before one of the guys at the door strolled toward her, leaning to the side, rubbing his hands together, and smacking his lips. Her classy, sexy style was a big difference from the 'less is best' women standing around her and she stood out like a sore thumb. You don't have to expose yourself to garner attention and that point was proven when she was escorted into the building.

Once inside, the odor and heat hit her all at once. Apparently, everybody forgot to shower before leaving their house, and whoever owned this place couldn't afford air conditioning. Before her escort could ask for her number, Meme thanked him, stifling the desire to knee him in the balls for inappropriate placement of his hands. It was obvious that the women who frequented the club were used to being objectified and probably enjoyed it, but she didn't. After looking around, she was grateful she hadn't kneed him. Sagging pants and red rags hanging from back pockets were everywhere. All she could think of were gunshots, being hit by a stray bullet, or trampled in a stampede out the door. Instantly, her party mood faded.

*You have got to be kidding me.* She should've known when April gave her the address that it was not going to be her type of establishment. Imperial Avenue was a long street that took you from one rough neighborhood to the next. This club wasn't in the worst of the worst, but she surely wouldn't walk around at night by herself or even in the day for that matter. This gang infested shindig was definitely not her cup of tea.

Walking through the crowded room to look for April or Candice to let them know she was going home got her butt tapped, pinched, squeezed, or slapped every two seconds and she was heated. This was definitely turning out to be a glass of Moscato and a hot bath type of night. She was about to say forget her so-called friends and leave when she saw them walk through the door. April looked like she owned the place; Candice, like she was ready to bolt.

There was enough booty and cleavage hanging out to film a porno flick, but every male eye was on April and Candice. They also knew how sexy a beautiful woman with a banging body could be when she covered up, leaving a little something for the imagination. Being sure to let irritation show on her face, Meme greeted April with a weak hug and smiled at Candice who sauntered in behind April with obvious frustration on her face.

"Just one hour." April knew Meme was going to take one look at the place and be ready to leave before giving it a chance. "Stay for an hour. Forget about what the place looks like and just have a good time."

Meme rolled her eyes, refusing to respond.

A popular song started playing and just about every woman around started popping and shaking their way to the dance floor. April stood back and let them make a fool of themselves. Tossing a wink to Meme and Candice, she took her time getting to the floor. "Follow my lead ladies." The trio strutted out to the middle of the dance floor and guys were breaking their necks just to get a peek.

Meme danced for a few minutes. She tried to get into it, but it really wasn't her scene. All she kept picturing was stray bullets and stampedes. When April's attention focused elsewhere, she waved good bye to Candice and headed home.

The path to Meme's apartment was still dark, and that eerie feeling returned. The slight echo of foot steps behind her scared her to death and she took off running to her apartment. With high heels and all, she ran like her life depended on it. At her front door, her heart almost stopped. The door was cracked opened. Peering through the crack, she could see the overturned coffee table and broken glass on the floor. That's all she needed to see. Meme took off her shoes and sprinted back to her car like an Olympic gold medalist. Inside the safety of her steel panic chamber on wheels, she locked the doors and called her brother.

"Marlon." He had barely said hello before she started rambling into the phone. "Someone broke into my apartment."

"I am on my way." Marlon hung up the phone, told Cole what was up, and asked him to hold it down at the restaurant until he got back.

Arriving at Meme's apartment complex, Marlon found her locked up inside her car looking terrified. He knocked on the window and she screamed so loud that even with the window rolled up it pierced his ear. Seeing that it was him, she jumped out of the car so fast and wrapped her arms so tightly around him that he had to pry himself loose in order to breathe. "Meme, what's up?" Marlon could tell by her reaction that this fear was about more than just a break-in. He'd spent the majority of his life protecting her from boogey men, bad dreams, and bullies. He could tell something more was troubling her.

Meme watched Marlon's face distort from concern to fury as she told him about the notes, scratches on her car, and how the police had pretty much blown her off. She conveniently left out her interactions with Cole. Without a word, Marlon grabbed her by the hand and marched up to her apartment. The overturned table and glass on the floor were merely a small fraction of the damage. The sofas had been sliced opened and the filling pulled out. Soil from the potted plants was spread across the floor. Her flat-screen TV had been busted and knocked off the stand. It seemed as if every dish she owned was shattered on the floor. That was just the damage in the front of the house.

*Maybe it's punishment for not following through with all those promises I made at the hospital.* Oddly enough, being punished by the almighty God was a welcomed alternative from what she knew was really going on.

Without going further into her apartment, Meme called the police and plopped down on the arm of the couch. She couldn't take seeing any more damage, so she let Marlon continue looking. The destruction was consistent throughout the entire apartment. When he came out of her room and told her the word slut was written on the wall above her bed, Meme almost lost it. Who would hate her so much that they'd do all this?

There was a knock at the door and since the lock was busted, there was no need for anyone to open it. Assuming it was the police, Marlon yelled out for whoever was at the door to come in. In walked Latrice; Marlon was livid. He should've known when he called her that she would show up. That's the kind of woman she was. She would never let him handle a rough situation by himself. But there are just some places a man doesn't want his wife visiting after just giving birth, and a crime scene was one of them.

Closing the door as tightly as she could, Latrice ignored Marlon's chastising glare and went to comfort her sister-in-law. Meme couldn't help but laugh. She wrapped her arms around Latrice, whispering in her ear, "You are in big trouble."

Latrice whispered back, "Please, I am not scared of him." They shared a private laugh and Marlon eyed them suspiciously.

There was another knock at the door, and once again Marlon yelled for them to come in. The door opened and everyone froze. "What are you doing here?" Marlon and Latrice asked in unison.

Ignoring their question, Cole stepped further inside and as he did so, Meme was up off the couch flying into his arms. He lifted her off the ground as she wrapped her arms around his neck. Pressing her body against his, Cole carried her out of the living room and into the bedroom as he brushed his lips across her neck. "I am sorry for not being here for you."

Marlon had told Cole about the break-in and he immediately started beating himself up for not doing everything he could to keep her safe. He tried to stay put and close up the restaurant like Marlon had asked him to, but he was going crazy with worry. The only information he had was Meme's apartment had been broken into. He didn't know if she was home during the break-in or if she was hurt. Before he could stop himself, he was in the car and headed toward her apartment.

"Are you all right?" He asked just as his lips finally found hers. He kissed the reply off her lips and then some.

"I am a little scared, but I will be fine."

Searching her eyes, Cole saw the truth. She was terrified. Scanning the room and seeing the word scribbled across her wall confirmed his suspicions. This wasn't a random break-in; this was personal. Without giving her space to object, Cole commanded her to pack her things. "You are staying with me."

"No." Meme defiantly puffed her chest out as she took a step away from him. "I will stay with Marlon."

"He won't protect you the way I will." There was no way he was leaving without her and the sooner she understood that the better.

"Well, he has been doing a great job so far. At least I won't have to worry about him giving me mixed signals."

"It's not up for discussion. Pack a few things, so I can get you out of here."

"I am not going anywhere with you." Meme was in full sistah-girl mode, with a hand on her hip and neck rolling. "Until you admit your feelings for me."

His chest deflated and so did Meme's hope. She watched his eyes rake over her as he sighed in frustration. He turned his back on her to walk away and Meme wished he had never shown up. Seeing him was great and gave her hope that he was ready to be with her. That hope was short lived and was now being yanked from under her.

"I like you." Cole stopped just before reaching the door. *Stop being scared and be with her. Broken hearts do mend.* Janine's words picked the right time to float across his mind.

Meme held her breath.

"I like you a lot."

Meme was taken aback by his words and had to remind herself to breathe. She watched his back, waiting for his next move, word, or something. *Don't cry, don't cry. Breathe. Breathe. Breathe.* She wanted to touch him and tell him how much she liked him, but this was an important moment and it had to be all his.

Slowly, he turned around, and the sincerity in his eyes was too much for her to take. The tears she tried to hold back ran down her cheeks in full force. "I have never done this before." He wiped her tears with the pad of his thumb. "Never thought I'd want to, but I am all yours. That chemistry stuff you were talking about, I feel it and it is unreal. I want to see what's up with it, but it's over with anyone else you've been seeing and I will do the same."

Meme was so overwhelmed she couldn't speak. When she nodded her reply, Cole kissed her more tenderly than he ever had.

"Mmm," Meme moaned as their lips parted. "I've missed you."

Cole chuckled. "Yeah, I've missed you too." He tapped her on the rear end. "Now pack your stuff." On the outside he was smiling, but inside was a different story. This woman had the power to break him. He was terrified.

Marlon was in the living room jumping up and down, giving Latrice the, *I told you so* chant. She was so in shock that she couldn't care less about his ridiculous antics. Meme and Cole—the lesbian and the playboy—that's an odd couple. It wasn't just an 'I like you and you like me' type of connection either. The fire burning between them was pretty intense. If that electrical current was what Marlon saw at their reception, no wonder he kept harping on it.

Finally, Marlon's gloating started to grate Latrice's nerves. "While you're over there celebrating, you do know what playa playa is probably in there doing to your sister?"

Marlon stopped mid-dance and made a move to go bust up whatever was going on.

155

"Oh no." Latrice blocked him. "Mr. Matchmaker, your sister is a grown woman who can handle herself. You set these wheels in motion and you can't stop them now." Latrice laughed at his sullen expression, and when he plopped down on the arm of the couch, she sat in his lap—as much as the awkward position would allow—to tease him some more. That teasing morphed to playful little pecks to a full make-out session.

"Oh God, get a room," Meme groaned as she exited the bedroom.

Cole followed closely behind her and immediately made eye contact with Marlon, asking, "Are you cool with this?"

"Would it matter if I wasn't?"

"No." Cole slid his hand around Meme's waist and pulled her back up against him.

"You trying to hit it and quit it?" He knew of Cole's reputation, and any brother in their right mind would have kept their sister away from him, but Marlon knew what he saw at the reception. He recognized it as the same reaction he had to Latrice. Taking one look at Cole, Marlon knew the answer to his question.

Hunching over, Cole wrapped his arms around Meme, pulling her as close as he possibly could. His head slid over her shoulder and the stubble from his beard brushed against her cheek. "I couldn't if I wanted to." He mumbled as he rained kisses along the line of her jaw.

Meme melted into his embrace and was on the verge of kicking her brother and his wife out when there was another knock on the door. Once again, Marlon yelled for them to come in. Meme broke free from Cole's spell and greeted the officers as they walked inside.

Walking them through the house and giving them her statement seemed to take forever. Never in her life had she answered so many questions and repeated herself so many times. The whole process seemed a bit much, but she guessed they were finally taking her claims seriously. Whoever was harassing her was escalating, and the police were all ears now.

Once the police left, Marlon out right refused to let Meme leave with Cole, but once he was reminded of how he had rearranged his whole life to protect Latrice from her abusive husband, he understood why Cole wouldn't have it any other way. Latrice fled from her husband to friends who were more than willing and capable to protect her. Even though Marlon was dealing with the betrayal of his own wife, there was something about Latrice that made him want to protect her. Reluctantly, Marlon backed up and handed his little sister over to Cole.

## 15

Opening the front door to his apartment, Cole stepped to the side, allowing Meme to enter. As she walked by, her scent heightened his senses and every part of him was aware of the woman she was. His eyes took in her outfit and how the fabric caressed her curves. Each sway of her hips spoke to him, called him, taunted him, and dared him to come closer. Biting his bottom lip, Cole groaned at the thoughts running through his mind. The things he wanted to do. The places he wanted to savor. A sample wouldn't do. He wanted to feast over and over again.

She had no idea how her presence in his home was affecting him. At that moment, Cole decided he was done running from a relationship. He was going to let Meme into the parts of his heart that he normally kept hidden. He would enjoy her company and not push her away when it was time for the next level. If love happened, he'd embrace it.

Cole stood stuck in the same spot as he watched her make her way to the sofa. He needed to move, stop staring, and be a good host, but he couldn't focus on anything other than her. The blood from his brain had rushed to other parts of his body. Any task his manhood couldn't handle was neglected.

"Are you just going to stand there and watch me all night?" Meme smiled as she took off her shoes.

When he didn't respond, she shuffled her bare feet across the carpet to stand in front of him. Rubbing her hands up and down his chest, she encouraged him to relax. "Look, I know hearing the words *I love you* come out of my mouth the other night was a little scary, but I assure you it was the alcohol talking. I am not against the possibility of loving you. It's just too soon to tell. I am not here to intrude on your space. I will even sleep on the couch if that's what you want."

Pulling her closer, Cole explained. "Your intruding on my space is the furthest thing from my mind."

His grip was so firm, she couldn't pull away if she wanted to. His mouth descended upon hers with such an overwhelming intensity that she felt his kiss before their lips connected. An onslaught of passion washed over her and she was putty in his hands. Backing her up to the sofa, Cole gently laid her across the cool leather. The space between her thighs cradled him perfectly. Uninhibited, Meme moaned as Cole unleashed his desire for her. His mouth sought out her neck, searching for every spot that would drive her crazy.

Mustering up her strength, Meme pushed her hands against his chest, halting his pursuit. She wanted him—wanted this—but for the first time in her life, she was thinking about the consequences of her actions. "I am still a virgin. That hasn't changed." She panted, trying to stave off the blissful fury that was building. "I'm still the woman you claim not to be good enough for." She didn't want to give herself to him and then have him change his mind about being with her.

"Like I told you before, you make me forget all my rules," Cole whispered against her lips as he carried her to his bed.

For the first time, Cole was at a loss for what his next move should be. His body wanted Meme and his heart did too. His body said, "Take her and take her hard." His heart asked, "What's the rush?"

Reaching into his night stand, Cole pulled out a condom and placed it into her hand. "Are you sure this is what you want?"

He asked the question, hoping to make it her decision to slow down. If she changed her mind, there wasn't enough ice in the world to ease his condition. There was only one thing, with this one woman, that could bring him relief. For once, the sex wasn't his main focus. Lazily, his fingers caressed her shoulders and then trailed up her neck. He caressed the line of her jaw before stroking her lips with his thumb. Her skin was soft like rose petals and smelled just as good. He ached to replace his fingers with his mouth, but he had to take things slow.

"I want this with you."

"Why do you want it to be me?"

"For the same reason it's me you're allowing into your heart." Meme brushed her hand down his cheek and waited for him to look into her eyes. "Because there is no one else who can make me feel this way."

Cole rested his head on her chest. Any man in his right mind would take what she was offering and run with it. He guessed this was how it felt to really care about a woman and not want to take advantage of her.

"I don't want us to rush into this because we think we have to." He felt her stiffen and try to pull away, but he wouldn't let her go until he fully explained.

"Please believe me when I say this has nothing to do with you being a virgin. It's just that sex has always been the first stop in all my relationships and it was over shortly after. I'm just trying not to repeat past mistakes."

*Can't believe I'm putting on the brakes.* Truth be told, he was still concerned about the clingy virgin thing, but he'd wanted her so bad, he was willing to deal with the aftermath. Now he'd put a stop to it all and was sure he'd be mad as hell in a couple of hours when he couldn't sleep and her warm soft skin was brushing up against his. He should've just let her go with Marlon, but the thoughts that had run through his mind when he heard her house had been broken into had him on edge. If she had been home, he could've lost her, and he didn't want to waste any more time, possibly miss out on being with the one woman who made him feel something.

Meme was set to go off, but his soft spoken words and the obvious conflict between what his body and heart wanted softened her. She tossed the condom on the night stand and snuggled him close so they could talk.

In the morning, Cole woke to Meme standing on the side of the bed, hovering over him as she watched him sleep. His eyes fluttered open then slid back closed. He stretched and scratched the patch of hair on his chest.

"Should I be scared Meme?" His voice was raspy with sleep. "You're standing over me like you're getting ready to stab me or burn me with hot grits." Cole laughed as he yanked her onto the bed, rolling her onto her back. Holding her arms above her head, Cole used his free hand to tickle her.

Meme squirmed and bucked for her freedom. "I would never hurt you," She reassured him. She cried out in laughter. "I made you breakfast. I was just trying to decide if I was going to wake you."

That was a shock. His playfulness ceased and he released her. Most people found out he was a chef and expected him to cook for them. Meme had taken the time to prepare him a meal and from the smell of things, she had done a good job. His eyes scanned her face and his heart beat a little harder for her. Having her around was definitely going to be interesting. He lowered his head to kiss her and she squirmed even harder.

"No Cole, don't kiss me with your morning breath."

Her squirming was no match for the weight of his body. Trying to thwart his kiss, she violently shook her head back and forth. None of her efforts stopped him. Sure enough, he connected their lips and kissed the complaint out of her mouth. It wasn't until her squirming stopped and she moaned against his lips that he released her.

He stood from the bed and looked down at her heaving chest. Each rise and fall begged him to climb back into the bed, but he resisted.

"Give it to me like that every morning," he commanded as his eyes roamed the rest of her and landed on her lips. He fought off the urge to kiss her again and strode toward the door to go check out her cooking skills, but Meme stopped him.

"Aren't you going to put some clothes on?"

"Do you have a problem eating breakfast with a half-naked man?" Cole stood in the doorway only wearing boxer briefs. He was proud, virile, and more gorgeous than any man had a right to be.

"No not at all, but you're too tempting for me to ignore." Meme swayed her hips into the kitchen, trying her best to ignore Cole's penetrating glare. He sat at the table watching her every move as she prepared their plates. She tried to set his plate on the table in front of him, but he grabbed her wrist and guided her onto his lap. She straddled his legs and looked him in the eyes.

His desire for her nestled against her backside and she knew it was taking all his willpower to do right by her. She held the plate between them as a barrier. Scooping a spoonful of eggs, she placed it at his lips. Eyeing her warily, Cole's lips pressed together as he contemplated her actions.

"Open up," Meme prodded. Cole pulled his head back from the spoon with the words of refusal on the tip of his lips until her head drooped, eyes widened, and mouth pouted. "Please."

Cole's heart clenched and he knew he was a goner. Watching her move about his kitchen, in his home, like she belonged there already had him trippin'. That adorable look she just gave him could get him to do anything for her. He opened his mouth and sat there as she fed him bite after bite. By the end, he was starting to enjoy her tenderness. Meme fed him, wiped food off his mouth, brought his glass of orange juice to his mouth, and then kissed the lingering drops off his lips.

"Mmm," Meme moaned as she suckled the last drop of orange juice from his mouth. "I wish I could stay here with you all day." Meme thought about her first client for the day and groaned. "Ms. O'Neil." It was going to be a long morning.

"Who's Ms. O'Neil?" Cole asked as he stood with her legs wrapped around his waist and carried her to the bedroom.

"She is a client who is always trying to fix me up with one of her sons. I just recently went out with one, hoping her persistent match making would stop, but it hasn't. Now she insists that Scott was just all wrong for me and one of her other sons are more suited for my needs."

"Is this the same guy you brought to the restaurant?"

Meme devilishly smiled as she patted his stubbly cheek. "Yes, and he is the guy who made you crazy jealous."

Cole opened his mouth to deny it, but couldn't. He had been jealous. It was that jealousy that propelled him into action. "And also the guy you tried to impress by ordering something you really didn't want to eat."

"Oh please," Meme scoffed. "That jerk ordered for me like he was my daddy. He pissed me off, but the look on his face as he watched me eat the meal you prepared gave me much satisfaction and made the food taste ten times better." Meme slid her hands around his neck, guiding his lips to hers.

"Trust me, as soon as I realized where he was taking me, I knew what I was going to order. Regardless of how mad I was at you, my heart skipped a beat knowing that you were going to prepare it for me. I knew your hands were going to be in it and thought it was going to be my last time to taste you. With each bite, I searched for your taste and found contentment in the fact that even though I couldn't taste you, you were in there somewhere."

Cole tried to swallow the lump that had formed in his throat. Each word she spoke chipped at the stony wall he'd erected around his heart. He pulled her even closer as their mouths succumbed to each other.

"Do me a favor," Cole said, once they finally parted for air. "Tell Ms. O'Neil you got a man."

The intensity in his eyes and the sincerity in his voice almost stopped Meme's heart. He was reaffirming his words from last night. He wanted her and wasn't going to share. That revelation made words clog in her throat and all she could do was nod in agreement.

Making love would've been perfect. Being tangled in his arms, pressed to the mattress by the weight of his body, and covered in his sweat seemed like the obvious next step. He kissed her, suckled from her lips like they contained the air he needed to breathe. The electricity surging between them amped up a few volts. Meme shook from the electrical current. Her hands roamed down his already bare torso, acquainting themselves with the hard ripples of his chest and abs.

"Stop touching me, or I won't be able to stop."

She bit his neck and suckled the tender spot. She didn't want him to stop. She rotated her hips, grinding her core against his hardness, hoping to coax him into giving her what she wanted. His hands slid up her thighs and gripped the fleshy part of her backside that hung out of her boy shorts.

"Meme, please get up and go to work." There was only so much a man could take and he was well past his normal limit. With each second, the crack in his will power got wider and longer.

"What's wrong? Don't you want me?" Her breathy whisper traipsed across his neck. The simple act drove him insane and he groaned in frustration.

"Yeah, all of you." He gripped her hips to halt her movement. "You are the only woman I've ever wanted beyond sex. I've been running from you for almost two months. Let's not rush things and ruin this." *Can't believe I just said that...can't believe I'm putting on the brakes again.* He didn't have enough fingers to count the times women tried to halt his sexual advances by giving him the *let's not rush things* speech. He'd simply turn up the heat, and within minutes, she'd be begging him to give it to her.

"Okay." She leaned back to look into his eyes and cupped his cheek in her hand. "I can't believe I'm finally here with you."

*I can't believe it either.* Cole watched as she walked away. Those boy shorts perfectly framed the fleshy mounds of her backside. He had to be out of his mind to keep turning that down. Just watching her move was an aphrodisiac. Gripping his hardness, he groaned out his unquenched desire. Meme stopped walking. She smiled at him over her shoulder and seductively swayed her hips. She dipped and swirled, bouncing her body to her own beat. Cole gripped himself harder.

She dropped it down low and gyrated it all the back up.

Cole lost his mind.

She was about to get what she was asking for. Meme heard him get up off the bed and screamed as she took off running into the bathroom.

Cole could hear her giggling behind the bathroom door. His sweet, innocent, little Meme was sexy as hell and liked to play games. "Open the door."

"No," she giggled. "You told me to go to work. I'm just doing as I'm told."

"Meme..."

"Did you like my dance?"

"Hell yeah."

"If you had stayed put, I would have continued."

"Come out and finish. I won't touch you."

"Too late, the mood has left me. And I need to go to work."

Cole groaned.

Meme chuckled again.

*Hahaha, very funny.* Slowly, he backed away from the door. He had to get out of there. If that bathroom door opened and he was still in his current condition, the innocent vixen was going to lose her innocence. He grabbed his gym bag, told her he'd see her later that night, reminded her that he'd left her a key on the night stand, and was out the door.

## 16

**W**ithout question, Sundays were the best. Meme wasn't rushing off to work and Cole wasn't off to the gym. They could spend a lazy morning in bed, cook breakfast together, go for a walk, or even play video games. It didn't matter what the activity was, as long as they were together. Today, she had plans. Cole's laundry basket was overflowing and she was sick of it. She slipped quietly out of bed, grabbed the basket, and headed toward the laundry room. The sun hadn't risen yet and she stood in the dim light of the wash room separating his clothes.

The weeks they'd been living together were perfect and it was hard not to imagine forever with him. She tried to keep herself grounded by telling herself that Cole didn't want love, marriage, or children, and that one day their relationship would be over. In her last relationship, she made the mistake of expecting the impossible. The result was catastrophic and she didn't want to feel that kind of pain again. Being realistic was her best option. Cole may never love her, and would eventually move on to someone else. She'd accept what he was offering for as long as he offered it. When it was over, she'd try her best to move on. A broken heart was inevitable since she'd already fallen in love with him, but she figured expecting it would soften the blow.

A few weeks ago, she realized she'd fallen in love with him. She fell asleep on the couch, waiting for him to come home from work. She woke up to him lifting her from the couch to carry her to bed and she looked up into his eyes. At that moment, she knew she'd lost the fight of not loving him. His tenderness, the soft 'I missed you baby' he whispered in her ear, and the kiss on her forehead sealed the deal. She simply gave into her feelings, rested her head on his chest, wrapped her arms around his neck, and told herself he could never know how she felt.

Midway through folding the first load, Meme felt a pair of arms circle her waist. Her breath caught in her throat and she dropped the shirt she'd been folding.

Cole chuckled. "What are you doing?"

"What does it look like I'm doing?" She stepped out of his grasp, picked up the shirt, and continued folding.

"You know you don't have to."

"I know. Why are you up?"

"Can't sleep without you."

The corners of her mouth turned up at his small admission. Slowly, she lifted her eyes to his and the look she encountered was priceless. He hadn't meant to be so candid and she decided to let it pass without making a big deal out of it, but inside she was grinning from ear to ear and doing somersaults.

"Well, try to get some rest. I will come back to bed as soon as I finish this load."

Cole leaned his shoulder against the doorframe and studied her. Living with her was the complete opposite of what he'd ever thought it would be. She was fun to be with, easy to talk to, liked to play video games, and had cleaned and organized his house to the point where he didn't recognize the place. His eyes roamed up and down her body, taking in every curve. *And she's fine.* His eyes lingered on her backside and within seconds it was in his hands. This woman had been in his bed for weeks and he had yet to indulge in the pleasure of her body. It was becoming harder and harder to resist.

As he cupped the round mass, his lips found her neck. One hand grazed under her shorts, brushing against her bare skin, while the other traveled up the front of her shirt, caressing her stomach. This was the furthest he'd allow himself to go. If he felt the flesh of breast in his hands or the folds of her femininity, his libido would take over and reenact every fantasy he'd had about her. He wasn't ready for what a sexual relationship with her would entail.

"Cole," she managed to find clarity amid the sensual haze. "Please don't tease me. I don't know why you've held back and denied us both what we want. I'm here for you. You can have all of me." She felt him tense up and she turned in his arms to look into his eyes. "Is it still the virgin thing?"

His eyes dropped to avoid hers.

"Cole…"

He felt her pulling away from him and refused to let her go. "Yes and no, but not for the reasons you think."

"I think you're just sitting around waiting for us to break up and don't want to deal with the guilt of taking my virginity."

170

"That's not it at all. I'm feeling you Meme. For the first time, I want more than sex." The look on her face let him know she needed a better explanation. "Okay," Cole sighed in exasperation. "I do have my reasons, but they are definitely not what you just said."

"Baby, talk to me. I just want to make love and connect with you. Don't you? Is it because I am your friend's sister?"

"It's none of that. Trust me when I say I'm into you. When the time is right, I'm going to make love to you so hard and deep you won't know whether to beg me to stop or to never quit."

"Well, just so you know, every time you get me all worked up and refuse to follow through, I go into the bathroom and take care of what you refuse to do." With that said, she tossed a shirt in his face, pushed past him, and headed in that direction.

Cole let the shirt slide down his face and to the floor as he processed what she said. Never had he left a woman unsatisfied. The thought of her pleasing herself when he was very well capable of doing it didn't sit well with him. He turned on his heels and followed after her. He found her in the room rummaging through her night stand. "What are you looking for?"

She balled up her hand and spun around, hiding something behind her back. She was totally bluffing. She tried pleasing herself a few times, but she wanted Cole so bad that the techniques she'd mastered years ago didn't cut it. Maybe a bruised ego would propel him into action. "Tell me why we have to wait. Are you still sleeping with someone else?"

"No." He tried to reach for the hand behind her back, but she moved away from him. "Please trust me."

"I'm trying to, but this is not normal. I should be refusing you, not the other way around."

He grabbed her free hand and brought it to his lips. He kissed her knuckles and tried to pull her into his arms, but she locked her knees and wouldn't budge. Her unrelenting glare let him know she wasn't letting it go this time. He was going to have to fess up. With a deep breath and a frustrated eye roll he started talking. "I think about your relationship with Damien. If he hadn't turned out to be such a punk, you'd either be married or still saving yourself for your husband. Who am I to take that away from you? You've waited a long time to give that special gift to your husband."

*Who are you to take that from me?* Meme tried to stave off the pang of rejection his words caused. She could have won an award for her performance. Her words came out sounding light and carefree. "That's really sweet, but I don't know if I'll ever get married. I want to experience this with you."

"Of course you'll get married, you're perfect."

*Yeah, perfect for everyone, but you.* "I know you're adamant about not getting married. So when this relationship is over, what will I have to remember you?"

*When this relationship is over.* He'd never considered forever with any woman, but didn't like those words coming out of her mouth. "We have other memories. You can't tell me all this time we've spent together has meant nothing." He stepped forward to embrace her, but she backed away and snatched her hand away.

Feeling the dam of her emotions beginning to crack, Meme turned her back to Cole and strutted with as much dignity as possible to the bathroom. Once behind the shield of the door, the dam ruptured. Tears flooded down her cheeks like a rushing river. Meme vowed that would be the last time she offered herself to him. She felt like a fool for thinking he felt something real for her. *Joke's on me.*

Deciding a shower would soothe her anxiety, she turned on the water and stepped out of her clothes. As she stepped into the stream of the shower, she allowed the water to trickle down her face, mingling with the already free flowing tears.

*Maybe I really am unlovable. Damien couldn't have possibly loved me, Alicia out right said she never loved me, and now Cole.*

Her shoulders trembled under the weight of that thought. Was it so wrong to want to be loved unconditionally with someone's whole heart? She'd given just that twice, and Cole made three. Each time, it blew up in her face. She should have stuck with her first admonition and followed her head, not her heart, because the latter seemed intent on shattering itself.

Now she needed to determine her next step. Was she willing to wait for Cole to really be into her? Was he even capable of giving more or feeling more than what he already had? Maybe she should leave now while she still had the strength to walk away. Just thinking of walking away made the sobs come stronger. *Why did I get myself into another situation like this?*

"Baby, don't cry."

Meme spun around at the sound of the deep voice behind her. Her eyes widened in fear and shock. Her thoughts were so loud, she hadn't heard him enter the bathroom. "Cole—"

He kissed the words off her lips as he wrapped his hands around her waist, pulling her intimately close. When her bare flesh touched his, all sorrow was forgotten and the fire that had burned between them since

Marlon's wedding reception blazed to a roaring inferno. His lips abandoned hers, trailing along her jaw and down the column of her neck. The tenderness in his kiss made her feel treasured for the first time.

"Always know that I want you. I've wanted you since the day I met you. I want you so bad that it scares the hell out of me." That admission shattered his control and he gave into his desires.

His hands walked the plains, curves, hills, and valleys of her body as his eyes took in the depth of her beauty, which ran deeper than his fantasies ever imagined. Her body boasted of round, firm, full breast, a flat stomach that panned out to curvaceous hips, and toned thighs that he dreamed of wrapping around his waist. He couldn't believe the treasure he'd been holding all this time and had yet to unwrap. His mouth joined his hands, causing a soft moan to escape Meme's mouth. He kissed the swell of her breast, giving each equal attention, nipping and suckling until her knees buckled.

"Stay with me baby." He lifted her and hooked her legs around his waist as he leaned her against the wall. The cool tile against her skin did nothing to douse the trail of heat Cole was leaving across her body. His teeth nipped and tongue licked in places that she'd never imagined could take her higher into euphoria. She'd never known such a pleasure.

Cole's heart pounded wildly against his ribs. If she wasn't a virgin, he would have plunged in and rode her hard to completion by now, but he had to prolong her pleasure. He had to prime her body for his entrance to minimize her discomfort. When his name rolled from her lips in short hiccupping pants, he knew she was ready. He positioned himself at the doorway to her haven and recaptured her lips in a searing kiss as he slowly sheathed himself within her. Meme tore her lips away and cried out. Her screams echoed through the shower. Cole froze, questioning with his eyes if she wanted him to stop. Her head lolled to the side and her eyes rolled back giving him the only answer he needed.

Feeling him press forward, Meme moaned with satisfaction. She didn't have the breath to beg him to continue and she wasn't ready for the connection with him to end. Her body parted for him and her heat surrounded him, causing beads of sweat to pebble on his brow. As he filled her to the hilt, their eyes met. For a moment, they gazed at each other, both sinking further into the spellbinding abyss that sucked them in from the day they met, causing them to disregard rational thinking and surrender to what their hearts wanted.

A few deep breaths to maintain control was all he needed. Recapturing her lips, he kissed her in the same slow rhythm that he rode her against the wall. Her body tensed and her breathing became more rapid and he released her mouth. He wanted to hear her pant and call his name as he drove her to ecstasy. With each breathy moan of his name, she seeped further into his heart. He was worried that deflowering her would make her possessive and clingy, but it was he who was taking possession. "You are mine. I'm your first and your last."

"My only!"

Meme cried out as an orgasm hit her, sending her body quaking like a California fault line. Her tremors and contracting muscles pushed him over the edge. Her name rolled from his mouth on a strangled growl as he ground out his release. She nuzzled her face against his neck as she tried to regulate her breathing. Sated purrs tickled Cole's neck and he smiled at how her limp body draped over him. Securing her tightly to him, he walked them into the shower stream to wash away all traces of her ruptured hymen. He washed her with such adoration and reverence it took her breath away. She fought back tears as she struggled to contain the three little words that her heart was screaming. They had moved forward in their relationship, and she didn't want to scare him off by speaking those words. After he washed her, he carried her to the room, laid her on the bed, and massaged her back until she fell asleep.

## 17

Meme woke up again a little after ten. The day had just begun, and her life had already drastically changed. She rolled over and smiled at the soreness between her thighs. Not only had she and Cole made love, but the ray of hope that he actually felt something for her made the room glisten. She was no stranger to sexual gratification, but what Cole had done to her body totally transcended her expectations. She'd been told that no one knows a woman's body like another woman. Sure, the logic made sense, but in practice, it was clearly a lie. Cole knew her body like he'd created it himself. She'd also been told that her first time would be too painful to enjoy; wrong again. Yes, there was some pain, but the pleasure overshadowed all discomfort.

"Mmm," Meme moaned as her recollection of their morning tryst in the shower reawakened her senses. As her body began to hum for him, she crawled out of the bed to find the source of relief.

She found him in the kitchen sitting at the table nursing a beer. He was fully dressed in a pair of dark jeans, a white polo shirt, boots, and a hat cocked to the side. He looked dressed for his morning-after disappearing act, but he realized this was his house. He had to stick around. His solemn mood sent dread creeping up her spine. He barely acknowledged her presence as she stepped to his side. He took a long swig of his beer, stood up, and walked away without saying a word.

*Oh God, not so soon. Please not now.* She watched him walk away and couldn't help but feel he was giving her the brush off. Hadn't he told her his relationships ended shortly after sex? She should've listened and waited until he was ready instead of pushing him. Now he was pushing her away. *Calm down and get a grip. You knew this wasn't forever. Now go in there and talk to him.* She gave herself a pep talk, put her emotions in check as best she could, and went after him.

He sat on the couch, still nursing his beer. Their eyes met and stayed connected as she moved toward him. Even as he took another gulp of his beer, his eyes never left hers. She kneeled in front of him and placed her hands on his knees.

"Do you want me to leave?" It was a hard question to ask and she barely got the words out, but she had to ask him.

Cole leaned forward and reached around her to place his beer on the coffee table. He gripped her hips and rested his forehead against hers. For several minutes they sat in silence. She took his silence as a good sign that he wanted her to stay. She still wished she could read his mind and prepare her heart for whatever he was about to say.

"There is something I have to do today." He slid his hands up her back and used his shoulders to lift her arms around his neck. One hand gripped her backside, guiding her onto his lap. His other hand slid into her hair holding her steady for his approaching lips. "Will you come with me?" His lips brushed against hers as he demonstrated how much he wanted her to stay.

"Since I've already showered," Meme giggled, causing a break in Cole's sullen attitude. "Just let me throw some clothes on."

"How do you feel?"

"Amazing. My body is still tingly."

Cole smiled as he placed a finger under her chin and lifted her eyes to meet his. "I'm glad you enjoyed, but that's not what I was asking. Are you sore?"

Leaning forward, she placed her head on his shoulder. "I am a little sore, but I will be fine. I was hoping we could spend the rest of the day making love."

He wrapped his arms around her and she settled in to his embrace. "Your body needs time to heal. That's the only reason I haven't laid you on this couch."

"Well, I guess I'll get dressed. Maybe when we get back I can persuade you to rethink the whole waiting for my body to heal stance." Before getting up, she cupped his cheek in her hand. "Are you okay?"

"Yeah, I'm good." He brought the palm of her hand to his lips and gently kissed it. "Now get dressed."

As she walked away, she looked back at him. He'd grabbed his beer off the table, leaned his head back against the sofa, and guzzled the remaining contents of the bottle. There was something definitely bothering him. She'd never seen him like that. "Cole, is it me? Is making love to me what's bothering you?"

"Hell no." She waited for him to expound, but he didn't. She slowly walked away and got dressed.

The ride was quiet. Cole seemed deep in thought as he maneuvered the car up and down the streets. Meme just let him be. She figured wherever they were going would explain his mood. She was just glad that he wasn't pulling away from her. Meme's eyes widened when he pulled up in front of a cemetery and made the right turn into the gates. Her mind was running wild, but she kept her mouth shut. He drove up a few narrow winding streets and then slowed his car to a stop. He assisted her out of the car, leading her to a marble stone that read Phillip Monroe. The name didn't ring a bell, but what stood out the most was the date of birth. Whoever this person was, today was their birthday. Suddenly Cole's sullen mood made sense.

For a few moments, they stood in silence, holding hands. Meme squeezed his hand, letting him know she was there.

"He's my father." His soft spoken words caught Meme by surprise.

"Oh baby, I am so sorry." She placed an arm around his waist and the other hand on his chest.

"No need to be sorry. Thanks to my mother, he was dead long before he passed away." Meme waited for him to explain, but he didn't. "So, today's his birthday."

He nodded. "Every year since he passed, this day has been the worst day of my life, except for today. You helped me forget. Not only is this his birthday, but it's also the day he died."

Even weeks before the date arrived, Cole would shut down and block everyone out. His father had his flaws, but all the lessons he'd taught were out of love. He didn't want his son to experience the hurt he did. Cole obeyed everything his father told him, so he wouldn't leave him the way his mother did. No matter how flawed his father's instruction seemed, Cole obeyed. Eventually, his father's thoughts became his own. His father was proud of the way he jumped from woman to woman. Until the day he died, he'd encouraged him to continue his philandering ways. "I was supposed to be there. If I had been there, he'd still be alive."

"Don't say that. You have no idea what God's plan was." She held him a little tighter.

"It was his birthday, and we made plans to celebrate. I blew him off for some chick I'd met the night before. I was laid up in some woman's bed while my dad laid on the side of the road breathing his last breath. He was driving drunk. Not only did he kill himself, but he also took the life of the woman whose car he rammed into."

"Baby, it wasn't your fault. Your father made that choice, not you."

"That's the same thing Janine said. She's the daughter of the woman my father killed. We spent a lot of time together after the accident. She was the closest I've ever come to being in a relationship until now. Even with her, I've never felt what I feel with you. I've never even told her that I was supposed to be with my father that night. I've never told anyone."

Meme pressed her head against his chest and squeezed him compassionately. Cole stood at his father's grave doing exactly what his father spent years teaching him not to do, giving his heart to a woman. He accepted the comfort she offered and gave her another part of him. A day that had once given him so much grief was now marked as the day he'd made love to the amazing woman in his arms.

"Janine and I usually go to our parents' gravesites then meet up for lunch. Thanks to our shower this morning, I forgot today was that day until Janine texted me and asked to move lunch back and hour. Will you go with me?"

Meme nodded then followed him to the car. She tried to ignore the feelings that came over her about Janine texting him. She also tried to ignore how she felt about him still seeing a woman she was sure he'd slept with. There was no doubt that Janine was more experienced and able to satisfy him in ways she couldn't. Images of Damien and the scene Meme had walked in on flashed across her mind and she tried to swallow the lump of fear that formed in her throat.

They rode to the restaurant in silence. Cole held her hand while driving, occasionally bringing it to his lips. All the while, Meme stared out the window. Her thoughts ran wild. *Does he see her more than once a year? When's the last time he saw her? Does he have feelings for her? Does she have feelings for him? Are they still sleeping together?* By the time they arrived at the restaurant, she'd become so sick with worry that she had to excuse herself to the restroom. She patted her face with a wet paper towel and then made eye contact with her reflection in the bathroom mirror. "Stop it." She pointed at her reflection with calm admonishment. "You are not going to be an emotional basket case again. You are walking into this relationship with your eyes wide open. He is only capable of so much. Don't expect too much from him." Having thoroughly gotten her mind back on track, Meme walked back to the lobby.

The scene she walked into took every word she'd spoken to herself in the bathroom and jammed it back down her throat. Cole stood with his arms possessively wrapped around some woman she assumed was Janine. She cleaved to him like he was the last life jacket on a sinking ship. Forgetting that bathroom pep talk, her emotions swirled out of control.

She pretended to be calm, but a storm was brewing internally. He was her man. He initiated the relationship. The least she could expect from him was fidelity, even if he did have a fear of relationships.

Her presence was finally acknowledged and Cole made the introductions. Meme tried hard not to appear as the jealous new girlfriend who suspected her boyfriend was sleeping with his ex. But Janine was gorgeous, funny, and more experienced. Meme spent the majority of lunch trying to figure out why Cole wanted her when he could have Janine. By the end of the meal, she couldn't find a single reason to hate the woman, and that pissed her off even more. Infidelity in her past relationships still made her feel inadequate. This day was an eye opener. She questioned whether she really had what it takes to be with Cole.

The ride back home was even quieter. When he reached to grab her hand, she scratched her head and turned away from him, folding her hands in her lap. When they arrived home, Meme went straight to the bathroom. A long, hot bath was in order. If she was lucky, he'd be gone to work before she got out. She soaked in the tub for almost two hours, refilling the water every time it turned cold. By the time she got out, her mind was set. She had to get out of this relationship before it destroyed her. She'd been hurt in the past and barely survived. If things got crazy with Cole, she might not survive. What she felt for him made her realize she never knew what the word love meant. How could she recover if he betrayed her? It was better to walk away now, on her terms, before things got ugly.

Meme poked her head out of the bathroom door and was glad Cole was gone. She threw on a shirt and panties, preparing her mind to leave him. Her empty suitcase was under the bed. She pulled it out and proceeded to pack her things.

Cole walked into the room. "What's going on?"

Meme was running around the room, collecting her things, and throwing them into a suitcase. She kept moving like he hadn't said anything. When he stood in her path, she simply walked around him, never acknowledging he was in the room. She grabbed the pair of pants to finish getting dressed and he'd had enough.

"I'm leaving. I can't do this." Her fragile emotions shattered and tears rolled down her face. She hated herself for crying. "I can't compete with her."

"Can't compete with who?" He checked his pockets for his cell phone. Maybe someone called and Meme answered. *No, it's in my pocket.*

"Have you slept with her?"

"Who?"

"Janine!"

*Damn...* Just like that, the lights came on in Cole's head. He'd introduced the current lady to the ex. Even with his limited relationship experience, he knew that was a big mistake. "There is no competition."

Meme gasped, her eyes widened with shock and she spun around to grab her suitcase. Cole rushed forward to stop her. His hand gripped her wrist as soon as she reached for the handle. "That didn't come out right."

She snatched her hand away and tried to move away, but he grabbed her by the waist and pulled her back up against his chest.

"I've slept with her a few times and that one time with you was better than everything I've done with her. She can't compete with you. She's my friend and I care about her, but even with her sex was just sex."

She wiggled to get free, but he held her tighter. He was probably crazy for telling her all this, but he had to make her understand. "This

184

morning was incredible. I made love for the first time. Even with the horrible memories this day holds, I can't stop thinking about your legs wrapped around my waist, your nails digging into my back, and you moaning my name over and over again."

She felt his hardness pressing into her backside and she had to bite her lip to keep from moaning his name again.

"Besides, we tried being apart." He gripped the sides of her skimpy panties, ripped them at the seams, and let them fall to the floor. "It doesn't work for us." Her flimsy shirt met the same fate as her panties. She stood bare before him, and he kissed her exposed flesh with reverence. He removed her suitcase from the bed and laid her in its place. He left her trembling on the bed while he unpacked her things. As he returned to the bed, he removed his own clothing. When his warm skin touched hers, she could no longer contain her moans.

"Teach me how to please you." Just one touch of his hand caused her to abandon all thoughts of leaving him.

"You already do. You please me very much."

"Show me what you like and teach me how to do it right."

Cole began a lesson that lasted well into the night, leaving their bodies drenched in sweat and exhausted from exertion. He hoped Meme understood exactly how much he wanted her and hoped that it was the last time he saw her jealous side. Moreover, he hoped it was the last time he'd make her cry.

## 18

The past few weeks they'd spent together had been heaven on earth. The lazy days, lounging around the house on her days off, going to the movies in the middle of the day before he went to work, and talking late at night when he came home were perfect.

Waking up Saturday morning to her man's lips trailing across her body as the sun rose was the best. He spoke to her without uttering a word. She felt a shift in their relationship that could be discerned through the intimacy of his kiss. He was pouring his heart out, saying the things through a kiss that he was too afraid to say with words.

As they lay intertwined, neither uttered a word. His arm wrapped around her waist, anchoring her to him. Her eyelashes fanned against his chest as she blinked, letting him know she hadn't fallen asleep. They were content to stay there forever, but they both had busy days ahead of them. Meme watched the digital clock on the nightstand. Time ticked by way too fast for her liking.

Cole was quiet, still fighting off fear and ignoring the voice in the back of his mind telling him to run for his life. He had never felt so complete in all his life, and that scared him. His father loved his mother, and her betrayal destroyed him. Cole had let down his guard with Meme. He was done offering excuses as to why he'd done it. He finally accepted the truth. He was attracted to her the moment he spotted her sitting across from him at the reception. When she invited him to the restroom, he assumed she was like all others, a quick-and-easy lay. Her virginity shocked and intrigued him. This woman and what he felt for her contradicted every relationship lesson his father had ever taught him.

Meme lifted her head. "It's getting late. We have to—"

Before she could finish, Cole plundered her mouth, robbing it of words. Although she was in the dominant position where she should have controlled the kiss, his massive hands—one on her waist the other on the back of her head—restrained her. His demand on her mouth forced her into submission.

Ten more minutes rolled by before he released her. Meme brought her fingers to her swollen lips as she stared into Cole's eyes. Seeing the look in her eyes, Cole knew she wanted an explanation. Not ready to give one, he rolled her over and crawled out of bed. "Let's get dressed. You don't want to be late for work."

~

Meme bounced into work without a care in the world. Never in her life had she felt so happy. Life was perfect. She hoped karma didn't come back to bite her. That was the pattern of her life. Things would be going great and then out of nowhere, disaster would strike. She pushed aside those fears and decided to just enjoy her happiness while it lasted. Cole was turning out to be everything she wanted: kind, considerate, fun to be around, and had a great sense of humor. The right amount of tenderness sprinkled with a little aggression and his masculine strength kept her spinning. She kept telling herself that it was too soon to love him, but with each passing day she spent with him it was harder and harder to deny that he had captured her heart. She loved him and didn't care how soon it was.

She knew he didn't reciprocate her feelings. There was something keeping him from giving her his whole heart. In his eyes, she sometime saw confusion and sadness. It was obvious he was struggling with something that had been eating at him for years, and she resolved to love him until the pain of his past was diminished. Whatever it was, she'd love him through it.

"All right, that's it, to my office, right now!" Wayne's voice came from out of nowhere and scared Meme so bad she almost dropped the container of shampoo she was carrying back to her station.

She fumbled around with it until she was able to firmly grasp it to her chest. "What is wrong with you? You almost scared me to death."

Wayne simply pointed to his office then crossed his arms over his chest as he waited for her to get moving. "Okay Missy." Once behind his desk, his demanding demeanor faded and a smile spread across his face. "For the past week, I've watched you shuffling around here smiling and humming to yourself. You are glowing and I want details. Who is she and why all the secrecy?"

*She? Oh God! How is he going to take it when he finds out she is a he?* "You will meet her soon enough. Our relationship is still so new, I don't want to jinx it by bringing her around just yet." Okay, changing the gender was a total lie. But it was drama prevention, or at least that's what she told herself so that deceiving her friend didn't seem so bad.

"I hear you on that, but we don't hide from each other. With all the crap you've done, I have never judged you or sabotaged any relationship you've had, even the one you shouldn't have been in. So, I expect to meet your new love real soon."

Meme nervously chewed on her lip, trying to hold back the smile tugging at the corners of her mouth. He was right. Wayne had never looked at her cross-eyed. Since his suicide attempt, they'd grown even closer. Their other friends definitely wouldn't understand and would have all kinds of negative feedback, but not Wayne. "I promise you guys will meet soon." Meme left his office humming her heart's contentment as she went to finish her last client before Cole picked her up.

~

Cole dropped Meme off at the salon and instantly started missing her. He was on a slippery slope to love. He was sliding in head first and there was nothing he could do to stop. Crazy thing was, he didn't know if he wanted to. Suddenly, the idea of being in love didn't seem so horrific. He still had his fears, but was more willing to learn for himself instead of taking other people's word for it.

Walking onto the basketball court ten minutes late, everyone was standing around waiting on him. There was Pastor Richard Hawkins, was the youngest and coolest pastor he'd ever met. Not that he had met many, because he out right refused to go to church. Every man on the court was an adamant Christian and he considered them all good friends. On several occasions, they tried to coerce him into attending one of their services, but thanks to good ole Dad, Cole believed churches were filled with liars, cheaters, whoremongers, and thieves. This group of men and their integrity challenged his beliefs, but it was hard to let go of something that was instilled in at a young age. There was also Paul and Tim, the brothers who married cousins. Paul was a lawyer; Tim, an accountant. They were both very successful business men who built their businesses from the ground up and now lived on easy street. Jaleel, who also played ball with them, was Marlon's cousin. He was married to Tim's wife's sister. Cole used to envy their crazy family circle, but now that he thought about it, if he married Meme, it would put him into that circle too.

*Marry Meme.* Cole shook that thought off and finished stretching. There was no way that was happening. Relationship, cool; marriage, not a chance. A basketball bounced off Cole's chest, knocking him out of his musings.

"So, which one of your little conquests had you so hemmed up this morning that you would leave your boys waiting on the court?" Tim laughed.

Cole looked at Marlon and couldn't help but smile.

Marlon groaned. "Change the subject." His sister hooking up with his friend was more than he bargained for, and he wasn't about to stand around listening to Cole talk about his conquest when he knew it was his sister.

"You said you were cool with it." Cole saw the look on Marlon's face and didn't understand the attitude.

"I am, but I'm not going to let you stand around talking about what you are doing to her."

"Who is she?" Tim saw the heated look between the two and drew his own conclusion. "Please don't tell me you're sleeping with his ex-wife."

They both gave Tim a look like he was crazy and walked away. "Marlon, we need to talk." They walked away from the group for some privacy. "You got to know I would never disrespect Meme like that," Cole pleaded. Because of Cole's reputation, Marlon had every right to doubt his intentions with Meme. "I know I have a bit of a negative rep, but this is different."

"How so?" Marlon was purposefully being difficult. He worked with Cole every day and noticed how different he'd become since Meme started staying with him. He noticed Cole frequently sneaking around low-key spaces in the restaurant to talk to Meme. Even long after the calls, he would still be grinning from ear to ear. Cole may not admit it or even recognize it, but Marlon knew his friend was in love with his sister.

Dragging his hand across his face, Cole mumbled, "I'm really feeling her. She challenges all my hang ups about relationships. I like being with her."

Patting Cole on the back, Marlon chuckled. "Looks like I'm getting the brother I always wanted."

"What? You are crazy. I am not getting married." Cole marched back to the group shaking his head, grabbed the basketball, and declared, "For everyone's information, I am not dating his ex-wife. I'm dating his sister. Now let's play." Cole dribbled the ball to the hoop, shooting an easy jump shot, leaving everyone sitting with their mouths hanging open.

Cole kept shooting the ball until it was obvious no one was going to join him. Looking to his right, he saw five pairs of eyes watching his every move from the sideline. Shaking his head, Cole, with the basketball tucked under his arm, marched over to his friends. "What?" Looking at their expressions, he knew for the first time since they started their monthly basketball games not a lick of basketball was going to be played. Men could be just as nosy and gossipy as women. "Look, I know my reputation precedes me, but I really like this girl. Marlon, I know she is your sister, and because of that I tried to stay away from her."

"I told you I was cool with it, and I am. She is my sister. I don't want to see her hurt. You're my boy and I don't want to see you hurt either. Make sure you guys are upfront and honest with each other about everything. I'm sure you both have secrets." With raised eyebrows and concern, Marlon regarded Cole. He didn't want to put his sister's business out there and hoped she was smart enough to tell Cole the truth.

"If you are referring to her lifestyle, yes she told me." Looking around, Cole saw relief wash over everyone's face. "You all know about her preference?" One by one they nodded, but Cole noted a hint of something else in their expression. He couldn't quite put his finger on it, but something wasn't right. "Well, she told me. She didn't go in to detail; however, she did say that I was the only man she'd been attracted to in a long time. She also told me what happened to make her switch teams." As soon as the words came out of his mouth, Cole felt like an idiot. He had promised not to say anything and he knew Marlon was not about to let it slide.

"What happened?" Marlon had always suspected something happened to his sister. There was a period in her life when she just seemed to shut down, like she was running on autopilot. She was so detached from life. Marlon had pleaded for her to tell him what was wrong, but she denied all claims of there being an issue. Shortly after, she seemed to liven up a bit, but was still distant. The closeness they once shared never resurfaced.

"She made me promise I wouldn't tell you. I'm not about to break a promise to her. Just know that it happened years ago and it was horrible. She is an amazing woman for having handled it on her own. I can't tell you anything else."

Marlon was in Cole's face before he could even blink. Pastor Hawkins saw the fury flash on Marlon's face and moved just as quickly. "Come on, Marlon. Cole is your boy. You don't want to go there. Put yourself in Cole's shoes. You aren't going to betray Latrice's trust for anyone either." Conceding his point, Marlon apologized and slowly backed down.

Cole grabbed Marlon's hand, shaking it and bringing him in for a shoulder hug. As they released each other, Cole revealed, "Believe me when I say I took care of it." With that statement and a fist bump, they were back to being boys again.

To Cole's surprise, Marlon picked up the ball that had been knocked out of his arms during their brief standoff and dribbled it onto the court. "Let's get a quick game in before somebody's wife calls."

"I got twenty bucks on it being my little brother's wife this time." Paul swept his foot across the heel of Tim's foot to trip him up as they all walked onto the court.

"I'll take that bet. Nine times out of ten it's your wife anyway." Tim recovered quickly from the little trip up and tried to wrestle his brother to the ground.

"Aww, don't be jealous that my wife misses me more than yours misses you." Paul joked as he struggled to free himself from Tim's grasp.

With that said, the trash talk was initiated. Paul and Tim automatically took opposing teams without waiting for their customary selection process. Whenever that happened, Jaleel always teamed with Paul, and Marlon partnered with Tim. Jaleel always felt more like an older brother to Marlon than a cousin, so he and Paul were more than happy to issue the big brother beat down on the court. This left Cole and Pastor Hawkins to decide which team they would join. With little hesitation, Cole stepped next to Jaleel and Paul.

Marlon feigned like he was hurt. "So, my boy is siding against me?"

"Might as well, seeing as he's soon to be your older brother anyway." Pastor Hawkins chuckled as he slapped hands with Tim and joined their team.

"The pastor has jokes. I'm not getting married."

"I'm not a gambling man, but care to put your money where your mouth is?"

The *oohs* echoed around him as he tried to swallow the nervous lump that formed in his throat. The look on his face made Cole uneasy. His eyes gleamed liked he had information that Cole wasn't privy too. Instead of answering, he directed his team to a spot on the opposite side of the court so they could get the game underway. Cole was obviously rattled by Pastor Hawkins' statement and it showed in his game. He missed shots, rebounds, and didn't guard well enough to save his life. He was more than happy when a phone rang on the sideline.

Everyone stopped playing and looked at Tim. "That's not my phone." Tim shook his head and looked at Paul, as did everyone else.

"It's mine." Cole pushed passed the shocked expressions to grab his phone and smiled at the name on the display. "You ready to go already?" Cole said by way of a greeting as he clicked the phone open.

Everyone watched and listened in on Cole's conversation. He was never the one who ended the game early, and they all assumed it was Meme on the phone. Whatever she was saying had him grinning from ear to ear. When he ended the call, they tried to act like they weren't listening.

"All right fellas, I will see ya'll in a couple of hours at the baby shower. I have to go pick up Meme."

"Aww, Cole's in love," Tim, Paul, and Jaleel chimed in unison, barely containing their laughter.

Cole spun on them, grabbing Paul, the first one he could reach and put him into a headlock. They wrestled and slap-boxed like a group of teenage boys. Marlon and Pastor Hawkins hung back, giving each other a look of relief. With a fist bump, they spoke what words weren't needed to say. It looked like Meme was finally getting herself together, they were grateful.

Pulling up in front of the salon, Cole called Meme to let her know he was there to pick her up. She told him to come inside. He walked into the place like he owned it instead of like it was his first time. He smiled at the receptionist. His dazzling white teeth and his finely cut body barely hidden behind his t-shirt and basketball shorts left her speechless. He walked into the styling area and everything stopped: conversations, walking, and flat-ironing. It should've been illegal for a man to look that sexy in nylon shorts and a cotton shirt.

Meme looked around and saw the heated looks of lust. Normally, she would've defensively jumped up to claim what was hers, but there was no need. Every eye was on him, but his eyes were on her. The intensity in his gaze heated her and she had a hard time feigning indifference. She gathered her things and placed them in his hand before he had a chance to touch her. Her sole purpose for inviting him in was to introduce him to Wayne and didn't want to risk him walking up on them hugging or kissing before she had chance to explain.

They walked around the salon looking for Wayne and finally found him in the lounge reading a magazine. "Hey Wayne," Meme hesitantly stepped toward him with Cole following behind her.

Wayne's eyes roamed up and down Cole as he smiled in appreciation. He may have finally been in the loving-committed relationship he always wanted, but he wasn't blind.

Meme had to kick him to get him to stop. "Cut it out before I call Kevin."

"Please do. Tell him to hurry up and get down here." Wayne chuckled. "Keeps me from having to explain how fine he is when I get home. We both know how to appreciate a good looking man when we see one."

Stifling a laugh, Meme kicked him again. She was so glad he was back to his normal fun loving self. Looking back at Cole, she tried to judge his reaction to Wayne's appraisal. Both men were a part of her life and she wanted them to get along. If Cole was homophobic, that would be next to impossible. Cole didn't look happy, but he didn't look disgusted either, and that she could manage.

"Well," Wayne stood and kissed her on the cheek. "I can tell by the look on your face that *he* is the reason you have been walking around here smiling all day. And I can't say that I blame you." Meme made the introductions. Wayne embraced Cole in an awkward hug that he reluctantly returned.

"So, you're not mad?"

"Mad, please; it's your heart. If he makes you happy then forget about what everyone else thinks."

Cole slid his arm on to Wayne's shoulder and pointed at him with the other hand. "This is a very smart man. You should listen to him." He saw the look on her face while making the declaration. For the first time, he realized how hard this must be for her. Most of her friends might not accept her sudden change of sexual orientation. "Now, can we go before we're late to the party? I still have to shower."

He walked out of the salon feeling more at ease. He recognized Wayne's name as the friend who tried to kill himself. He was also the guy Cole once felt was the competition. He no longer felt there was a threat, but he could tell Meme cared very deeply for this man. He'd respect that just as she respected his relationship with Janine, but the next time Wayne's sexual innuendo was directed toward him, he'd most definitely get put in his place.

## 19

They walked up to Cole's front door and Meme began to hyperventilate. Her heart thumped erratically and sweat poured from her pores. She gripped Cole's arm, seeking his strength to stave off the meltdown that was approaching. Trying to hold back her emotions suffocated her to the point where she had no choice but to let them out. Slut was spray painted on the door. She'd gotten comfortable with Cole and had let her guard down. Whoever was taunting her was reminding her that it wasn't over. Cole didn't say a word, but she could feel tension radiating behind her. He grabbed the keys from her hand and opened the front door. It wasn't until after he looked inside and saw the front of the house was normal that he let her in. This freak had found her, which meant he'd probably been following her everywhere she went.

"Hey, come here." Cole pulled her into his arms and kissed the top of her head. "Don't let this fool get to you. We are going to the baby shower, you are going to play with your nephew, and we're going to have a good time. I'm going to keep you safe."

As they showered and got dressed, Meme tried to relax, but was still a little on edge when they left the house. Anxiety over being stalked and going to a party full of people who couldn't stand her mounted in her stomach. She felt queasy and silently hoped she'd throw up so she'd have a reason to stay home.

As they stood at the door waiting for someone to answer, Meme tried to put her nerves in check. Besides Marlon and Latrice, she was pretty sure everyone would treat her the way they had at the hospital when the baby was born. His little church friends had acted like she'd been declared unclean. Her parents were so caught up in their grandchild that their errant daughter didn't exist. But today she had Cole. There would be one person at this party whose only focus would be her wellbeing. Sometimes she wondered why he didn't know about what she'd done. Maybe since he wasn't a church boy like the rest of them, Marlon didn't seek his help in praying for his sinful sister. Maybe he knew, but just didn't care. Whatever the reason, she was glad for it. His presence was going to make this day a lot easier.

April answered the door and Meme felt bad. She'd been so caught up in Cole that she hadn't made time to visit. To be honest, she didn't really know if April wanted her to. She'd left her at the club without saying goodbye. She hugged April, vowing to try to be a better friend. As April escorted them through the house and into the back yard, Meme berated herself for being so self-absorbed. The self-chastisement stopped as soon as she stepped into the backyard.

The yard was filled with family and friends she hadn't seen in years. Her self-imposed exile after Damien's attack and her banishment after betraying Marlon had kept her from the people she loved. Meme timidly made her rounds, greeting her family and introducing them to Cole. Her reception chased away nervousness, anxiety, and thoughts of banishments and spray painted doors. She was happy and giddy until she spotted her parents. They were walking to where Latrice sat with her nephew. Not wanting a confrontation right now, Meme turned on her heels and marched around the yard to get to her nephew.

Stepping next to Latrice, Meme greeted the circle of her brother's closest friends. She received the warmest welcome she'd ever received from them. She was sure it had something to do with the man at her side being a part of that circle. Camilla sat in her husband's lap, so Cole or Meme could have her chair. Meme took little Marlon from Latrice and propped him up on her shoulder. The image of her smiling and talking to the baby as she patted his little back captivated Cole. Everyone else faded into the background as he imagined Meme pregnant with his baby. He'd never given much thought to having kids, but the thought of having them with this woman seemed so right.

"Cole!" Marlon clapped his hands in Cole's face. "Stop eyeballing my little sister and pay attention."

The circle erupted with laughter, but Cole didn't care. He touched Meme on the elbow and guided her on to his lap. As she made herself comfortable, he whispered in her ear. "You look beautiful holding that baby. Are you going to give me babies as beautiful as you?"

Meme smiled and softly kissed his lips.

"It's not polite to whisper," Marlon scolded them, advising them to break up their lip lock before it got too fierce.

"I heard what he said." Camilla smiled as bright as day. "He asked if she was going to give him babies as beautiful as her."

The circle fell quiet and all eyes were on Cole.

Cole and Marlon locked eyes. "When's the wedding, because I know you're not trying to make my little sister your baby mama."

"Marlon!" Meme was shocked, embarrassed, and pissed. "Mind your own business."

Cole fought the smile tugging at the corners of his mouth and looked away.

"Are you done?" Tim waited for Cole's nod before he continued. "Like I was saying, you were nowhere to be found a few weeks ago when we went to visit Jason…"

"I'm sorry. It was my dad's birthday and kind of got caught up that morning."

Meme giggled and Cole smiled.

Marlon groaned, shook his head, and walked away.

Meme passed the baby back to Latrice, grabbed Cole's hand, and followed Marlon.

Gloria and Marlon Sr. watched her from across the lawn. When she was close enough, they made their move. There was no way to avoid them. As they approached, Meme searched their faces for how they felt about seeing her, but their expressions were not forthcoming. She was always daddy's little girl, but since her secrets had been exposed, she felt like daddy's heathenish little whore, which only made her interactions with them all the more tense. Yeah, she knew her parents loved her. However, sometimes the disappointment in their eyes was unbearable.

"Mom, Dad, it's nice to see you," Meme said as she timidly hugged her parents. To her surprise, her dad squeezed and held her for a while.

"I miss you, baby girl. When are you coming by the house?"

Cole almost swallowed his tongue. His relationships never reached the point of meeting parents, and although he'd met Gloria and Marlon Sr. at the wedding reception, he wasn't quite sure he was ready to be introduced as the boyfriend just yet. Ready or not, it was happening. He cleared his throat, wiped his sweaty palms on his pants, and tried not to overanalyze why he wanted them to like him. Meme turned toward him and smiled. His nerves kicked into overdrive. Combine that nervousness with the tension he felt between Meme and her parents, Cole was a mess. His exterior posture gave no inkling to the flight of the butterflies taking place in his stomach.

"Have you guys met Cole? He works with Marlon."

*Works with Marlon.* Quickly, Cole swallowed the disappointment of being introduced as Marlon's coworker and extended his hand to greet them. "Yes, we met at Marlon and Latrice's wedding reception."

"Nice to see you again." Marlon Sr. shook Cole's hand. "Were you able to hold it down at the restaurant while Marlon was gone?"

"Daddy," Meme interrupted before Cole could answer. "He's my boyfriend." She waited for the words to sink in.

*Boyfriend, now that's more like it.* The corners of Cole's mouth turned up. He grabbed Meme's hand and brought it to his lips. Their eyes locked, which totally left them off guard for Gloria's reaction. She wrapped Meme into a hug and screamed so loud, Meme probably wouldn't be able to hear for a week. She didn't care; hearing be damned! This was the most affection she'd gotten from her mother since the morning all her dirty laundry was aired at the kitchen table. Meme leaned in and accepted all the love Gloria had to offer.

Cole watched in amazement. He had never seen a mother so happy her daughter had a boyfriend. Even though he had never been a boyfriend to have the experience, he still found it fascinating. Until it dawned on him, they were probably happy she was no longer a lesbian. That thought made him suspicious of Meme's true motive for wanting to date him. He waited for the celebration to die down then gripped Meme by the elbow.

"Excuse us for a second, please." Cole guided Meme to the side to get some answers. "Are you with me to make your parents happy that you're no longer a lesbian?"

"Don't be silly," Meme giggled. "I am with you because you invaded my personal space at Marlon's wedding."

"What?" Cole couldn't help but laugh. "You invited me to that restroom for one reason."

"Yeah, and I was perfectly fine sitting at the table trying to ignore you until you came into my personal space, put your hand on my thigh, and set me on fire. If you hadn't touched me, I could've ignored you all night."

"You mean like this?" Cole's eyes darkened with desire as he slid his hand down Meme's thigh.

Even through her jeans, she felt that familiar fire that only Cole could kindle. "Yes, just like that." Her voice was wispy with the same desire reflected in his eyes. Before she had time to reconsider her actions,

Meme stood on her tippy toes, wrapped her arms around Cole's neck, and pulled him down to meet her lips. She leaned into him and he placed a hand on her waist, pulling her as close as possible. Intensely, they kissed as if they were alone.

"Get your hands off my little sister."

Gasping at the curtness she heard in her brother's voice, Meme spun around, pressing her back up against Cole to shield him from Marlon. The voice brought back distant memories of how Marlon used to threaten her potential boyfriends in high school, and most of them went running for safety. She was not about to let Cole run away. She was prepared to give Marlon a piece of her mind, but she looked up and the smile on his face took the words off her lips.

"Hate to tell you this, but your little sister belongs to me now, and I will put my hands anywhere I want." Hunching over her shoulders, Cole placed his cheek against hers, slid his hands around her waist, and caressed her stomach just to prove his point.

"How possessive of you. I don't recall you ever being this possessive of a woman."

"I've never met a woman worthy of possessing until now." His words shocked all three of them. His hands dropped from around her waist, Meme spun around to look him in the eye, and Marlon almost choked on his soda. Cole caressed Meme's cheek and walked away. He desperately needed to regroup and get his mouth under control.

As he walked away, Meme turned back toward her brother with tears in her eyes. "I'm in love with him. Is it too soon to love him? My emotions have always gotten me into trouble, and I don't know if I can trust how I feel."

Grabbing her by the hand, Marlon led Meme into the house, so they could have an overdue, private talk. Once inside, Marlon directed her to have a seat. "Cole is a good guy. I don't think he will intentionally hurt you like whoever this guy is that's had you running scared for the past few years." His conversation with Cole this morning had confirmed some of his suspicions. "I don't know what happened to Cole to make him run from relationships, but I do know that I have never seen him look at a woman the way he looks at you. I saw it at my reception, I saw it at your apartment, and I saw it today."

"What do you mean you saw it at your reception?"

"You and Cole weren't fooling anyone. I saw you guys come from the same direction, both wearing the same expression. Even though you came out at different times, acting like you didn't know each other, I knew something went down between you guys." Meme opened her mouth to speak, but Marlon stopped her. He didn't want any details.

"Cole is hard working and has a big heart. He cares for the employees at the restaurant. When I'm ready to fire someone, he comes running to their rescue and then takes the time to help them become a better chef. Even with this guy, Jason, we've been visiting in prison. Months ago, Pastor Hawkins asked us to start visiting him in prison so that when he got out he would have some brothers he felt close to. Cole won't step foot in a church, but he volunteered to help and was right there with the rest of us when it came time to visit."

The more Marlon talked, the harder Meme fell for Cole. "I know he's wonderful, but the last time I went after what my heart wanted, it destroyed my life and yours." Her head sagged and shoulders slumped with shame.

"You didn't destroy my life. You helped me see what I had been trying to ignore, and because of that I found and married Latrice. I wouldn't change that for anything in the world."

"Marlon stop!" Meme's voice was stricken with sorrow and shame. "I slept with your wife. How can you act like that isn't the most horrible thing in the world? You are my brother and I slept with your wife. Not only did I sleep with her, but had a relationship with her for months behind your back."

Marlon pulled his sister into his arms and she sobbed into his chest. Stroking her head in comfort, he shushed her sobs away. "If it makes you feel any better, if it hadn't been for Latrice, I would've tried to kill you." Marlon chuckled, drudging up a slight laugh from Meme. "Truth be told, I was miserable with Alicia. We were two people occupying the same space, not husband and wife. Like I told you before, she admitted to cheating on me before anything went down between you and her. I agree, you should've never slept with her, but I am just too happy right now to be angry and holding grudges. I want you to be happy too. Get over this and be happy with Cole."

"If you're over it, then I am over it." Meme grabbed a paper towel and dried her face. She gave her brother one last hug, stepped out of the kitchen, and stopped dead in her tracks.

~

Marching around the yard, looking for a quiet place to think was an impossible mission. There were so many people in attendance, it seemed as though every inch of the yard was taken. Cole's best bet was to go inside the house for some privacy. Walking through the living room and toward the kitchen, he heard voices. The closer he got to the kitchen, he recognized the voices as Meme and Marlon. Their discussion halted his footsteps. Eavesdropping was wrong, but there are just some conversations you couldn't pull away from and this was one of them. He listened to every word that came out of Meme's mouth and couldn't believe the trifling things she'd done. The woman who made him break all his self-imposed rules, demanded he opened his heart, and invaded his life turned out to be exactly what his father told him all women were. He got caught slipping. She fooled him, but never again.

Standing his ground, he waited for the footsteps that were headed in his direction to round the corner just so he could look her in the eye. He wanted her to know that he heard everything and whatever they had was over.

Meme almost passed out when she saw Cole standing outside the kitchen looking like he was on the verge of a massacre.

"Cole..."

Beads of sweat formed on top his brow, muscles in his jaws twitched, and a vein in his neck bulged. Without him saying a word, Meme knew he'd heard their conversation. Everything they'd been working to build was getting ready to crumble.

Confusion tilted Cole's head and his eyes squinted as he tried to make sense of what he just heard. *I couldn't have heard her right.* "You slept with your brother's wife?" Cole asked, hoping for a denial. When she didn't answer, he backed away, shaking his head in disbelief. He needed to get out of there as soon as possible.

Meme was right on his heels. She was not going to let him run from her. Having Marlon talk to him crossed her mind, but this was something she had to handle on her own. She practically had to run to keep up with Cole's long strides. Throwing herself between him and the car, Meme pleaded for him to let her explain. He tried to reach around her, but she put her rear end up against the handle and refused to budge. Finally, he just picked her up and tried to set her to the side, but Meme wasn't going without a fight. She wrapped her arms around his neck, legs around his waist, and held on for dear life. She peppered his face with kisses and then plundered his mouth. Cole stood stiff as aboard, refusing to participate until she stroked that spot that only she could reach. Of its own volition, his tongue danced with hers.

Every emotion Meme owned was wedged into that kiss. With desperation, she devoured his mouth like a starved woman who hadn't eaten in days. When it was over, she imploringly looked into his eyes. "Please don't throw this away. Let me explain."

Cole's only response was, "Get in the car."

The entire car ride, Meme racked her brain for the right words to say. How do you convince someone who already has relationship and trust issues to stay with you after they find out your worst secrets? There was no doubt in her mind that all Cole's relationship fears or hang-ups were playing out in his mind. The eyes that had looked upon her with such adoration were now filled with revulsion.

"How could you do something like that?" Cole asked as soon as they stepped into the house. He put forth no effort to hide the disgust in his voice.

"I was lonely, I was needy, and I was stupid, but there is no excuse for what I did." Meme's voice cracked and she gave way to her tears. "She came onto me and I immediately put her in her place. We started hanging out, strictly platonic at first. Then, I developed feelings for her. I backed up, stopped calling, and stopped accepting her calls. I hadn't felt anything that strong since Damien. Soon, she was all I could think about. Then one night we went out and it felt so right, but a couple days later, I went to see her and everything had changed. She was distant and that playful side was nonexistent. I could tell she was getting ready to end things and I panicked. I pleaded and seduced her for a chance to prove I could make her happy. She gave into me and Marlon walked in and caught us in the act."

"If you could do something like that to your brother, who's to say you won't do worse to me?"

Meme placed her hand on his heart. "Trust your heart. Just as it told you to let me in, I know it is telling you that I am not that same person and I'd never hurt you."

Cole's heart was racing and his mind was spinning. His father was right; women weren't worth the air they breathed. She was manipulative, selfish, and deceitful, just like all the other women he'd heard about. He should've listened to his assumptions and all the dating horror stories he'd heard. Meme was like all the rest. He turned his back on her and walked away.

Choking on her sobs and wiping away tears, Meme followed behind him. "Cole, please give me a chance to prove myself."

"I am not giving you a chance to destroy me the way you did Marlon. I remember those days clearly. He never gave me details, only said he caught his wife cheating, but I remember how devastated he was.

So excuse me if I don't want to sit around and wait for you to do that to me. I don't know why I even bothered. My father told me that all women are just as manipulative and deceptive as my trifling mother. I caught my mother cheating on my father. At the time, I was too young to know what was going on, but I walked in on her laid on the couch with some man between her legs. Her betrayal destroyed my father, but he quickly learned that the nature of a woman was to be deceptively conniving. That's a lesson he taught me until the day he died. The really messed up part is she has never tried to contact me." His voice cracked with emotion and Meme tried to hold him, but he quickly recovered, staving her off with a look of repulsion.

"I guess I should be thanking you for proving my father right and making me come to my senses before I wasted too much of my life on you." With that he walked away. His chest constricted with grief, but he refused to give in to it. How could he have been so blind to the woman she really was?

His words cut deep. Long after he walked away, Meme stood rooted in the same spot, her heart bleeding. *This cannot be happening.* Their relationship seemed to be moving to the next level. Now it had diminished, dwindling to nothing. Reluctantly, Meme uprooted her feet and went to pack her bags.

Minutes later, she stood at the front door with her bags packed. Cole sat at the kitchen table and didn't even acknowledge her as she walked by. With each step toward the door, her heart broke into tiny pieces. She was expecting something to happen to ruin the happiness she was feeling. Karma always seemed to find her. Would she ever be rid of the guilt and punishment for her actions?

Putting her hand to the knob, Meme allowed the tears to flow down her cheeks. As she turned the knob, she heard a chair scoot across the kitchen floor and within seconds felt his heat behind her.

Hovering over her, Cole placed his hand on the door, pressing it closed. "You can't leave."

Meme's heart hammered against her ribs as she awaited his next move.

"I promised I would protect you, and it isn't safe at your apartment."

Her little spark of hope fizzled. "I will stay with Marlon or my parents," Meme choked out as she turned the door knob and waited for him to remove his weight.

When he did, she slowly opened the door and stepped through. One last time she turned to him. "You're throwing us away again. I'm not the same person I used to be. You are going to realize you made a mistake. This time, I won't take you back."

Cole watched Meme walk out of his life and was conflicted. Did he have the right to be mad over something that didn't involve him? Should he discard their relationship over something that happened before they met? Coming home to her in his bed after a long night at the restaurant, making her breakfast before she went to work, and just hanging with her was better than he could have imagined. Laughing and talking with her far exceeded the pleasure of all his one night stands combined.

Even with all that he felt for Meme, being with a woman like her meant suffering the same fate as his father was inevitable. He wasn't willing to risk it. A woman with such a low moral standard that she would sleep with her brother's wife doesn't change that easily. *Once a dog always a dog.* "Guess it applies to women too."

Cole erased all thoughts of chasing after her and decided to head to work. It was one of those rare occasions where he and Marlon were both off, but he needed the distraction of work to take his mind off Meme.

## 20

**M**eme's heart shattered as she drove away from Cole's apartment. Her soul ached with the love she had for him, and the pain oozed out in tears. That morning, they'd woken up in each other's arms and life had seemed perfect. No words needed to be spoken. His heart spoke to her through his touch. His fingers stroked her flesh, speaking the words his mouth was too afraid to verbalize. She wanted to hold on to those words, but the disgust that had just rested on his face now diminished their effect. Is it possible to go from such intense adoration to complete hatred within minutes?

Sitting at the red light, Meme tried to wipe the tears away with the back of her hand. The more she wiped, the faster the tears fell. Why didn't she listen to herself and not follow her emotions? She should have never gotten involved with Cole. It was obvious from the beginning that he had issues. Those issues were deeper than what she first believed. He was rejected by the one woman that should have loved him unconditionally, and then reared by a man who taught him to believe all women were trash.

No wonder he pushed her away. Granted, her past did confirm what he believed to be true about women, but she had to find a way to convince him she'd changed.

Yes, she promised she'd stay at Marlon's or her parents' house, but they were still at the baby shower. There was no way she was going back over there to sit around a bunch of smiling happy couples when her heart was breaking. So, with nowhere else to go, she drove to her apartment.

Between the thoughts that clouded her mind and the tears that clouded her vision, Meme had no idea how she made it home safely. Walking through the front door, she almost passed out from the shock. It was her first time back since the break in. She didn't remember the destruction being that horrific. Taking tiny measured steps around the living room, she took in all the damage. Someone had definitely been back and added to the previous damage. That thought made the fine hairs on her arms stand on end.

"I've been waiting for you to come home."

*Oh my God.* Fear seized Meme, temporarily immobilizing her. Her pulse accelerated and pounded with such force she feared it would leap out of her chest. Cole's warning flashed through her mind and everything within her wished she'd followed his advice to not return. Like every other situation in her life, she did what she wanted without considering the consequences. It happened with Damien, with Alicia, and now she was doing it again. Maybe Cole was right in pushing her away; she hadn't changed. She was still making stupid mistakes. At least this mistake would only affect her.

With her eyes, Meme searched the debris on the ground for something she could use as a weapon. Whatever this person wanted, they'd better be prepared to fight for it. Not finding anything, she prepared for some hand-to-hand combat. Damien's attack flashed across her mind. There was no one here to rescue her this time. She'd fight for herself.

Meme began to turn around slowly, with terror-filled eyes, afraid of who she might see or what would happen next. Her entire body throbbed from the pounding of her pulse. Out of the corner of her eye, she saw a figure throw a punch, and before she could react, it connected to her ear. Sound was muffled with a dull whistle ringing in her head. She stumbled back, grasping for something to steady herself. Her head was spinning. All attempts to maintain her balance were futile and she fell to the ground.

~

Work was a welcomed distraction and Cole threw himself into it, but with every spare second, his mind wandered back to Meme. Thinking about the things she'd done to her brother outraged him, and then remembering the tears in her eyes as she walked out of his apartment softened him. All his life, he had avoided serious relationships and all of the drama they bring. The one woman he'd let into his heart turned out to be the epitome of why he avoided relationships. The deceitful, manipulative, selfish ways of beautiful women would be the downfall of men all over the world. Forget AK-47s, M-16s, stealth bombers, and weapons of mass destruction. Construct an army of beautiful women and any nation would crumble at their feet. Of all the women in the world, why did she have to be an untrustworthy, devious, self-seeking fraud?

It just didn't seem fair. He had been dealt a hand in life that most black men would've used as an excuse to become a statistic. Thug, addict,

215

abuser, convict, baby daddy—he was none of that. He never laid a hand on a woman to hurt her, never cursed her out, or called her out of her name. Although he had relationship issues, he was an all-around good guy. Didn't he deserve to be loved and to love in return? Or, was this repayment for pushing away all the women who wanted to love him? If he had felt the tiniest bit of the chemistry he felt with Meme with any one of them, he might have given them a shot. Meme was the only woman to make his heart race. She fit perfectly in his bed, in his heart, and in his life. Now he had to decide if he could live without her.

That thought withdrew him from the kitchen. Could he live without her? *Yes*. Did he want to live without her? *No*. But never being one to follow his heart, Cole pulled out his cell phone and called Marlon. He had questions and knew his boy would give him honest answers.

"Tell me what went down with your ex and your sister." Cole spoke over Marlon's greeting, skipping all pleasantries. He needed answers.

"How did things work out after you left?"

"Not well." Cole's response was curt. He called to ask questions not answer them.

"Sorry to hear that. You guys seem good for each other." Marlon looked at his wife and shook his head. Just when he thought things were looking up for his sister, everything seemed to fall apart at the seams.

"I thought so, too. Now tell me what went down." Cole's voice was curt and harsh. He didn't want to think about how good she was for him.

"Cole, you're my boy and all, but Meme is my sister. This is a conversation you should be having with her."

216

"I did, now I want to hear your side. How can you forgive her?"

"If I expect to receive forgiveness from God, how can I not forgive?"

Cole groaned in response. That groan was laced with frustration and torment, Marlon knew the biblical approach wasn't going to move him.

"Look, I love my sister unconditionally and there is nothing she can do to change that. When I first found out, it took my parents, Latrice, and the power of God to keep me from killing Meme. If we had been alone, I know I would have hurt her. She crossed a line that siblings should never cross, but once I learned the whole truth, it was easy to forgive. Meme sought friendship; Alicia sought revenge. She wanted me to hurt for neglecting her. She manipulated Meme for revenge. Yes, Meme should've recognized when her feelings changed and backed off, but the heart wants what the heart wants." Marlon knew you didn't talk about what your heart wanted with your boy, but he had to do something before Cole threw away the best thing in his life.

"Just like your heart still wants her. In spite of the things she's done, the things your pops taught you about women, and your mom being absent, your heart wants Meme. Now go wrap your arms around her, tell her you love her, and get over your hang ups. Find your mom and hear her side of the story. Maybe you'll learn something that will cut through all that crap your dad told you. Do what you got to do to be free to love Meme. If you walk away from her, you will regret it for the rest of your life."

Marlon ended the call and Cole sat there with the phone still to his ear. *Find your mom.* That was definitely something he'd thought of in the

217

past, but not recently. Mulling over their conversation, Cole tried to make sense of everything and come up with a plan of action when it donned on him that Marlon didn't know how things went down with him and Meme, which meant she never went back to the baby shower. Knowing her, she probably went to her apartment. Cole's internal rationalization and debate over to call or not flew out the window. He called her cell. There was no answer, and without a second thought, he pulled out his keys, hopped in the car, and headed to her apartment.

~

Meme laid in the bed, grappling to stay conscious. Whenever she became alert enough to open her eyes, the pain in her head sent her scrambling back to the darkness for comfort. The tranquility it offered was preferred over the overwhelming throbbing pain that met her when she tried to wake up. This time was different. The shadow that she'd felt lingering over her was back. Gone was the soft, caressing voice pleading for Meme to wake up. There was a gruffness that crept into its tone. With it came an eeriness that urged Meme to fight for consciousness.

Her eyes fluttered and the throbbing in her head intensified, but she continued to fight. The shadow came closer; it was no longer hovering, but sitting next to her. *Come on Meme wake up.* The urge to get up was even stronger. She didn't know why she was afraid, but she was. She had to wake up and defend herself. The fog over her mind lifted and she remembered the notes, remembered her car being vandalized, and her apartment being destroyed. Finally, she remembered someone walking up behind her. As her mind recalled the blow to her head, her eyes shot open. Right there, hovering over her, was Sahara.

Sahara caressed Meme's thigh and instantly, Meme registered the naked state of her body. *Where are my clothes?* Her mind raced, trying to figure out what Sahara had done to her. Fear gripped her as she watched Sahara lower her head. The moment their lips connected, Meme bucked and squirmed in an attempt to fight her off. Her efforts were futile. Both of her arms and both of her legs were tied to the bedposts. Each buck and pull on her restraints magnified the swelling sensation in her head, but she knew if she gave in to the pain and slipped back into the darkness, her fate would be far worse. She held on to consciousness and refused to give in.

"Don't fight. I know you want this as much as I do." Sahara pleaded as she continued to pay homage to Meme's body. She watched Meme lying motionless in that bed and feared the worst.

Hitting her was not part of the plan. She was only supposed to be tied up to keep her from leaving the apartment. Before she could do anything, her partner punched her on the side of the head. She stumbled around for minute, but couldn't remain upright. On her way down, her head hit the overturned coffee table. Her brow split open and blood oozed down her face. Pinching the gash shut, Sahara tried to stop the bleeding, but it just kept gushing. For a minute, she thought to abandon the plan and call an ambulance, but her partner shot that idea down and quickly silenced all Sahara's thoughts of mutiny by pulling out a gun.

The plan was to immobilize Meme long enough to tie her up and then confess how long she'd been in love with her. She needed Meme to sit still long enough so she could pour her heart out. There were so many things Meme didn't understand, and if she would have just given Sahara a moment to explain, things wouldn't have gotten out of hand. They were perfect for each other, and if Meme would just hear her out she would think so too.

Grunting and sweating profusely, Meme tried to thwart Sahara's advances, but her limited movement left her victim to the assault. Sahara's fingers brushed pass Meme's mouth and she wanted to bite them off, but the movement of her jaw intensified the pain in her head. Groaning with the pain, her eyes rolled back and her body stilled as the darkness moved in on her. She stopped fighting and focused all her energy on staying conscious.

Taking Meme's stillness as concession, Sahara lightly brushed their lips together as she explained. "I didn't mean for you to get hurt like this. I just wanted to get you alone and get you to listen to me without walking away." Meme continued to lie still even though Sahara's touch was repugnant. "I was there your first time at the Golden Stone. You walked in with Wayne and you took my breath away. I wanted you then, but you looked so fragile and broken that I wanted to give you time to heal. I sat in the background and tried to keep my distance, because I didn't want you while you were on the rebound. I wanted you to want me, not come to me because you were hurting. Trying to look out for your best interest, I waited too long and someone else got you before I could."

That night was a distant but clear memory. Meme searched her brain and couldn't recall Sahara even being there. There were a few unfamiliar faces, but none of them resembled Sahara. She opened her mouth to speak, but was shushed.

"I have waited too long to say this. Please let me finish. I just want you to take the time to see how great we'd be together."

*You have got to be kidding me.* Meme tried to keep the disgust from showing on her face. *Do you actually think I'd ever consider dating you after this?* Meme kept a passive expression as she cursed Sahara out in her mind. It was obvious this woman was mentally unstable, and Meme didn't want to rock the boat and knock her over the deep end.

"I love you so much and I know you'll love me if you just give us a chance. We can even move away together and you wouldn't have to pretend to be something you're not anymore. If no one knows where you are, they can't force you to be something you're not. When I first saw you with that guy I was angry. I was angry that once again I was going to have to take a back seat, but then I realized that you didn't want him. It was probably just your family trying to control you again."

"If you love me, then let me go. I need a doctor. My head hurts." Meme had to think fast and play on Sahara's weakness. "If we are meant to be together, it will happen."

"You can't leave!" Sahara screamed slamming her hands on the bed beside Meme's head. Meme cringed, more so out of pain than fear. "It's not part of the plan." Pacing around the room, Sahara grabbed handfuls of hair and pulled as tight as she could. Mumbling incoherently to herself, Sahara marched around in circles.

Tired of being a victim, Meme didn't let Sahara's instability faze her. Her outward composure gave no clue as to the scheming taking place in her mind. There had to be a way out of this situation. If Sahara hadn't already crossed the line between sanity and insanity, she was flirting with it. Whatever Meme decided to do, she needed to do it quickly and carefully. Once again, Meme sought the God she had abandoned. This entire situation was probably because she hadn't followed through with her promises to God for sparing Latrice and her son. There would be no empty promises today. She prayed with sincerity and asked the Lord for His help. Sahara might have the upper hand right now, but Meme knew that God was greater than any obstacle.

No sooner than she said amen, her doorbell rang. Relief washed over Meme and praise to God tumbled out of her mouth. She feared that no one would know where she was. Marlon assumed she was with Cole and vice versa. No one would look for her at her apartment, but someone was there. She couldn't have been happier.

Sahara froze mid-stride when the doorbell rang. She had anticipated someone coming to look for Meme, but not so soon. Plan B— if Meme didn't reciprocate her feelings—was to move to a more discreet location where she'd have the privacy and the time to persuade Meme to love her. Either way, Meme would never go back to life as she knew it. She didn't want to leave San Diego and take Meme against her will, but Meme not loving her and continuing to see Cole would lead to a far worse fate. Sahara refused to let that happen.

Seeing the look of triumph on Meme's face, Sahara rushed over to the bed and clasped her hand over Meme's mouth. She tightened her grip, making sure not even a whisper escaped. Meme fought hard to get free. All she needed was one scream. If she could move Sahara's hand for one second, she could scream loud enough to be heard. She opened her mouth to bite and once again pain shot through her head. The fight left her body as she succumbed to the pain. A river of tears flooded her face. She was going to miss her only chance for freedom and was about to give up hope until she heard his voice. He came for her. Surely he wouldn't give up until he talked to her.

## <u>21</u>

Seeing Meme's car when he pulled into the parking lot took the edge off of his worry, but Cole wanted to hear her voice and see her face to make sure she was all right. Ringing the doorbell, there was no answer. His ringing turned to banging and his banging to calling out her name, still no response.

"Meme," Cole pleaded again for her to open the door. "I know you're upset. So am I, but let's be rational. It is not safe here. Just come back to my place and we will work something out."

Meme's tears flowed in great succession. Her breath came in hiccups, the pain in her heart superseding the pain in her head. Her mind pleaded for him not to leave. She tried to tap into that connection they developed, hoping he could feel her agony and sense her distress.

*Baby, I am here. Please help me!*

Sahara scowled when she heard Cole's voice. She hated everything he stood for. Men who thought they had the power to convert a lesbian.

She looked into Meme's eyes to let her know she no longer had to pretend, and that's when she saw it. Saw it in her eyes and felt it in her body. There was no pretense or farce of a relationship to get friends and family off her back. Shining in Meme's eyes was the hope that he would save her. Her body awakened at the sound of his voice and exuded an energy that Sahara had never felt before. Meme's heart belonged to this man and the love that was shining in her eyes would not be easily overthrown. She'd have to use Plan B; they'd relocate.

Telling himself that she was just pissed and didn't want to talk to him, Cole tried to shake off his concern. As he walked to his car, uneasiness crept up his spine. He looked back toward her apartment and couldn't shake the feeling something wasn't right. He started to head to her apartment again and his father's adage hit him in the gut. *Chasing after a woman gives her the power to break you.* If she didn't want to talk to him, he'd respect that. Cole sent a quick text to Marlon telling him to call Meme just to check on her and then hopped in his car.

Not wanting to go home, Cole drove around for hours trying to clear his mind. Replaying his conversation with Marlon opened his mind to something he had never considered. Could there be another side to the story? Could there have been something that drove his mother away? For so long, he'd hated her for leaving and never considered there was a reason she left, besides the fact that she was selfish. In his mind, mothers didn't leave. They were the ones who stuck around until the end, come hell or high water. Maybe he should talk to her and find out why she'd left and never called.

Cole finalized his decision regarding his mother, but what to do about Meme was another story. How could he go back to how he used to be after what he experienced with her? She had changed him, made him open up, made him trust her, and then shattered that trust. But, did she really? She didn't lie or cheat on him; hadn't broken a promise or mistreated him. So why was he so upset? She was up front and honest about her sexuality, even told him about Damien when she hadn't even told her family. Their relationship was still new. Maybe she would have gotten around to telling him about this.

Pulling up at a stop light, Cole finally had to be honest. He was mad because his innocent diamond in the rough was a little flawed. His precious jewel had a blemish. His heart suddenly saw her in a new light. As if looking through a magnifying glass, everything that was wrong or could go wrong was overstated. She could break his heart and the thought scared him. Could a broken heart make him bitter like his father? Would he be able to get over her or would he be stuck loving her? Maybe their relationship wouldn't end like his parents' had. Maybe she would return his love.

*Wait a minute; do I love her?* Cole groaned in frustration. His mind was running a hundred miles a minute. He had no idea how to spot love or if it was even possible to be in love this soon. Over the next hour or so, Cole drove around analyzing every couple he knew that claimed to be in love. There were those who argued every second they were together, those who got along only between the sheets, those who barely touched each other, and the worst, those who claimed to be in love, but had someone on the side. Then, he thought about his basketball buddies. He'd never heard them utter a negative word about their wives, assumed everything worked well in the bedroom, and they were more faithful than he ever believed a man could be. He compared their actions toward their wives to his interactions with Meme and a lump formed in his throat. He was definitely in trouble.

The clock on the dashboard read one o'clock. Cole couldn't believe he was still out driving around. Although he wasn't tired, he thought it best to head on home. His gas tank was just about empty, so he stopped at the nearest gas station and filled his tank. He took a detour past Meme's apartment and saw her car still sitting in the same spot, but didn't have the nerve to stop.

Walking through his front door, his mind instantly went to the nights Meme greeted him when he came home from work. Some nights a foot massage, other nights a back rub, but they talked almost every night. Almost twenty-four hours ago, things couldn't have been more perfect. If he had known how the day would end, he wouldn't have let her out of bed. He would've blown off the basketball game, begged her to call in sick, and made love to her all day.

As he walked into his room and saw his empty bed, he found clarity. He didn't want to sleep alone nor did he want to live alone. He no longer wanted to be alone. He wanted Meme, flaws, indiscretions, and all.

~

Sleep eluded him. For hours, Cole tossed and turned. The uneasiness he felt from not being able to contact Meme and the confusion of unanswered questions regarding his mother battled for dominance in his mind. He was minutes from losing it. In a last ditch effort to maintain his sanity, Cole hopped on the computer and pulled up a web browser. Going to his favorite search engine, he typed in his mother's name and sighed at all the results that popped up. After finding a comfortable position, Cole refined the search by typing San Diego next to her name and hoped it made the list shorter. It helped a little, but the list was still extremely long. One by one, he started clicking the links, hoping one led him somewhere.

The hours ticked by, the sun had risen, streaks of light peeked through the partially closed mini-blinds, and the birds were chirping their morning melody. The noise of garbage collection trucks had rattled through the neighborhood about an hour ago, and Cole was still in the same spot, clicking on links. He was no closer to finding his mother than when he first sat down. Only things he had to show for his perseverance were a sore back and bloodshot eyes that were now out of focus and on fire. With squinted eyes, he kept clicking.

Trying to keep his frustration at bay, Cole stood, stretching his legs to get his blood flowing properly. He flexed his hand to get his fingers to loosen up and relax after hours of being stuck in the same position. It wasn't until he stood that he realized how exhausted he was. His body demanded sleep, but his mind wasn't ready to concede. Coffee was what he needed. Jogging to the kitchen, Cole made a large cup of instant coffee with no cream and three teaspoons of sugar. He made sure he warmed it to the perfect temperature, hot enough to warm his body and cool enough to drink without blowing.

The liquid flowed through his body, instantly making him immune to the slight chill in the room. Coffee was his drug. He never smoked weed, shot anything into his veins, took anything to stay awake, or even took anything to fall asleep. He didn't even mess with energy drinks or dietary supplements. Of course he drank occasionally, but his drug of choice was coffee. The legal addictive stimulant was all the fuel his body needed to get going. Even now, as the caffeine seeped into his blood stream, his mind perked up. He was ready to put in a few more hours at the computer and he did just that.

Feeling defeated, Cole resigned himself to finish this page and call it a day. Upon the second to last link on the page, his eyes widened and his heart accelerated. This had to be it. The link was a church website. What little fond memories he had of his mother were all of her taking him to church. Chills ran down his spine as he clicked on the link and waited for the page to load. The link took him directly to the First Lady's page of the website. The last thing to load on the page was her picture. Images in his mind of her were fuzzy, but there was no way he could deny their resemblance. He had found her.

His emotions waged a war. Excitement, joy, anger, resentment, sadness, regret, and fear bombarded him. After all these years of wondering who she was and where she was, it took only a few hours to find her. She'd been in plain sight all this time. Regret for not looking sooner won the battle of emotions, and resentment toward her for her not looking either was a close second.

Cole read her bio and indescribable satisfaction rose within him. Her husband had passed away a few years ago. *Good, maybe it was the same bastard she left me and my father for.*

At least her life hadn't been a bed of roses while he had to grow up without a mother. With the next sentence, his breath caught in his throat and he almost fell out of his seat. He rushed through the rest of the bio and frantically searched the rest of the website for more pictures. What he found confirmed his thoughts. Shutting off the computer, Cole paced around his living room. What were the odds of something like this happening? He needed answers, but he had to have a plan first. He couldn't just storm out of the house and start banging on a woman's door that he hadn't seen since he was a child. There were new factors to consider. Innocent people could get hurt.

In deep thought, Cole walked to the bathroom off of the master bedroom. He figured a shower and a few hours of sleep would refresh his mind so that he could think clearly. Being irrational and flying off the handle would get him nowhere. Stepping into the shower, the hot water cascaded down his broad shoulders and thoughts of Meme came flooding back to his mind. Just yesterday morning they were in this shower together. If she was here with him now, she'd help him sort through this mess. Cole tried to keep thoughts of her at bay, but he failed miserably. His mind kept drifting from one problem to the next, and it was probably best if he just went to sleep. If he was asleep, he could escape reality and not deal with any of it for a few hours. Cole hopped into bed and, thanks to his long night of web surfing, sleep no longer evaded him.

Cole had been asleep for what seemed like only minutes before the phone rang, waking him up. He checked the display and, without pause, sat up to answer. Marlon calling this early had him on full alert and he mentally prepared for bad news.

"What's up man? I just got your text from last night. Is something wrong with my sister?"

"I don't know." He hoped Marlon was calling to say he talked with her and she was all right.

Something was wrong. Dread mounted his shoulders, and this time he couldn't shake it. Cole climbed out of bed, determined to talk to Meme or at least see her. Putting on his clothes, he tried to stave off the anxiety that was rising as he continued talking to Marlon.

"She left me yesterday." He conveniently left out that he did nothing to stop her from leaving. "She said she was going to stay with you or her parents, but after talking to you, I realized that she hadn't talked to you and probably wouldn't talk to her parents, so I went by her place to see if she was all right. Her car was there, but she didn't answer and I got a weird feeling like something was wrong."

Marlon chuckled and Cole laughed with him, hoping his inner turmoil didn't show in his voice. He didn't blame Marlon for not taking him seriously. If the shoe was on the other foot, he would laugh, but that feeling he had leaving Meme's apartment—the same one that was now overtaking him—was strong. He couldn't ignore it.

*Guess I have to handle this one myself.* "You know what, now that I think about it, she is probably just upset and doesn't want to talk to me."

"Well, if it will make you feel better..." Marlon tried to hide his amusement, but his boy had it bad for his sister.

Cole might as well turn in his playa card, burn his little black book, and start shopping for engagement rings, because his days as a bachelor were numbered. Marlon knew exactly how his sister felt about Cole, and listening to the despair in Cole's voice that he so desperately tried to hide, Marlon now knew how Cole felt too.

"I will swing by after church."

"That's cool." Cole had his shoes on and was stomping out the door before the call ended. Marlon could stop by whenever he got good and ready. Cole was heading to Meme's apartment now, before he went crazy worrying.

## 22

Sahara jumped up off the couch when she heard banging on the front door. She checked her watch and couldn't believe how long she'd slept. She needed sleep after being up for over twenty-four hours, but she knew that Meme wouldn't sit quietly. Although Meme squirmed and protested, Sahara had gagged her. Now she was glad she had the foresight to silence her.

Walking back into the room to check on Meme, Sahara racked her brain for a way to get rid of the person at the door. As long as Meme's car was parked out front, everyone would assume she was home and would keep banging on the door until someone answered. Her sanity was slipping by the second and all the banging was rattling her nerves.

"Meme, baby, open the door."

*Him again.* A scowl spread across Sahara's face as she listened to Cole's voice pleading for Meme to let him in.

She was all set to make her move on Meme and then he stepped into her life. She was sitting outside Meme's apartment, trying to come up with a plausible explanation for being there and knowing where Meme lived when he had showed up with breakfast. They had partied at Wayne's the night before and Meme seemed to loosen up around her. She dared to hope that it was now their time. Cole ruined that. They spent the entire day together, locked up in that apartment, doing only God knows what. It ate at her as she sat outside watching the front door. Nervously, she chewed her lip and bit her nails until they bled. She was on the verge of getting out of her car and busting through the door when Cole finally stepped out. That day brought her more trouble than she could handle; but if in the end it got her Meme, it would all be worth it. She'd make Cole pay for taking what was hers.

Once again, Sahara watched Meme respond to the mere sound of his voice. Hope, desperation, and love mingled in the depths of her eyes as her soul pleaded with his.

"Meme, I'm sorry for how I treated you. It's just that you're the woman I've been running from my whole life—the woman who makes me feel something, makes my heart beat, takes my breath away, and makes me love. Your past scares me. I don't want to end up like my father, loving and hating a woman so much it drives me crazy. Someone who has so much power over me is capable of some terrible things. All I could think was to push you away before you destroyed me the way my mother destroyed my father. My mind told me to run, but the heart wants what the heart wants. My heart wants you."

Tears flowed from Meme's eyes, cascading down her cheeks like a waterfall. She wanted to go to him and throw her arms around his neck, kissing him with all the love she had for him. She wanted to reassure him that her heart beat for him as well. She wanted to connect with him and feel the fire that had burned between them since the day they met.

Sahara watched the sickening display of emotion; she'd had enough. It was time to put an end to whatever was going on between Cole and Meme. This time she refused to lose; refused to sit in the background and watch Meme build a relationship with someone else. Although her method was extreme, she finally had Meme all to herself and no one could change that. In time, Meme would forgive her and come to love her. Confident in that fact, Sahara marched to the front door and yanked it open.

"What do you want?" Sahara snapped at Cole. "It is too early in the morning for you to be banging on the door and yelling."

"I'm sorry. Is Meme here?" Cole asked, confused and taken by surprise. His brain tried to process why this woman answered Meme's door, hair disheveled, looking like she'd spent the night. He stepped back to look at the apartment number to make sure he was at the right place, even though he already knew he was.

"Yes, but she doesn't want to see you. You hurt her and she is done with you. I guess I should thank you, because now she is where she's supposed to be, with me." Sahara watched with satisfaction as shock and resignation flashed across Cole's face. She had no idea what she was talking about, but took her cue from the things he'd yelled through the door. From the looks of things, it was working.

"I'm sure you don't mind if I let her tell me that to my face." Cole tried to walk past her, but she blocked his path.

"She specifically told me not to let you in here and unlike you, I like to make her happy."

Cole wouldn't normally hurt a woman, but this woman was pressing her luck. He opened his mouth to warn her of such and she stopped him.

"Look," Sahara saw the look of malice on his face and decided to dial back the attitude, "I'm sorry. I'm just doing what she asked me to do. Getting upset with me only makes things worse for you and better for me. Don't keep calling, hounding her, coming by here, and groveling. She is done. Just leave now while you still have your dignity." With that said Sahara stepped back and closed the door in his face.

Cole stood outside that apartment enraged. He wanted to break down that door and have it out with Meme once and for all, but his hurting heart wouldn't let him. He had opened up and bared his heart, only to have it snatched out of his chest a few seconds later.

*How can she run to someone so quickly after all we've shared? She just let it go the next day.*

Now he knew why he had such a sense of dread, only it was for the destruction of his heart and the desolation of their relationship, not for Meme's safety.

With slumped shoulders, Cole walked back to his car. Even though he was hurting, he couldn't be mad at Meme. If she felt just a fraction of what he was feeling now when she walked out of his apartment, he completely understood why she ran to someone else. Being alone right now was the last thing he wanted to do.

He sent a quick text to Marlon, *Meme is fine no need to stop by,* and then drove off.

By the time Sahara returned to the room, Meme was sobbing uncontrollably. The scarf tied around her face to muffle her screams was saturated with tears. Her face was red and covered with a mixture of sweat and tears. With each sob, her body shook with anguish. Her stomach churned and mouth filled with spit. Her eyes widened as she felt the bile rushing up her esophagus. Sahara rushed over to remove the scarf when she heard the muffled retching. The contents of Meme's stomach splashed onto Sahara's hand as they projected out of her mouth, saturating her sheets.

"Why are you doing this?" Meme pleaded through labored breaths once her stomach stopped convulsing. "You can't force me to love you. I love Cole. It may seem odd to you, but I can't help it. The heart wants what the heart wants. One day you will meet someone that will love you as much as you love them. But, you have to let me go. Let me be happy with Cole." Her eyes begged for compassion and her heart hoped for an answer to the prayer she'd prayed all night.

Sahara watched Meme's agony and tears fell down her face. She wanted that love, wanted someone to hold her, appreciate her, and cherish her. Most of all, she wanted that person to be Meme, but at what expense? She loved Meme and wanted her to be happy. She hated seeing her in pain; most of all, she hated being the cause of that pain. The truth of the matter was that the situation was out of her control. She couldn't let Meme go. "I'm sorry, but you have to stay here. It is the only way I can protect you."

Sahara walked out of the room without looking back, leaving Meme yelling. "Protect me from what?"

~

Cole drove away from Meme's apartment, determined to take his mind off of her. The only thing capable of that was his mother. He entered the address for her church into the GPS app on his cell phone and headed in that direction. He had absolutely no idea of what to say or do once he saw her, but he needed some type of diversion to keep him from stressing over Meme.

Pulling up to the front of the church, he spotted her immediately. She looked good, smiling and laughing without a care in the world. She was shaking hands and greeting people as they entered the church. Some walked out of their way to greet her. Everyone seemed to love her.

*I wonder if they'd still love her if they knew what I knew.* She'd cheated on her husband and abandoned her child. Would they still think their precious first lady was worthy of all this adoration?

For a few minutes, Cole sat in his car, watching his mother with anger and hatred, but also with a sense of loss. The child that always wondered where she was or if she thought about him rose to the surface. As a child, he couldn't help but love her, despite all the negative derogatory things his father said about her. She was his mommy and he wanted her back. Once he entered his teens, that's when the hatred showed up and he started to buy into his father's theories about women. The two people who were supposed to nurture, guide, and help develop him into a man had done more damage than good. All of his stupid hang ups over what his parents did or said caused him to allow the best thing that ever happened to him to walk out of his life.

Cole couldn't bring himself to shut off the engine and get out of the car. So, instead of approaching his mother and getting some much needed answers, he drove off. Turns out, going to see his mother wasn't the greatest idea. His mind and heart were once again in turmoil over the woman who had given him life and the woman who was his life now. His temples throbbed with tension and he gripped the steering wheel so tightly his fingers turned white from the pressure. He was on the verge of a breakdown and sought the quiet private comfort of his apartment to do so.

The silence of his apartment catered to his depressed mood, giving him the atmosphere needed to amplify his pain. Had he not wasted that bottle of tequila, it would definitely be his healing balm. He didn't care what time of day it was. A drink was what he needed, but seeing that alcohol of any sort was the one thing missing in his refrigerator, he'd have to find something else to numb his pain.

His cell phone rang, and without checking the caller ID, he sent it to voicemail. He wasn't in the mood to talk to anyone. It rang again, and once again he sent it straight to voicemail. He plopped down on the sofa, prepared to sort through his chaotic life, and the doorbell rang. Incessantly, it rang. Releasing an exasperated sigh, Cole jumped to his feet and marched to the door; snatching it open with such vigor he almost snatched it off the hinges. His mouth was poised for a good cursing out, but the look of terror on Vanessa's face halted the words on his lips. The way he snatched the door open obviously scared her enough. He saved his words for another time.

"What do you want, Vanessa?" Cole asked, barely hiding his irritation.

She pushed her way into his apartment before he had the mind to close the door in her face. "I am worried about you."

"Vanessa, I don't have time for this right now. We can talk…" The words died on his lips as Vanessa lifted her sundress over her head, revealing her naked body.

"Don't kick me out. Let me make you feel better."

Cole's eyes scanned the body that he neglected to appreciate the last time they were together and didn't argue when she shut the front door, took him by the hand, led him to the couch, and straddled him. She pulled his shirt over his head, giving her lips and hands freedom to roam across his bare chest. Meaningless sex should do the trick. If he couldn't drink his sorrows away, he'd sex them out. He knew his choice in sex partner would have far greater consequences, but didn't have time to analyze them. He'd deal with the backlash later. Right now, he just needed to forget about Meme.

Cole sat back, resting his head against the cool leather of the sofa, awaiting the pleasure sure to bring peace to his mind. Vanessa connected their lips, snaking her tongue across the threshold of his mouth. Moaning in pleasure, she crushed her mouth to his and pressed her bared flesh against him. She prepared her mind for ecstasy only to whimper at the immediate disconnect. Cole abruptly ended their kiss, lifted her off his lap, and placed her on the couch beside him.

He couldn't do it. The taste, the feel, her scent, it was all wrong. There was no spark or chemistry, no rush of adrenaline. He couldn't believe he settled for meaningless sex in the past, but he was done settling. Vanessa wasn't Meme, and he refused to settle. Without a word, Cole walked over to her dress. Picking it up, he tried to formulate an apology, but she snatched the dress out of his hand. She slipped it on and was running out the door before he could utter a word.

Cole shook his head as he plopped back down on the couch. He was one step closer to being like his father, so stuck on one woman that all others were irrelevant. The only difference was he had the foresight to see how bitterness over losing the woman you loved could destroy you, and he wasn't going out like that. He'd give Meme a few days to calm down and then she and her little girlfriend were in for a rude awakening. Yes, he screwed up and let her go, but he wasn't about to screw up by not fighting to get her back. With all the confusion in his mind, there was one thing he was certain of; his heart still wanted Meme. He'd given part of himself to her and he'd never be the same without her.

## 23

Sahara reluctantly went to answer the ringing doorbell, hoping that it wasn't Cole again. If he was back after the performance she put on earlier, she knew there would be nothing stopping him from coming in this time. She checked the peephole and breathed a sigh of relief. It wasn't Cole.

"What are you doing here?" She asked as she opened the door. "I thought you didn't want her to know we were working together."

"Shut up!"

Sahara's eyes widened with shock. She'd never seen her that riled up before. She was crazy, that was a fact, but the look in her eyes made Sahara uneasy. Seeing the direction she was heading, Sahara chased after her. Meme was defenselessly tied up in the bedroom and Sahara wouldn't let anything happen to her. Grabbing the crazed woman by the arm, Sahara spun her around. Before she knew what was happening, the woman slammed Sahara against the wall, pressing a nine millimeter gun into her cheek.

"Don't ever put your hands on me," the woman barked with a trail of spit following, eyes devoid of compassion and alive with fury.

The woman marched into the room, gun leading the way, and pointed it directly at Meme. "I should've gotten rid of you a long time ago. That first night I saw you guys together, I knew you were going to be a problem." Her hand shook as she inched closer to the bed.

"Vanessa?" It took Meme a second to register her presence. *This is who Sahara keeps referring to.* "What are you talking about?" Meme trembled with fear, but refused to give in to it. After Sahara convinced Cole that she no longer wanted him, she lost hope of being rescued and prepared her mind for the worst. If death was her fate it was better than living without Cole. "I have never done—"

Before Meme could finish her sentence, Vanessa was on top of her, pointing the gun to the center of her forehead. Her legs straddled Meme's chest, her weight making breathing nearly impossible. The gun pressed so firmly into Meme's forehead that her head pounded from the pressure. Shutting her eyes, Meme braced for what was next. She had made so many mistakes in her life, had so many regrets and things she wished she could do over. Silently, she made her peace with God.

"Wait! Wait!" Sahara pleaded in a panicked frenzy. "This is not a part of the plan. You said if I get her away, you wouldn't hurt her." She tried to wedge herself between them, but Vanessa's legs were locked around Meme.

"It's too late. She has ruined everything. She had to come along with her pretty little face and make him fall for her."

"It's not too late. Just help me get her to the car and you will never see us again."

Vanessa's hand shook uncontrollably as her finger rested on the trigger. "I love him. He belongs with me." She chanted over and over.

"If you do this, you'll be in jail, and you'll never see him again." Sahara watched Vanessa's sanity return as she considered the consequences of her actions.

Slowly, she raised the gun and pointed it at Sahara. "Untie her and get her out of here now."

Meme sat quietly still as Sahara untied her. When Vanessa barged into the room waving a gun, she was too shocked to comprehend her involvement in this craziness, but now her mind replayed the past few weeks. All the notes, her scratched car, flowers to her job, and her ransacked apartment. Vanessa was the mastermind behind it all. One thing she couldn't figure out was how they met. They were from two different aspects of her life. How and when did they join forces to destroy it?

Watching Vanessa pace around was terrifying. Meme thought Sahara was mentally unstable, but it was obvious she was the more stable of the two. Vanessa had always been this pretty, bubbly girl. Meme never would've guessed she was capable of something like this.

Finally free, Meme massaged her bruised wrists and, for a second, thought about making a run for it. Vanessa must have read her thoughts and raised the gun toward her with eyes that said don't even think about it. Quickly turning her attention to Sahara who was kneeling before her, Meme stepped into the pair of pants she was offering. When she pulled the sweatshirt over her head, Meme found her eyes. Remorse briefly flashed across Sahara's face as she read the silent message in Meme's eyes.

Pulling Meme to her, Sahara embraced her, whispering in her ear that she would make everything better. Oddly enough, Meme returned the embrace as a tear slid down her face.

They were moving her to God knows where. No one would have a clue as to where to find her. Her prayers went unanswered, but at least this time she deserved what was coming to her. This must be the ultimate pay back for turning her back on God. She didn't deserve what Damien did to her, but that was no excuse to betray God. Up until that point, God had been good to her. She had a loving family that believed in her and wanted what was best for her. Then, she allowed a single day, although horrible, to separate her from the love of God. Then, she made promises to return to Him and didn't follow through. Yes, she was getting what she deserved.

"All right!" Vanessa busted up their embrace, flailing her arms in between them, knocking them both upside the head with the gun in the process. "I don't need to see all your lesbian interactions. Now get moving before I change my mind."

As she followed every command barked at her, Sahara couldn't help but feel the tables had turned. The victor had become the victim. She wasn't the brains behind the whole scheme, but she felt like what little authority she did have was taken away the moment the gun showed up. As they walked to the front of the house, she felt her life was in danger just as much as Meme's was.

"Try anything and I will put a bullet in you."

The threat sent chills down Sahara's spine. Sahara grabbed Meme's hand and escorted her to the car, hoping she got the message. They climbed into the car, Sahara in the driver's seat, and Meme in the back with Vanessa sitting so close that the gun dug into her ribs. Looking out the window, Meme recognized the car pulling into the parking lot as they pulled out.

*Marlon.* Tears flooded her face and she was powerless to stop them. She reached for the door to jump out, but it was locked. She moved to unlock it and the gun dug deeper into her ribs. Meme cried out in pain, terror, and despair. *God don't let them take me.*

~

Marlon stood on his sister's porch ringing the doorbell, the same ominous feeling Cole described now crept up his spine. It was not like Meme to not answer the door, especially for him. He'd parked next to her car, so he was 100 percent sure she was home. He'd received Cole's text that he no longer needed to come over, but the brevity of his message let him know that things hadn't gone well. Marlon just wanted to make sure she was all right.

Becoming more and more apprehensive by the minute, Marlon pulled out his key to Meme's apartment. Normally, he wouldn't use his key. He didn't want to mistakenly walk in on something that he didn't want to see, but today he'd make an exception. Turning the key inside the lock, Marlon crept inside the apartment. Immediately, alarm bells rang out. The apartment was still in disarray from the break in. There was no way his neat-freak sister would've spent the night in this apartment without cleaning it.

Standing in one spot, Marlon scanned the room. Tables were still overturned, glass scattered across the floor, and the stench of fermented garbage permeated the air. Something definitely wasn't right. Slowly, he started toward the bedroom, glass crunching with each step. The last time he felt this much anxiety, his wife was being attacked by her ex-husband while he was on the phone with her, powerless to help.

His hand stilled on the door knob as he prepared his mind for what he might find on the other side of the door. As he turned the knob, each click accelerated his pulse. If the images of Meme slain and sprawled across her bed that were stampeding his mind were real, he was going to lose it. She was his only sibling. And although they had issues, he loved her.

*The room is empty.* Marlon didn't know whether to be relieved or terrified. Searching the rest of the apartment, he came up with the same results. She wasn't home, but her car is outside. Where could she be?

*Maybe things worked out between her and Cole.* Rereading the text Cole sent him, he concluded that he must have miscalculated somewhere. Nowhere did it say things went bad. *Maybe they kissed and made up.* Finding that to be a viable explanation, Marlon sent Meme a quick text, *Call me if you need me,* and figured he'd get the details of what went down from Cole at work.

Normally, he wouldn't get involved, but he'd lost too much sleep and prayed long and hard for his sister to get over whatever happened in her past. He'd prayed just as hard for her to find happiness. He saw a glimpse of that happiness at the baby shower and wasn't going to sit idly while his sister lost what could turn out to be the best thing in her life. He'd check with Cole, make sure they reconciled, and make sure they stayed that way. It's the least he could do, seeing that it was Meme's meddling that got him on a plane to Atlanta to find Latrice when she'd ran off.

Hopping in his car, Marlon made the quick drive to the restaurant. He was pretty early, but he could always find something to do to kill some time. Cole's car was in the parking lot when he pulled up. That definitely wasn't a good sign. They were different in so many ways, but the one thing they had in common was cooking. Just like him, the restaurant was Cole's sanctuary. Cooking helped him escape the world.

The kitchen was quiet. Flipping on the light chased away the darkness and Marlon scanned the kitchen for any sign of Cole. Nothing; there was no movement, no sound of dishes clanking, water running, or chopping. Marlon knew exactly where Cole was. Sometimes life was so crazy that even cooking couldn't calm the beast in him and he had to find alternate means to keep his sanity. When dealing with his ex-wife's infidelity, Latrice was that place of solace for Marlon. Cole couldn't find comfort in a woman, because he refused to allow anyone near his heart. So when cooking wasn't enough, Marlon new exactly where to find him: the freezer.

Maybe the cold slowed his adrenaline, made his mind stop running a hundred miles a minute, or gave him something else to focus on other than his problems. Sure enough, Marlon opened the freezer and there sat Cole, brows knitted together in deep thought. Cole didn't even notice Marlon until he spoke.

"Where's my sister?" Marlon, on the other hand, didn't like the cold. The walk in freezer wasn't the place for beating around the bush.

"She's fine. I checked on her." He was not about to admit to his boy that his sister played him.

"If she is fine, why are you sitting in the freezer?" Impatiently, Marlon waited for a response, and when there wasn't one, he turned to leave. This wasn't the end of the conversation, but unlike Cole, Marlon didn't do his best thinking when he was freezing. So, when he came to his senses and retreated out of his frostbitten think tank, Marlon would get to the bottom of things.

Marlon plopped down behind his desk and had just begun reviewing a stack of invoices when he noticed Cole lingering in the doorway. He continued looking over the paperwork as if he hadn't seen him. He was on the verge of spilling his guts and Marlon didn't want to say anything to make him stop.

"My whole life I've tried to be a good person." Cole spoke slowly as he made his way into Marlon's office. "Yeah, I could treat the ladies a little better, but I have never misled them. I'm upfront about what I want and they accept it. I treat people right, try to help them whenever I can, but God seems to be punishing me for something. Don't I deserve some type of happiness?"

Marlon, taken aback by Cole's sudden openness and vulnerability, didn't respond. He sat looking stunned.

Cole continued, more so talking to himself and needing to voice his thoughts than actually talking to Marlon. "I saw my mother today. It's been well over twenty years with no visits, phone calls, birthday cards, or Christmas presents. She just vanished without a care in the world. Just a couple hours on the internet and I found her. If it was that easy, why hadn't she looked for me? What kind of woman leaves her son and never gives him a second thought?"

Cole fought hard to hold back his emotions, but as his thoughts steered more toward the real source of his anguish; it was next to impossible. "Thanks to good ol' mom and dad, I've spent most of my life keeping people from getting close to me. I don't know when the hell I got caught slippin', but I am in love with your sister." Sighing in surrender, Cole ran his hands down his face as the confession sank in.

"Vanessa showed up at my place today." Cole saw the look on Marlon's face and hated the disapproval he saw, but knew it was best to tell him now, before Vanessa showed up and gave some dramatic altered version of the truth. "She stripped down, climbed into my lap, and offered herself to me. After the day I had, it might've done me some good, but…" Cole made eye contact with Marlon. Not only was he talking to his boss, but the brother of the woman he just professed to love. He wanted Marlon to completely understand, no matter what story Vanessa told, that nothing happened. "I couldn't do it. I couldn't just sex the wrong woman after meeting the right one."

"Have you told Meme that you love her? If not, go home and tell her now."

Just like that, Marlon snapped Cole out of his euphoric grandeur of love and all that he felt for Meme. She wasn't at his home. She went running back to her past and left him shattered and alone, trying to pick up the pieces of his heart. But she warned him didn't she? As she walked out, she warned that if he let her go it would be for good this time.

Marlon saw those emotional walls popping back up and quickly changed the subject before he missed a rare opportunity to witness to Cole while he would be receptive to what he had to say. "We've all been through things that would give us just cause to lose faith in God. Lord knows I have, but we can't allow those things to win. At some point, you have to let go of the hurt. You said God seems to be punishing you. I would say He is trying to get your attention. Maybe He is trying to get you to see that your life doesn't have to be so empty."

Cole's eyes overflowed with tears. Marlon watched him catch a tear in the corner of his eye. Cole was up and out of his seat, fleeing the room before Marlon could say another word. Marlon wanted to follow after him, but knew if he pushed, Cole would shut down. It was best to leave it in God's hands. Marlon said a quick prayer that God would continue to soften Cole's heart and heal wounds inflicted by his absent mother and lunatic father. Then, Marlon turned his attention back to the invoices.

## <u>24</u>

Wayne watched the empty station, wondering what was going on. Meme never missed work without calling in. He was able to squeeze in her clients who didn't want to reschedule with other stylists, but this was so unlike her. He called her, but her line went straight to voicemail. After the third time, he stopped trying. Worry gnawed at the pit of his gut. The more people asked if he'd spoken to Meme, the more concerned he became. He couldn't shake the feeling that something was terribly wrong.

It was the longest work day of his life. Every idle minute was spent obsessing over Meme's whereabouts. When the last client and stylist left, Wayne was right behind them. Shelves and supplies would get restocked another time. He had to get over to Pavoli's and talk to Meme's brother. He was breaking the unwritten code of being in the closet by approaching Meme's family, but he had to do something. That's the thing about their lifestyle, most wanted to keep it from their family. On the rare occasion the family knew, there was rarely someone you could call that cared enough to be concerned. If Marlon didn't care, Meme had Cole, and from the look in the man's eyes when they met, he cared. He had no idea where to find Cole, but hoped he didn't have to go that far.

By the time Wayne arrived at Pavoli's, it was the middle of dinner rush. He circled the parking lot twice before seeing a couple leaving and followed them to their parking spot. He was so nervous and worried that he was nauseous, but he surprisingly held it together. Having always been dramatic, Wayne had to remember to keep the hysterics under control. Any minute, he was bound to breakdown crying, but gave himself a pep talk before getting out of the car.

All the pep talking and telling himself to stay calm flew out of the window the moment he stepped into the restaurant and asked to see Marlon. The seating hostess telling him it was not customary for the chef to come to the front of the restaurant to speak to patrons unless it was to discuss their meal lit a fire in him. Before one more, *"Stay calm, Wayne,"* could cross his mind, he was in her face, having a full-on neck rolling, finger-pointing diva fit.

Apparently, one of the other employees must have decided it was better to break a rule than to have an altercation in the restaurant, because mid-rant, Wayne was interrupted by the deep timbre of a voice laced with anger and frustration.

"How may I help you?" Though the words were inviting, the look on this man's face was not.

Extending his hand, Wayne introduced himself. "Hi, I am Wayne, Meme's friend. Can we go somewhere private to talk?"

251

Without saying a word, Marlon led him to his office. When he plopped down on the sofa, it finally donned on him who Wayne was. "It is good to see that you are feeling better." Seeing the confused look on Wayne's face, Marlon explained. "I sat with Meme at the hospital when you were in the emergency room. So how is Kevin?" Marlon asked, hoping to get the conversation moving, but the question seemed to further stun him into silence.

Wayne stared at Marlon for a while before finally answering. "He's good." He was unaccustomed to families caring. The fact that this man cared so much for his sister that he sat in a hospital—concerned for someone he didn't know—just because his sister was upset was a little shocking.

"That's good to hear. When you see him again tell him I said what's up." Feeling his patience slipping, Marlon tried to guide the conversation to a conclusion. "Now what can I do for you?"

"Well, I wanted to see if you had talked to Meme." Wayne paused to clear his throat and put a little bass in his voice. He knew he was a little on the feminine side, accepted it, and never apologized for it, but the masculinity radiating off of Marlon would make anybody want to man up. "She didn't come to work today, and she didn't call in either. That's so unlike her."

Marlon thought for a second, and then excused himself from the room. He had to agree. Meme loved being a stylist and would never leave her clients hanging without cause. Something was up and he went to get the one person who should have the answer. A few minutes later, he returned to his office with Cole trailing behind him.

Wayne was up, out of his seat, and heading toward Cole before Marlon could get the introduction out of his mouth. "Where is Meme?"

Cole didn't like the accusatory tone and immediately jumped on the defensive. "Why would I know where she is?"

"Maybe because she is your girl and lives with you." Marlon jumped in before Wayne could respond. He didn't understand what was wrong with Cole. He had been acting strange for the past two days and Marlon had assumed it was because he was in love, but now he wasn't so sure. The question he'd just asked and the way he'd asked it was not sitting well with him.

"I told you she left me," Cole said.

"Yeah, but Sunday you texted and said she was fine. I assumed you guys worked everything out and she went home with you," Marlon shot back.

Cole explained how some woman answered the door, said she was Meme's woman, and dismissed him. While he talked, Marlon and Wayne sat silently listening and thinking.

Marlon was the first to speak. "If she didn't go home with you then there is a problem. I still went by after church. I read your text and assumed things didn't go well between you guys. Her car was there, but she wasn't. I went inside and there was still a mess everywhere. Being the neat freak that she is, I thought it was a little strange that she was sitting around in that filth." Marlon was up on his feet, pacing around as he tried to put everything together. "Seeing that she was nowhere in the apartment, I reread the text and assumed I misinterpreted its meaning. I told myself you must have taken her back to your place."

"Yeah, there definitely is a problem," Wayne interrupted. "If she had a new woman, I would be the first to know about it. And, it still doesn't explain why she was a no-show this morning and didn't call in."

The room fell silent as they all tried to come up with an alternate conclusion than what was blaring right in front of them. The notes, vandalized car, the break in, and now no one had seen or heard from Meme since Saturday. Cole plopped down on the couch, cursing himself for not pushing his way into that apartment and demanding Meme to tell him to his face that she didn't want him. At least then he'd know she was all right; but no, he let someone convince him that Meme was done with him, even though his heart told him otherwise. If anything happened to her, he would never forgive himself.

"What does this woman look like?" Wayne hovered over Cole, for the first time in his life, controlling his hysterics. Being dramatic would not help them figure out what happened to Meme.

"We can discuss this in the car," Marlon said, grabbing his keys off the desk.

"Where are we going?" Cole managed to ask, even though his mind was in a whirl with regret, rage, and guilt.

"To her apartment to make sure she is not there before we start jumping to conclusions."

During the ride to Meme's house, Wayne grilled Cole about the woman who answered Meme's door. He wanted to know height, width, and weight; skin complexion, shade, and texture; hair length, color, grade, and style; big nose or small; eye color and circumference. By the time they arrived at the apartment, Cole felt like he'd been grilled by the FBI.

They stepped out of the car and as their feet hit the pavement, they were running toward Meme's apartment. One would've thought the three of them were in the Olympic trials for the hundred-meter dash to Meme's door. Marlon opened the door and Wayne gagged from the stench of rotting garbage. Cole pulled out his phone and called the cops. There was no way Meme was living in this filth. In just the short time she stayed with him, he knew how much of a neat freak she was. No matter how depressed or upset she was, she would have cleaned.

Wayne got sick, Cole had the job of calling the cops, but Marlon had the hardest responsibility of all, calling his parents. After all the things Meme had done, Marlon knew his parents still loved her, just as he did. If something happened to her before they had a chance to truly reconcile, his parents would never forgive themselves. Before he could finish his sentence, his mom was wailing and the loud clanking noise let him know she'd dropped the phone. Having a hard time holding it together while his mom sorrowfully mourned her daughter's existence, Marlon simply hung up.

Cole was busy walking himself through possible scenarios, none of which sat well with him, when the cops showed up. He greeted them and Marlon instantly appeared at his side. Cole had a hard time hiding his disgust for the idiot cops standing in front of him. They were the same ones who came down to the restaurant when he made Meme file a report, and the same ones that showed up when her apartment was vandalized. If they had done something or taken the situation more seriously from the beginning, Meme would still be here. He had to find someone with whom he could place the blame to ease his guilt. They were suitable candidates.

Between Cole and Marlon, the cops were filled in on everything that had taken place since the break-in. They listened and asked questions.

When it was all said and done, they turned to Cole with an accusatory tone. "Looks like you were the last one to see her."

"What the hell is that supposed to mean?" Cole stepped toward the officer. He had a lot of emotional tension to unleash. If the cop had to catch it, so be it. He would deal with the consequences later.

Marlon saw where this was heading and put a stop to it. "Let's not even go there. Cole loves my sister and would never hurt her."

The officer shook his head. "You need to seriously think about whom you align yourself with, Mr. Wright. I would hate for you to later find out that you defended the man who hurt your sister."

Before the cop could finish the last word, Cole was in his face trying to rip his head off, but Marlon wasn't letting him go out like that. He jumped between them, scuffling with Cole, trying to ensure he didn't catch a case, but the officer just wouldn't shut up.

"You see there, Mr. Wright? Look at that temper. You said he and your sister had an argument. Are you sure it didn't escalate, and he hurt her?"

Cole went after him again. This time with a force Marlon couldn't contain. Luckily, the cavalry had arrived. On cue, Marlon Sr. and Pastor Hawkins jumped in and helped wrestle Cole away from the cops. The cop tossed a couple of business cards at Cole, admonishing him to give him a call if he felt like coming clean and walked away to take a look at Meme's apartment again.

Marlon, along with his dad and Pastor Hawkins, held Cole back until they were sure he was calm. Getting arrested for assaulting a police officer would only make matters worse. They needed everyone calm and level headed so they could figure out their next move. Cole nodded that he was good and they let him go.

Cole looked Pastor Hawkins up and down with a scowl. "Why are you here?"

He tilted his head in confusion. "Well for one, I am Marlon's pastor, and when my members are in need, I try to be there." He looked in Cole's eyes and could tell that this was more than just a hurt man lashing out because he was scared. Something else was going on. "And for two, I thought we were boys. Where else would I be when my boy needs me?"

"Well, I don't need you here."

Cole walked away and Marlon started after him, but Pastor Hawkins stopped him. "I got this. Go take care of your mother."

Marlon looked toward the car at his mother who was obviously crying her heart out and didn't budge. Everyone had better get themselves together and quick. He couldn't keep putting out everyone's fire while trying to contain his own. He was hurting like everyone else, and if someone else stepped out of pocket, he was going to lose it.

Like she could sense his pain, Latrice pulled up into the parking lot. He should've been upset that she was out of the house, but he needed her more than ever. He jogged over to her, opened the driver side door, kneeled down, and laid his head in her lap. His tears soaked through her pants and she stroked his head, praying for his strength and the safety of his sister.

Cole heard footsteps behind him, assumed it was Marlon, and turned around to complain about Pastor Hawkins being there, but was face to face with the new source of his frustration.

"What's up Cole? Did I miss something? Are we not cool anymore?" He waited for a response, but all he got was a nostril-flared menacing glare from someone he presumed to be a friend. "I am not going to stand here and assume you are lashing out at me because you're upset. It's obvious that I did something to upset you, so be a man and spill it."

Those might have been the wrong words and the wrong tone to take with an already volatile man, but they were out there now and Cole was burling toward him with a vengeance. Just because he was a pastor didn't mean he was a punk. He stood his ground.

"You want to know why the hell I don't want you here?"

"First of all, don't disrespect me, and get out of my face."

Cynically, Cole laughed. "Respect you? How can I respect you knowing she gave you everything and didn't give a damn about me?"

*What in the world is he talking about?*

Cole cursed himself. The words were out there now and he couldn't take them back. The look on Pastor Hawkins' face let him know he wanted an explanation. Silently, they stood toe to toe. Cole's rage dissipated as he searched for the words to explain and Pastor Hawkins' confusion escalated as he watched the emotions playing across his friend's face.

Opting for the direct approach, Cole started talking. "I think you're my brother."

He laughed until he saw the seriousness on Cole's face. "Are you saying my dad had a child he didn't know about?"

"No, what I'm—"

"So you're saying he knew about you, but was a dead beat? He died years ago. How do you know for sure he was your father?"

Sighing in frustration, Cole braced for the fallout that was sure to come. Pastor Hawkins was on the defensive and no matter how much he sugar coated his words, they wouldn't be received well. "When I was four my parents separated." There was no need to discuss why they separated. Pastor Hawkins would get even more defensive and Cole would never get the answers he deserved. "I never saw my mother after that until a couple nights ago. I Googled her name, and after hours of searching the links, I came across a link to your church. I think your mother is my mother."

Before he could respond, they were interrupted by the screeching shrill of Wayne's voice.

Wayne had been scanning through his mental rolodex, hoping the features Cole described matched someone in his memory. There were very few things Meme kept from him and relationships weren't one of them. He knew without a doubt the woman who answered the door when Cole had come by was responsible for Meme's disappearance.

When the images running through his mind didn't match up, Wayne pulled out his cell phone to search through his pictures. He used to get frustrated when his phone froze up due to all the photos he stored, but was now glad he was one of those people who never deleted pictures. He studied each image carefully. He didn't want to rush and mistakenly overlook someone. He had tuned out the world and everything going on around him. His gut told him to keep looking, and he didn't stop until his finger slid across the screen to bring up the next image and he almost fainted. Smiling cheek pressed to cheek with Meme, at the margarita party he'd thrown a few weeks ago, was Sahara. His heart rate sped up then slowed down as he compared Sahara's image with the features Cole recounted. Finally putting it together, Wayne screamed for Cole to come take a look at the picture.

Once Wayne reached Cole, he was so out of breath and grief-stricken, he couldn't find his voice to speak. Fighting to hold back his temperament, Wayne turned the phone toward Cole, allowing him to look at the screen. The look on Cole's face when he viewed the picture was all the confirmation Wayne needed. Sahara was responsible for what ever happened to Meme.

"What's her name and where can I find her?" Cole impatiently watched Wayne taking deep breaths to calm himself. Cole didn't have time for emotions, not even his own, so he surely wasn't going to put up with Wayne. He barked out again, this time with the intensity of a raging bull. "What is her name and where can I find her?"

The fierceness of his tone garnered everyone's attention, and when they looked up, Cole was about three seconds from having his fingers wrapped around Wayne's throat. If it wasn't for Pastor Hawkins being right there, Wayne would've already been gasping for air. The commotion drew everybody to them. Marlon, Latrice, Marlon Sr., and Gloria quickly surrounded Wayne.

Having his life threatened was a good way to get his vocal chords working. "It's Sahara, a friend of ours. From what I hear, she's in love with Meme and crazy as hell." He wasn't there the night Sahara went crazy, but he'd heard about it. No telling what else she was capable of. After giving everyone a chance to look at the picture, Wayne called Kanani. If anybody knew where Sahara lived, she did.

## 25

Cole and Marlon refused to let the cops drop the ball. They convinced everyone else to fall back and wait at Cole's house while they followed the cops to Sahara's house. Just like they figured, the cops knocked on the door, waited a few minutes, checked the perimeter of the house, hopped in their car, and then left. If Sahara was in that house, she now knew the cops were looking for her and would probably run. If she left with Meme, they'd never find her. They weren't about to let that happen.

Cole knew that without a search warrant, the cops were limited on what they could do, but they could've played it a little smarter. He and Marlon stuck around and just as they suspected, ten minutes later the garage door rolled up. Not leaving anything to chance, Cole started his car and pulled into the driveway, blocking the car from pulling out. He and Marlon were out of the car and walking into the garage before the driver had time to react and close the door. They had no idea what they were walking up on, but took their chances. Seeing Cole stalking toward her, Sahara's eyes widened with fear. Frantically, she fumbled to lock the doors. She was trapped and desperately racked her brain for a way to escape.

Sahara knew they should've been gone days ago. The longer they stayed, the more Vanessa teetered on the brink of insanity, and the more time it gave Cole to figure out what was going on. Sahara had a few things to take care of before relocating. The people helping her were dragging their feet. She never anticipated having to take on a new identity, but that's where she was headed. She'd already shaved her head and bought a few pairs of baggy jeans and some hooded sweatshirts. All she needed was the documents to make it official. Sahara Wilkins would cease to exist and Cedric James would rise in her place. Now, all her efforts were coming to a screeching halt.

"Open the door." Cole tried to keep his voice as calm and peaceful as possible. He had no idea of what she was capable or what kind of weapon she had in the car. He didn't want to push her into action.

Fear radiated in her eyes as she turned toward him. It couldn't end right here like this. Meme was alone with that monster. No telling if Vanessa would follow through with her threats. That thought alone propelled Sahara in to action. She put her car in reverse and stepped on the gas. She crashed into the hood of Cole's car, but didn't let that deter her. She stepped on the gas harder, inch by inch, pushing Cole's car back. The screeching tires and revving engine echoed through the hollow garage as it filled with exhaust fumes.

Choking on the smoke, Cole and Marlon frantically searched for something to break the window. Marlon spotted a wrench and, without hesitation, picked it up swinging it full force into the passenger side window. Glass shattered into Sahara face as she screamed in fear. The shattering glass halted all movement and the only sound was Sahara's sobs.

"Open the door, Sahara," Cole spoke with a calmness he didn't feel. The locks clicked and he wasted no time pulling her out. He would've loved to take her back to his apartment and use his own methods to persuade her to tell him where Meme was. However, due to the damage she did to both cars, he had to call the cops and wait for them to come back.

"You don't understand." Sahara tried to plead for understanding, but Cole shut her up. Grabbing her by the arm, he drug her into the house. He doubted Meme was in there, but had to make sure.

"The only thing I want to hear coming out of your mouth is you telling me where Meme is." He never wanted to hurt someone so bad in all his life. Her sniveling and whining were grating his nerves. She didn't have the right to cry or have a breakdown. She took his heart and had done only God knows what with her. If Meme was hurt in any way, Sahara would regret it until the day she died. Marlon must've sensed that this woman's life line was running short, because he stepped in to intervene, but her fate didn't fare much better with him. He glared down at her, hoping for the compassion of God to help him see her as a human being. "Where is my sister?"

The question only made Sahara more hysterical. She wailed and finally lost her strength, collapsing to the floor. The past few days had been more than she bargained for. She hadn't slept for fear of what

Vanessa would do, hadn't eaten much, and felt like prisoner. "You have to let me go. She'll kill her if I don't come back."

"Where is she?"


"You don't understand. She gave me two hours to finish things up. If I don't come back, she will kill Meme."

"Where is she?" Marlon didn't have time for the ramblings of a crazy woman.

"I can't tell you." Sahara crumbled under the exasperating effort to get them to listen. "If she sees anyone coming besides me she will put a bullet into Meme's head."

That got Cole's attention, "Who is *she*?" He thought her talking in circles and mentioning this infamous *she* was her way of trying to clear her name or at least set up her insanity defense, but now he wasn't so sure.

"Vanessa." That name rolled out of her mouth and hit Cole in the chest. It couldn't be the same Vanessa. If it was, all of this was his fault, and he'd never forgive himself. He already blamed himself for letting Meme leave his house. If Vanessa was behind this, there was no doubt it was because of him. Cole couldn't even bring himself to look at Marlon.

Marlon knew exactly where his mind was headed. "This is not your fault. This is a crazy scheme cooked up by two crazy women."

Cole shook his head and walked away. There was no way anyone could convince him this wasn't his fault. He walked outside to clear his mind. It was dark out and the cops should've made it back by now, but why would they choose this time to start acting like they cared. He took a couple of deep breaths, inhaled some fresh air, and a light bulb went off.

Running back into the house, Cole yelled out, "I know where Vanessa lives." His excitement was met by Sahara's shrieks of objection, but he ignored every last one of them. Sleeping with Vanessa had gotten Meme involved in this and this experience was going to get her out of it. Because Cole had slept with her, she was obsessed with being with him. But also, because he'd slept with her, he was one step closer to finding Meme. By all the objecting, begging, and pleading Sahara was doing, he was right on the money. Meme was at Vanessa's house.

"Please don't go over there. Vanessa has a gun and will kill her. I am supposed to leave town with Meme. Just let me go get her and I will bring her to you."

"You think we should listen to her?" Marlon asked Cole.

"Don't trust a word she says. She lied to my face and convinced me she and Meme were in some type of relationship."

"I hear you, but what if she is telling the truth. I don't want to do something stupid and get my sister killed."

"What if she is lying, gets your sister, and disappears?"

"I know I seem crazy, and this whole situation is way out of hand. I never would've touched Meme if it wasn't for Vanessa. If I could end it, I would, but now I am just trying to keep her alive." Sahara took a second to get her emotions together. They were finally listening to her and she had to get them to see things her way.

"I have been into Meme for a long time. I kept waiting to make my move and someone always seemed to sweep in before I got a chance." She looked at Cole and he understood he was one of those people. "I was sitting outside her apartment the morning you brought her breakfast. We hung out the night before and had a great time. I was sitting there trying to

265

convince myself to go talk to her when you showed up." Sahara sighed as she plopped down on the couch. Stalking made her sound even crazier, but she had to tell him the whole truth to get them to trust her.

"I was sitting there trying to rationalize why you were there and hoping you'd leave soon when Vanessa showed up. She taped something to the door and ran to her car. Of course I stopped her, assuming she was there for Meme. That's when I found out she was there for you. We'd talked for a while; we understood each other. Just as I had been waiting for Meme to want me, she's been waiting for you. We hung out a few times and that's when she came up with this crazy notion that if I could get Meme away from you, she'd want me and you'd want her."

"For a minute, it looked like things were going to work themselves out. You and Meme stopped talking, and one night Vanessa called you. She asked what Meme had that she didn't. You hung up on her and she lost it. All she talked about was getting rid of Meme. I was afraid for her. Vanessa was out of her mind with jealousy and trashed Meme's apartment to scare her, but it only brought you two closer together. Every day we watched you guys come and go together. It broke my heart, but it did something else to Vanessa. She went from this love obsessed woman to a mad woman with homicidal thoughts. I agreed to get Meme away from you and she promised not to hurt her. That is the only reason I had her. Everything was going as planned until you showed up at her apartment. The way Meme responded to the sound of your voice, I knew she'd never love me that way. If I could have let her go with her safety ensured, I would have. Vanessa will not rest until she is gone. That is why I have to get back over there before Vanessa loses it."

Sahara desperately pleaded her case. Everything she endured over the past few days had come to an apex and she was on the brink of a meltdown. How could she have been so stupid to believe this insane plan would work? Her throat constricted, choking off her sobs. If they didn't believe her there was nothing else she could do. Meme would die because of her. Cole still regarded her skeptically. He wasn't moved by her display of emotion. She had put on a good show when she answered the door the other day. She didn't look like an innocent pawn caught up in someone else's wickedness. For her own selfish gain, she stood at that door and deceived him. There was no perceptible fear like she was being coerced into deceiving him. She acted on her own volition. This could be her encore performance, and that was why he didn't trust her. She had already changed her appearance. There was no doubt in his mind she'd bolt if they let her go.

Marlon, on the other hand, believed every word she said. He had seen that other side of Vanessa when she came into his office claiming Cole attacked her. If Cole hadn't already told his side of the story, Marlon might've believed her. Vanessa would go to the extreme to get what she wanted, and he didn't want his sister to be a casualty in the war for Cole's heart. He knew Cole had seen another side of Sahara that made him unwilling to trust her. However, Marlon's gut was telling him that she was sincerely remorseful and letting her go back to get Meme would be safer than waiting around for the cops to show up.

"Why are we even standing here listening to her? I know where Vanessa lives. Call your dad, have him pick us up, and let's get over there."

"If there is a possibility that she's telling the truth, I don't want to just go over there and bust through the door. Vanessa could fly off the handle and kill my sister before we get to her."

Roughly smoothing his hand down his face, Cole sighed in frustration. He was not one for the passive route, but he had to admit Marlon had a point. "So what? We let Sahara go, then we wait?"

"No. I have another idea." They stepped closer so they could talk without Sahara overhearing. Marlon explained that Paul had a group of friends who specialized in getting things done incognito. Paul had called them into action when Latrice's ex-husband threatened her. They got into the house undetected then, surely they could do the same for them now.

Despite the situation, Cole chuckled as he nodded his agreement to Marlon's plan. He liked Paul and always wondered how a church boy achieved the mob boss kind of clout that he had. Now he was even more curious. Within ten minutes, a black SUV pulled up and they jumped inside, dragging Sahara with them.

## 26

S o much for love," said Vanessa. Her sinister glare should've terrified Meme, but she was past the point of fear. She'd been malnourished and plagued by crippling thoughts of her fate for days. She'd seen far worse than Vanessa's stare in her nightmares. "Time's almost up. Looks like Sahara came to her senses and left you to fend for yourself."

Seeing her only opportunity to gain the upper hand, Meme gathered her strength and swung her legs at Vanessa. The effort was pitiful and in the end, all she managed to do was knock Vanessa off balance and further deplete her energy.

Vanessa chuckled. Looking down at the pitiful sight that was Meme caused her chuckle to morph into a wicked cackle. "I can't wait to get rid of you. For weeks, I've watched you prance around like the world belongs to you. Tell me, how does it feel to have the red carpet snatched from under you?"

"You tell me. How does it feel to love a man that will never love you back?" She knocked the smirk right off Vanessa's face.

"Shut up!"

"Look at you. You're pathetic. Kidnapping and assault, all for a man you will never have."

"Shut up!" Vanessa was agitated.

Meme didn't care. She was going to die anyway, so she might as well speak her mind. "He won't love you when I'm gone. You had your chance well before I came along and he never gave you a second thought."

"Shut up!" Vanessa pulled the gun out the back of her pants and pointed it toward Meme. Her vision blurred with unshed tears. Meme had spoken the very words that had taunted her since this thing began. "He's just keeping his distance because we work together, but I am going to quit and we will be together." Her voice shook with uncertainty.

"Are you sure about that?" It was Meme's turn to laugh. "Cole is a real man who wants a real woman, not some desperate psychopathic stalker."

"Shut up!" Vanessa furiously trembled under the weight of Meme's words.

"You think he won't find out what you've done? Sahara is probably with the police, telling them everything, placing all the blame on you. You're going to spend the rest of your life in a jail cell, not in the arms of the man you love." Meme chuckled again and the taunting rumble of her laughter was more than Vanessa could take.

"Shut up. Shut up. Shut up!" Vanessa's arms flailed as she shook the gun at Meme. A loud explosion echoed through the room. The loud firing startled Vanessa out of her psychotic rant.

*Silence.*

The gun had gone off. She looked at the gun, at Meme, and then back at the gun. "Oh God!" Vanessa dropped to her knees in utter shock. Her heart knocked against her ribs while her lungs constricted. She was prepared to go to the extreme to get Cole, but preferred for Meme to leave town and never come back. Now, she'd pulled the trigger and Meme was on the floor bleeding. It was too late to rethink the plan, but she had to do something and fast.

Meme gripped her side, moaning in agony.

That moan propelled Vanessa into action. She lifted Meme to her feet and helped her walk to the master bedroom. Meme winced with each step. Blood pooled in her hand as she clutched her wound. Vanessa propped her up against the wall inside the room and rushed to the bathroom for towels to stop the bleeding.

The excruciating pain and the loss of blood weakened Meme's body. She slumped to the floor, leaving a streak of blood down the wall. She tried to call for Vanessa, but couldn't muster the strength. Her attempt resulted in a shallow whisper. Oxygen was limited and all she could do to cope with the pain was succumb to the darkness that was creeping in on her.

~

Sahara fidgeted as the car stopped down the street from Vanessa's house. She waited for the signal that everyone was in their place. Paul and his henchmen had given her strict instructions to walk into Vanessa's house like everything was normal, though things were far from it. The house was surrounded by men decked out in surveillance gear, black painted faces, skull caps, and .9 millimeters on each hip. She'd been given two minutes, a mere one hundred and twenty seconds, to locate Meme and open the blinds to signal she was okay. One second over and they were rushing the house. God forbid Vanessa interfered. Any screw up could get them both killed. Paul promised that if things got gun blazing serious, his men would spare her, but the lethal glare in Cole's eyes warned that he would not be as lenient. In the midst of all her fear, Sahara couldn't help but envy the way everyone rallied together for Meme. There was no one in the world that cared for her that much.

Sahara received the signal from Paul and took a deep calming breath before stepping out of the car. *Showtime.* Her stomach was in knots over all the possible outcomes. It was fifteen minutes after the time allotted for her to get her affairs in order, and she feared the worst. With each step toward the house her pulse accelerated. Her clammy palms gripped the door knob. As she stepped into the house, time seemed to move in slow motion. The silence that greeted her was deafening. Although it had been quiet while they were in Meme's apartment, there was an eeriness to this quiet that unnerved Sahara. Her pulse throbbed in her ears and head swooned with anxiety.

Sahara reached the kitchen and her heart dropped into her stomach. Vanessa sat at the table with a crazed look in her eye. She mumbled incoherently to herself as her hands, stretched across the table, continuously clenched and unclenched. What was truly distressing were the blood stains on her shirt. Vanessa's head snapped up and her eyes connected with Sahara's. She gripped the handle of the gun that had been sitting on the table and scooted her chair back. The sound of metal scraping across the tile floor propelled Sahara into to action. Frantically, Sahara bolted down the hall toward the rooms.

272

The first room was empty as well as the room Sahara had left Meme in. She held onto hope as she turned toward the last room. As she put her hand to the knob, Vanessa rounded the corner with gun drawn. Sahara pushed through the door and all her fears became reality. The pounding in her head intensified. Meme lie motionless on the floor. *I'm too late.*

"I didn't mean to shoot her."

Sahara spun toward Vanessa and her eyes met the barrel of the gun.

"She kept taunting me and taunting me. She wouldn't shut up." The gun shook with the tremble of her hand. "I warned her, but she kept running her mouth. She said I was pathetic and that a man like Cole would never love me. She pissed me off and I pointed the gun at her to get her to shut up and it just went off."

*You killed her.*

Vanessa opened her mouth to explain some more and Sahara lost it. She lunged toward Vanessa and grabbed the gun. If she had the backbone to challenge Vanessa days ago, Meme would be alive. The image of her limp body was fuel to the rage brewing inside. She'd avenge Meme's death, even if it meant losing hers in the process. With everything they had in them, they fought for dominance. Each knew the outcome if the other had the gun. Sweat poured from their bodies as they pushed and pulled against each other.

"Let go of the damn gun," Vanessa growled through clenched teeth

Sahara wrapped her leg around Vanessa's and swept her legs from under her. She refused to let go of the gun and fell down with her. They landed side by side, but Sahara quickly tossed her leg over Vanessa's waist and pushed for the dominant position. Her grip on the gun slipped and that was all Vanessa needed. The gun popped and all movement stopped. Slowly, Sahara rose to her feet, clutching her side. She looked down at her blood covered fingers. *Oh my God!* Tears filled her eyes as she stammered backward.

Vanessa stood to her feet with the gun still aimed at Sahara. Before she could get another shot off, there was an explosion and glass shattered throughout the house.

~

Marlon and Cole had parked the car far enough down the street where they wouldn't be noticed, but could still see the house. They watched Sahara walk into the house and waited for the blinds to open. It was the longest two minutes of their lives. When they never opened, it seemed like all the oxygen had been sucked out of the car. With trembling fingers, Marlon sent a text to Paul, who was parked further down the street. He signaled for his men to move in. Cole's grip tightened around the steering wheel. It took all the strength he had to stay put. He was unarmed and had no idea what Vanessa was working with on the inside. Running in to save Meme could cost his life, which, he was willing to risk at this point, but it could jeopardize others as well. It was best to let the professionals handle it.

Shortly after Marlon sent the text, the loud pop of gunfire echoed through the neighborhood. Without a second thought, Cole and Marlon were out of the car and running toward the house. All the hours in the gym doing squats and leg presses still hadn't given Cole the power to move as fast as he wanted. The man hiding out by the front door had already attached a small explosive device and blown the lock off the door. Cole and Marlon followed him into the house.

Vanessa didn't have to think about what was going on. She knew exactly what was up. Sahara had betrayed her and brought reinforcement. She lifted her gun and sent another bullet flying into Sahara's chest and then spun around to handle whoever was creeping up behind her. She turned and came face to face with seven gun barrels. She froze in fear. There was no need to tell her to put her gun down. One simply reached out and took it out of her hand as he walked by to help Sahara.

Cole pushed his way to the front of the pack and stood before Vanessa ready to spit fire. "Where is she?" Her silence sent Cole's rage into a blazing inferno. Like the magma of a volcano, it was on the verge of rising up and spewing out of his mouth. "I am going to ask you one time and if—"

"She's in the room," Sahara managed to whisper.

Sahara was losing a lot of blood, and in any other situation, Cole would've been concerned for the well-being of another person, but Meme was his main focus. He stepped over Sahara and let Paul's men continue trying to save her life. He stepped into the room and all the scenarios that had played out in his mind didn't come close to what laid before him. The love he'd just come to accept, taken before it could fully develop. Vanessa's deranged obsession with him had cost Meme her life. Cole would never be able to forgive himself. He kneeled by her side with no attempt to restrain his emotion. Grief constricted his lungs and his hollow cries were unheard. He pressed his lips to the top of her head as he scooped her up into his arms.

In the distance, he heard the faint sound of emergency response sirens. *Too late.* As he prepared to stand to his feet, he thought he heard something else. He looked at Meme's face, placed her on the ground, and he heard it again only this time it was accompanied by the slight furrow of her brow.

"Meme." He caressed her cheek. Her eyes fluttered but didn't open. Without hesitation, he lifted her into his arms and sought out the sirens he heard moments ago. He stepped over Sahara, who lay motionless, covered with a bed sheet. Marlon and Paul rushed up to him, but he ignored their inquiries. He saw Paul's men retreating out of the windows before the cops arrived. There wasn't time to worry about any of them. Meme's life was his only concern.

"Don't leave me," Cole whispered as he sat beside the gurney in the ambulance. He watched the EMT checking Meme's vital signs and felt powerless. The only woman he had ever loved lay in front of him dying, and there was nothing he could do. She looked pale, fragile, and the only sound she made was an occasional moan. He couldn't do anything for her, but there was someone that could. He dropped his head and barely above a whisper begged, "God, please help her." Church wasn't his thing, but he'd heard of the miraculous things God would do if you had the faith to ask.

The ambulance pulled up to the hospital and Marlon was right on its tail. He wanted to push Cole out of the way and ride with his sister, but he tried to put himself in Cole's shoes. No one could stop him from being by Latrice's side. He jumped out of his car and fell in line alongside the gurney's procession into the hospital. They were greeted by doctors and nurses that had been notified of Meme's condition prior to her arrival.

Cole held onto her hand, hoping his love for her would give her strength to pull through.

"Sir, we need you to let go, so we can help her."

Cole ignored the nurse's plea. The last time he let Meme out of his sight, she walked into the trap of a lunatic and now her life was slipping away. There was no way he'd allow that to happen again. He had to stay with her to keep her safe.

"Cole, come on man. You have to let her go." Marlon gripped their joined hands and pried their fingers apart. He had to wrap Cole in a bear hug to keep him from going after Meme. He'd never seen his friend this distraught. He felt Cole's pain, but he was powerless to help him. It was only the grace of God that was keeping him from having his own break down. The sight of his sister lying on that gurney with the life draining out of her was more than he could bear on his own and he found himself inwardly chanting, *God, help my sister.*

Once Marlon felt Cole's body relax and stop pulling against him, he released him. They stood in silence for a moment, both trying to get their emotions under control. Cole looked to Marlon with a muscle twitching in his jaw. "Where is Vanessa?" Just thinking about all the damage her ridiculous obsession caused sent fire surging through his veins.

"Don't worry about her. Paul is taking care of her. You just focus on my sister."

"If Meme dies—"

"Don't talk like that! She's not going to die. You know how I know? Because I have faith in God." Marlon placed his hand on Cole's shoulder and looked him in the eye. "I am going to pray, and so are you.

277

You are going to get over whatever hang-ups you have with God and the church. You are going to pray like your life depends on it."

"My life does depend on it." Cole hung his head and walked away with slumped shoulders. His existence depended on Meme's survival. He tried to blame Vanessa for everything, but the truth was he felt solely responsible for Meme being caught in this mess. He let her leave his house when he knew she wasn't safe. His trust issues put her in jeopardy and he wouldn't be able to live with himself, knowing his actions caused the death of the woman he loved.

Marlon found Cole hunched over in a corner of the waiting room and took the seat next to him. "Are you ready to pray?"

"I have been praying since they put her in the ambulance." Cole leaned back and rested his head against the wall. They sat side by side candidly calling on God, not caring who saw or heard.

## 27

Sitting around, waiting to hear from the doctor was driving Cole crazy. Every time the doors to the ER opened, he'd jump to his feet, expecting to see Meme's doctor. When they walked in a different direction, he'd plop down in his seat and curse the hospital along with every doctor on duty. Paul had arrived and notified him that Vanessa was in police custody, and thanks to his powers of persuasion she confessed to everything. At least after all she endured, Meme wouldn't have to sit through a long trial and look the woman who had tried to take her life in the eyes.

Cole looked up just as Latrice walked through the door. Marlon must've seen her at the same time, because he sighed and the tension instantly left his body. Cole watched as she made her way toward her husband. Their eyes never left each other. When she reached him, she sat on his lap and pulled his head to her chest. Marlon wrapped his arms around Latrice's waist and held on for dear life. He continued to watch their interactions and couldn't help but feel a twinge of jealousy. Just her presence seemed to ease Marlon's anxiety. In her arms, he released his fears and her touch strengthened him. Cole didn't realize until then that he desperately wanted a connection like that, but with no one other than Meme.

He hopped to his feet and paced around the waiting room as his prayers intensified. He'd have that type of love with Meme. If he had to pray all day and night, he would. He'd be in God's face so much that He would heal Meme just to get Cole off His back. It's funny how he was now calling on God when he'd once rejected all thoughts of God, invitations to church, and even questioned if He existed. Pushing his lack of relationship with God to the side, Cole's prayers increased. He needed Meme to pull through, and believing that a power higher than these doctors was in control brought him a modicum of peace. Needing some reinforcement, Cole pulled out his cell phone and called the one person he was sure could get through to God, Pastor Hawkins.

"She's been shot. I need you here." Cole grumbled the words out before Pastor Hawkins could finish greeting him.

"I'm on my way." He shot to his feet, grabbed his keys, and headed out the door without a second thought.

Cole told him what hospital to go to and ended the call. He felt a little awkward talking to Pastor Hawkins, not only because they were brothers, but because of the way he'd treated him back at Meme's apartment. But just like the man Richard had proven himself to be over and over again, he disregarded his personal feelings to help someone in need. He was a pastor with integrity, and his character and compassion continually fought against Cole's expectation of a pastor's persona. *One more thing I've been wrong about.*

Footsteps shuffled behind him and Cole turned to see the nurse approaching. He rushed over and met her, Marlon, and Latrice in the center of the waiting room. The look on her face did nothing to ease his anxiety. He stood before her, a tall, menacing presence with balled fists and clenched jaws, daring her to tell him that Meme was dead. The look on his face scared the words out of the nurse's mouth. She turned to Marlon, but what she found there was no better. Finally, she turned to Latrice, hoping for a face that didn't say, *"I'll rip your tongue out if you give me bad news."*

"We need to see someone who can make medical decisions for Melanie Wright."

Marlon looked to Cole and knew exactly what he was thinking. "I know you love her, but right now it has to be me." He knew how it felt to be helpless to save the woman you loved, but Meme was his sister, any life or death medical decisions would be his.

As they stood watching Marlon and the nurse walk away, Latrice placed her hand on Cole's back. "Just keep believing God."

Her words did nothing to soothe his anxiety, but that is what he tried to do. Keep believing God.

~

Cole sat in the waiting room on the verge of exploding. Latrice sat next to him, no doubt sensing the impeding detonation of his internal time bomb. She firmly gripped his hand as she chanted, "Peace in Jesus' name."

Being back in this hospital, Cole couldn't help but think of the last time they were there when he'd been such a jerk. He'd hurt and rejected Meme at a time when she really needed him. More than ever, he believed she deserved better than him, but it was him she was going to get. He'd make sure of it.

Cole was in such deep thought that he didn't hear Pastor Hawkins approach. "How's it going?"

Knowing that the pastor was there brought a sense of comfort Cole willingly accepted. After hours of being on edge, the comfort felt good and he sighed with relief. *Now maybe God will listen.* He raised his head to thank him for coming and had to bite his tongue. Standing right next to Pastor Hawkins was he and Cole's mother.

"Just hear her out," Pastor Hawkins pleaded. The look of disgust on Cole's face was a dead giveaway that bringing his mother was a bad decision. This conversation wasn't going to go well. When he'd confronted her about Cole's accusations, she didn't even try to deny it. She cried and praised God for answering her prayers and then demanded to see him. When Cole called, Pastor Hawkins thought what better way for a mother and son to bond than supporting each other through tragedy. By the look on Cole's face, he couldn't have been more wrong.

"I can't deal with this right now." Cole attempted to get up, but Latrice held his hand tighter and pulled him back to her side. She had no idea what was going on, but she trusted Pastor Hawkins and his mother. They'd been there for her more times than she could count. Cole needed that kind of support.

"Cole, when Richard told me about you," Lillian kneeled in front of him, "I couldn't believe my fortune. I am not here to push myself on you, but I want you to know that I am your mother—"

"What!" Latrice jumped to her feet. Her shocked expression and loud voice drew everyone's attention to her. She quietly apologized, sinking down into her seat.

Lillian turned her attention back to Cole. "As soon as you're ready to talk about that, I'm here. As for right now, we are here to help everyone get through this."

"How can you help anyone when you abandoned your child?"

Lillian's head dropped as his words pierced her heart. "I know your father told you a lot of things about me. Please give me a chance to explain before you pass judgment."

"Too late for that." Cole's menacing, unflinching eyes bore into her, and without another word she stood and exited the hospital. Latrice, confused and shocked, but loyal to a fault, ran after her.

Pastor Hawkins watched his mother leave, knowing she was hurting, but didn't follow her. She made her bed and now had to lie in it. His mother and brother would have to work out their issues.

"I know you're angry with her. You have every right to be, but we are brothers. That means something to me. I hope you don't make me pay for her mistakes."

"I'll try, but our age difference proves that you're the reason she never came back. She left when I was four, and we are a little over four years apart."

"I hear you, but I had nothing to do with that. I know you're hurting and I'm praying God gives you the strength to deal with all this, but try to look at this from my perspective. All my life I thought my parents were perfect. I idolized my father and wanted to be just like him. Now I find out he was a home wrecker and I'm a product of their adulterous relationship. I'm having a hard time wrapping my head around that. On the upside, I get a brother out of this mess."

Cole couldn't help but laugh. The pastor is his brother. Although Pastor Hawkins was cooler than he ever thought a pastor could be, they were at opposite ends of the spiritual spectrum, so their relationship would definitely be different.

"Okay, since we are brothers and I am older, you have to do everything I say." Cole sat up rubbing his hands together as he searched the waiting room for a nurse. "I need you to throw your weight around and get me in to see Meme."

Pastor Hawkins tried to contain his laughter, but couldn't. "What rule book is that in? I am thirty, not three, get out of here with that *do as I say* nonsense." They laughed and Pastor Hawkins relented. "I'll see what I can do. Not because you told me to, but because I can tell not knowing how she is doing is killing you. You're in love with her?"

"Am I that obvious?" Cole rubbed his hand down his face as he sat back.

"No, I just know what love looks like."

Cole's brow rose with interest at the misty-eyed look that briefly passed over Pastor Hawkins face.

"Let's get you back there to see Meme."

"Oh no, don't try to change the subject now."

"You know I have to be discreet."

"Don't tell me you've been creepin'."

"You know me better than that, but let's say my heart wants this woman. I just have to wait for God's time."

"So, you're just ready to take the next step? Just like that, no doubts?"

"Of course. My heart knows what it wants. Why waste time? Seems like that's some advice you should follow."

"I don't know about that. I admit I love her. If she survives this, I'll probably never let her out of my sight. But marriage? I don't think I'm ready for that."

"You just said you're never letting her out of your sight, sounds a lot like marriage to me. The marriage license is just a formality. You've found the woman you don't want to live without. That's the hard part. Once you've found her, everything that marriage entails comes naturally: compassion, consideration, loyalty, honesty, selflessness, camaraderie, and passion. If you don't have all of that with Meme then walk away. By the look on your face, I can tell you do."

"This conversation is getting a little too deep. Let's go see Meme." Pastor Hawkins was right; Cole had all that and then some with Meme. He tried to hide the smile that crept on his face. *I'm getting married,* was his final thought before following Pastor Hawkins to the nurse's station.

~

"Lady Lillian, wait up." Latrice practically had to run to catch up to her. "Don't leave. He needs you." That was enough to get her to stop. Latrice stood in front of her, seeing a side of her she'd never seen. Although she wasn't the first lady of the church in the traditional sense, she ruled Zion Pentecostal with an iron fist. She was always well put together, demanded holiness, and was quick to reprimand anyone who stepped out of line. In spite of her hard exterior, Latrice adored her. The lady before her with tears streaming down her face and anguish in her eyes was not the woman she was used to seeing. On instinct, Latrice embraced her. "He needs you. He's just angry right now."

"I didn't abandon him."

"That's not what's important right now. What's important is my sister who's in this hospital fighting for her life. Cole loves her, and if he loses her, he is going to need you. So for right now, you are going to go into this hospital and deal with Cole's anger. You are not going to run."

Lillian took a few minutes to compose herself. Staying away from him years ago was what she thought was best for him. She wasn't about to make that mistake again. She'd wait it out and wear him down. Eventually, he'd have to talk to her.

~

Cole and Pastor Hawkins rode the elevator to ICU in silence. Neither knew what to expect; they gleaned joy from the fact they weren't riding down to the morgue. ICU was bad, but she was still alive.

The sight of Meme motionless on the bed with a tube down her throat constricted Cole's voice. He opened his mouth to ask Marlon, who sat on the side of the bed holding her hand, what the doctor said, but nothing came out.

"Marlon." Pastor Hawkins stepped forward to get his attention. "What did the doctor say?"

Marlon stood and accepted the brotherly embrace his pastor offered. "They said the surgery went well, she just won't wake up." He watched Cole take his seat, grab Meme's hand, and bring it to his lips. "They said something else." Marlon waited for Cole to look at him, and when he didn't, Marlon called his name. "She was pregnant and lost the baby."

"What?" That was all Cole could take. He'd done his best to control his emotion. An occasional tear escaped, but for the most part he'd held it together. He bowed his head, rested it on the edge of the bed, and unleashed every emotion he'd held in since the day he watched Meme walk out of his house.

## 28

The rest of the family had arrived and the nurses had long ago stopped trying to keep only two visitors in the room at a time. Wayne paced around in circles while Kevin tried to calm him down. Gloria and Marlon Sr. sat side by side at their daughter's bed. She had yet to wake up and they refused to leave her side until her eyes opened. Cole sat on the other side of the bed mourning the loss of his child, but trying to hold himself together for Meme's sake. Marlon and Pastor Hawkins stood by the window joined in a deep conversation.

"Before Latrice left she told me about you and Cole being brothers."

"Yeah, I'm still shocked. I have a brother. Not once did my mother try to deny it." He was having a hard time coming to terms with his mother's actions, but at least she hadn't tried to lie about it.

"Do you believe her story?"

"No reason not to. It's not like she made herself out to be a saint."

"I hear you." They stood in silence for a minute, both thinking about the situation. "This is crazy. It's one thing to find out you have a brother, but another to find out that brother is your boy."

Pastor Hawkins chuckled as he looked over his shoulder at Cole. "This is going to be interesting, the playa and the pastor, brothers."

"You mean ex-playa." Marlon watched Cole sitting on the side of Meme's bed, whispering in her ear. "It looks like we are going to be related real soon. Your brother has it bad for my sister."

"Who you tellin'?" Pastor Hawkins turned toward the sound of someone clearing their throat.

"Excuse me, Pastor. I know you said believe God, but I'm having a hard time. As you can tell, I've never really been one to go to church. So believing God is a little hard for me. Do you really think she is going to be okay?"

"Wayne, I told you God's got this, but if you can't believe God then trust the doctors. They said her vital signs look good. She just seems to be asleep. She will wake up when she gets good and ready."

"You're right. I just need to calm down."

"You know Wayne, the same God I serve wants to be your God as well."

"Oh please, don't try to convert me or save my sin-filled soul."

"I'm sorry that's the impression you have of the Church. Yes, the Bible speaks against your lifestyle, but it also says that we are all sinners and that there is no big sin or little sin. Who are we to judge anyone's struggle or deem them unworthy of God's grace? You, just like me, are a creation of God. We were created for His glory and it is our duty to serve Him. Everything else, God will handle."

"So, you are saying I can come to your church, be me, and no one will say anything."

Pastor Hawkins chuckled. "They are going to say something. I'm pretty sure you know that people are always going to have something to say. What I'm saying is that it is your duty to serve the Lord and all else is irrelevant. In the process of serving Him, you must seek to do His will, regardless of our personal desires."

"So, you're saying if I serve the Lord, I can't sleep with men?"

"I'm a thirty-year-old, single pastor. Living for the Lord comes with all types of sacrifices. Some single pastors choose to appease the desires of their flesh, I don't. The choice is also yours."

Pastor Hawkins saw his mother walk through the door and left Wayne to mull over his words. Before he could get to her and shuffle her out of the room, Cole saw her.

"I thought I made myself clear. I do not want you here." He stood and made his way toward her.

"I made the wrong choice and left you years ago. I'm not going to mess up again. God set us up to reconcile and I am not going to miss the opportunity."

"Who says I'm interested in reconciling?"

"You did when you found me on the internet. I know I hurt you and nothing I say or do can make up for it. The only thing I can do is help you understand what happened."

"I don't have time for this." Cole turned back toward Meme, but Lillian wouldn't let him shut her out.

"Please, just listen. Please." She held her breath as she waited for him to honor her request. Reluctance stiffened his shoulders, but gradually he stood and walked toward the windows.

Lillian smiled at him, but knew the hardest battle was yet to be won. "Yes, I screwed up and I cheated on your father, but I did not abandon you, at least not at first." That statement intensified Cole's glare and his nostrils flared with caged fury. Lillian finally had a chance to explain and she wasn't going to let his anger deter her.

"The night your father confronted me I left, but I came back the next day. I wasn't going to insult him by asking him to work things out, but I came to see you. I loved you more than anything else in this world and didn't want you hurt by what was going on between me and your father. He wouldn't let me see you, and when I insisted, he grabbed me by my throat and threatened to kill me if I ever came back. I could smell the alcohol on his breath. I knew he was hurting. He always loved me far more than I ever loved him.

"When I got pregnant, I was willing to settle, but after a few years it wasn't enough. I left that night, thinking I'd give him a few days to calm down, but when I came back, you were gone. The house was empty and you were gone." Her voice cracked as she remembered that day. Her voice echoed against the walls as she ran through the house calling Cole's name. Each room was as empty as the first. Everything was gone. There was no note or explanation; her husband had taken her baby and disappeared.

She walked closer to the window as she continued her story. "I called the police and was told there was nothing they could do. There was no custody arrangement, so there was no law broken. I called all of his friends and relatives that I had numbers to and no one would tell me where

291

he was. I spent all my savings hiring private investigators and they found nothing. I almost lost Pastor Hawkins because I was so stressed. I wasn't eating and I lost so much weight, the doctor finally admitted me into the hospital for the duration of my pregnancy."

"But once your precious little baby was born, you forgot all about me and went on your merry little way."

"You're wrong." Lillian looked at Pastor Hawkins. "You said you wanted the truth, so here it is. After I was released from the hospital, I was more obsessed with finding you than before. I was in that hospital for months and had to make up for lost time. I was out putting up flyers and talking to people at your father's old hangouts. I was so focused on finding you that I left the stroller in the store. I had pushed it up against a wall to get it out of the way while I talked to some of the clerks and showed them your picture. None of the clerks noticed the stroller until Pastor Hawkins woke up and started crying. They'd called the number on the flyer and his father picked him up and was waiting for me when I got home. I never even noticed I'd left him until I saw him in his father's arms. I almost lost one child while looking for the other. His father threatened to sue for custody unless I got help. I went to therapy and tried to move on with my life." She turned her eyes back to Cole. "I never stopped loving you or thinking of you."

"We moved in with my grandma in Virginia. I know you had her number. All you had to do was call."

"I did. She told me she had no idea where you were and promised to call if she heard anything."

"I moved back, why didn't you keep looking?"

"Well, like I said before, I didn't abandon you at first." She sighed and shook her head with exasperation as she rethought her past actions. "When you were ten, I received an anonymous message telling me that you were back. They gave me the address and I didn't hesitate to look for you. I pulled up in front of the house and you were outside playing in the yard. I hadn't seen you in six years, but I knew who you were the second I laid eyes on you. I approached you, asked if you knew who I was, and tried to touch your hand."

She reached out and cupped his cheek in her hand, touching her son for the first time in twenty plus years. Tears saturated her cheeks, emotion strangling her next words. "You ran from me, screaming for your father to come save you. It was then that I abandoned you. I figured you were better off without me. Six years was a long time for me to come along and interrupt your life. I had no idea what your father had told you about me. I didn't want to confuse you any more than you already were. So, that time I disappeared."

"How could you give up so easily?" Cole stepped away from her touch. "I needed you." He spun away from her to get his thoughts together and his eyes locked with a set of eyes he'd never thought he'd see again. "Meme!" Every eye in the room turned toward the bed.

Within seconds, Cole was at her side. He pressed the button to call the nurse and practically yelled through the intercom that Meme was awake. He scanned the room for his mother and she was gone. He didn't have time to dwell on where she'd run off to. Meme was alive and awake. That's all that mattered. The doctor came in and Cole backed up long enough for him to remove the breathing tube and check Meme's vitals. As soon as he finished, Cole was right back at her side, caressing and kissing her cheeks.

"Baby, I'm sorry you had to go through all of this." Tears leaked from the corners of her eyes and he tried his best to catch them. "I never should've let you go. I was upset over something that had nothing to do with me."

Meme raised a shaky hand to his lips to shush his apology. Her voice was raspy from the tube that was down her throat, but she forced the words out. "I love you." She'd told herself if she made it out of this ordeal alive, she'd tell Cole how she felt.

"I love you too." Cole rested his head against hers and cuddled her as gently as possible.

"Who's that woman you were talking to?"

"Don't worry about that right now. You just focus on getting better, because as soon as you get out of here, I want you to become my wife. I don't want to live another day without you. So can you do that for me? Will you be my wife?"

"Yes baby." Her tears fell so fast, Cole stopped trying to wipe them away. He peppered her cheek and neck with kisses. The sweet romantic moment was interrupted by Wayne sniveling across the room.

"Come here, you big crybaby." Cole stepped out of the way, so Meme could hug Wayne and the rest of her family. He watched her smile. After all she'd been through, it was still as bright as the day he'd met her. It still brightened up his heart. He'd been through a lot, and for the first time, his heart finally knew what it wanted. Meme was his and he'd never let her go. He'd spend the rest of his life making up for everything she'd endured over the past few days. Her love would give him the strength to face his mother, brother, and anything else that came up.

"I told you that you were going to marry Meme." Pastor Hawkins gave Cole a congratulatory slap on the back. "I better be the best man."

"No! If you're the best man, what other pastor can we get to marry us on such a short notice?"

"Always the pastor and never the best man."

Cole couldn't help but laugh. It felt good to be able to laugh. He embraced his brother and they agreed to get to know each other better. Then, he reclaimed his spot next to his soon-to-be wife. He never would've thought that the innocent little flower he followed to the restroom a few months ago would turn his life upside-down. She infiltrated every barrier he had around his heart, made him break all his rules, and he couldn't be happier.

Meme leaned as far into Cole as she could. Just being in his arms helped to drown out the torture she'd experienced over the past few days. She'd been through hell—stalked, vandalized, attacked, kidnapped, starved, and shot. She'd endure it all again just to have Cole love her. She couldn't figure out what it was that kept drawing them to each other. Now she had the rest of her life to figure it out.